THE STRANGE CASE OF
MADELEINE SEGUIN

To Mark and Rachel

with warm wishes

William (Lindsay) Rose

THE STRANGE CASE OF MADELEINE SEGUIN

A Novel

William Rose

KARNAC

First published in 2016 by
Karnac Books Ltd
118 Finchley Road
London NW3 5HT

British Library Cataloguing in Publication Data

A C.I.P. for this book is available from the British Library

ISBN-13: 978-1-78220-440-4

Typeset by Medlar Publishing Solutions Pvt Ltd, India

Printed in Great Britain by TJ International Ltd, Padstow, Cornwall

www.karnacbooks.com

For Margaret Madeline W.

CONTENTS

CHAPTER ONE

A night at the Salpêtrière

From a Historical Archive of Hôpital de la Salpêtrière, created and maintained by Father Pierre Lambert, Chaplain to the hospital in the years 1874–1886.

Item: An extract from the diary of Jacques Bignan, blacksmith and resident of the faubourg Saint-Marcel, Paris. Dated 5th September 1792.

Two days ago we set out to free a goodly number of women from Salpêtrière. It was not difficult to gain access. A hundred men and some of our women too, well-armed and wearing our clothes of the revolution, our red caps and our honest coats and trousers—who in these days would dare to stop us? The guards were expecting us anyway, and clearly too were the governor and his assistants as they had removed themselves and were nowhere to be seen.

We had fortified ourselves well and some of us had been preparing our plans in Madame Bonnet's tavern. There was much refreshment thanks to the generosity of our hostess, herself a great supporter of the Revolution, and for a small charge whole jugs of wine were set before us. For me the first cup was sufficient. For a man to perform his duty the warmth and encouragement of strong, hearty, blood-red wine is a tonic indeed. But too much and we may err in the performance of those duties, ones that we carry out for the sake of our great and now free nation. Freedom has been our goal and freedom was our aim last night. To free the women, our sisters in affliction, who have been shamefully locked away—and for what? For selling their bodies when there was no other way for them to buy food or pay the few sous for a miserable leaking roof over their heads. The old rulers treated them with disdain, cleared them from the streets as if they were rubbish, prosecuted and incarcerated them and then sent many onto the boats, expelled to slavery in new lands, never to return. Now we were to march upon their gaol to free them. I saw some of our men who were looking to have instant reward for their actions and if some of these freed ladies would wish to show their gratitude through the skills of their profession, so be it. We live in times that are raw and many acts not even imagined by ordinary men are carried out in the streets now before our very eyes. I though am a man with a family and my dear Madame Bignan was awaiting my return to our home and my aim was to see our task through, deliver the women safely from the cells and be sure that I had carried out a goodly work for our cause and for freedom.

So we marched on to Salpêtrière. By the time we arrived our number had grown to more than a hundred. Most of us were armed. I carried my pike, but there were some axes and clubs and a sword or two as well. For me the pike is not really a weapon to be used. True, it can be, the staff is strong and the steel point sharp enough, but more than that it is the token of our new state, one carried by true soldiers of the Revolution. It is the pike that we march with in unison, a sturdy and visible sign of honest resolve.

Axes and swords, these are not for me, especially the swords. Too much a weapon for those that we have overthrown and when I think about the sword I think not of the need to show our new power and authority, but of killing, and dear God there is enough of that. Sometimes necessary I know, but now

2

these streets and squares where we walk with our children show the actual stains of blood, seeped into the very stones on which we tread.

So as we marched to Salpêtrière I for one had no killing in mind. My aim was to put right the sad injustices carried out within the walls of that grim building. But as our numbers grew there was other talk. Some were greatly fearing the war with Prussia. The invaders will soon be in Paris, they said. They will free the aristocrats and it will be we, the sans-culottes, who will be thrown in the dungeons with those now in them our gaolers. "Kill the priests and the royalists," they were crying, and "Kill the criminals who are their lackeys!" And some said that Danton himself would wish it so.

I myself have little power. Yes I wear the insignia of a sans-culotte, and when all is calm and we discuss and plan our purpose and gather together for the task, my voice is heard and considered and carries its own weight. I spoke now to some around me and asked how poor, miserable women locked up in Salpêtrière, most for trifling crimes, could be a danger to our Revolution, or be allies of the Prussian army! But there was a madness starting up and the muttering became shouting and the women that some had come to free had for others now become the new enemies of the state.

And what can I, Jacques Bignan, do when our force of men swells in the street to a small army, when some have drunk so much wine that they sing and curse in ways that suit no true militia? Where is the pride? And the singing and cursing were nothing to what was to come. There were some amongst us, and I know them and have heard their views, who are most ruthless. They believe that if a mortal existence impedes the cause, then that human life should be snuffed out with the ease of fingers on the wick of a candle. But there are some who are more dangerous still. When we talk amongst ourselves, when we debate on the society we will forge, when we cry out aloud against injustice and the acts of those tyrants who have ruled

3

us, these others are the ones who sit quietly. They are waiting there with their swords, axes and daggers, hoping for the only part they want to play, the only reason for them to be there at all: a time for torture and killing. They were there with us now. One or two I recognised as they grouped together. They know each other from their previous deeds and their own shared lust for blood.

We came to Salpêtrière and some were singing, some chanting and already I feared we were less a band of dedicated men and more a rabble in the making. So I cried out loudly for our Revolution and for our purpose of honour and there were those whose voices joined with mine. Real comrades in arms and we marched through the outside gate and to the main doors and there we stood and demanded that we should be given entry to that place and that it should be done in the name of the Republic. Such demands have their strong effect. Who would dare resist and be seen to be against the Revolution and the Commune? So the doors were opened to us and we required that those who had been within remain and serve us as guides and that they should bring with them every key to every lock for doors and chains alike.

It had been agreed that I, who had also been there at the Bastille, would be one of those to enter, but all order and plans were cast aside and many burst through those doors ahead of me and some of them were the quiet ones with the swords and the daggers and the glint in their eyes. I and a group of comrades had a Salpêtrière guard as our guide. Now we were in we ceased to shout and it was a pure, grim purpose that drove us through those corridors. Very long corridors they were with locked doors side by side and dim lights, and because our voices had ceased there was a strange and unnatural quiet. Those women, cowed behind the locked doors, listening to strange footfalls, could not have guessed that we wished them freedom, but when the doors were opened, we declared ourselves for just that and what a wonderful sight to see their relief and joy.

But there were others whose views were against us. "No one to be released!" they cried. And their group, more numbered and grown strong through wine and their fear of Prussians, held sway. "There must be a trial," they said. "Tomorrow we will find the traitors within, the degenerates and the enemies of France."

It makes me sad to think of our sisters shut away. But to see the very site of their captivity, with its filth and stink and the bodies all huddled together—it showed me that we would have done well to set those women free. True, the next day some would be released, but many bad things would come before.

It was then that one of those quiet ones—his name is Giraud and no brethren of mine—came out of the main doors and into the courtyard where we were and behind him was a woman and he had hold of her by her long hair and he was pulling her like she was a dog on a leash. He was laughing but she was crying in a piteous way and she looked all unkempt and uncared for and with a strange, wild look in her eyes. I could see that she was no normal woman, and for sure that was why he had picked her. So helpless, and she could only make the strangest of sounds, a sort of wittering, and there were no words I could make out that belong to our own good language. So he pulled her out and left her there cringing and making her strange sounds with her eyes swivelling around and I could see that she was as frightened as anyone can be. He, the quiet one, went back inside and came out with two more, and I could tell that these were the same as the first and these were not women of the streets, but were from the mad women of Salpêtrière. The ones locked away because there is nothing that any caring person can do to bring them back to the world we all share. No, they live in a world that is all their own and what

5

a terrible place that must be. But no worse than the one they were dragged into on this terrible night.

Then a henchman of Giraud, another quiet and sinister one, came out through the doors and with him was a young girl. Still in her teenage years, and I straight away had to avert my eyes because she was naked and whatever tatters of clothes she had were now stripped from her body, and the only thing still attached to her was the chain that had held her to the wall inside and which was now the leash used to drag her into the night and into the full view of us all. And there was much muttering of disgust amongst us at these shameful things carried out by so-called brothers-in-arms. But there were also those who looked, and without doubt they looked at this poor girl with lust, and there was laughing too, and some were gathering round and mocking these poor creatures and making noises in that same sort of gibberish that mad women speak. And so there were four of them there and one of these women was screaming, screaming so terribly that I will never forget that sound, the worst cry of fear that a man could hear. And I think that that is what made the difference—that is what brought about the first death because the sound was too horrible to hear and one of those there, one of those drunken henchman of Giraud swung his axe and the screaming was no more. Then two of the others, scared as they already surely were, were taken with a terror that jumped between them, wailing, screaming, clanking their chains, sprawling on the ground, tearing at their hair. It was as if those cries were the very summons to murder, because the louder they became the more those amongst us struck out, with clubs, axes, swords, and even with pikes. And then standing there in the middle of it all was that same girl who had been pulled out with her modesty so usurped, but she, and I can see it now and will forever, just stood there upright and calm as could be as if she was in another world, and I glanced, God forgive me for I could not help but look, and I saw her eyes looking far off into some other place, certainly some other

6

place that was far from that scene of carnage, and there she was, the last of them still alive. In a way too strange to kill, or were they just saving her till the last?

I do not write here to keep a record for myself, to have something to stir the memory in later years, or to keep the history for those who will follow us. I need not do that for the pictures in my mind, the things I saw that night, will never leave me and no single day will pass when I am not compelled to remember the scene of those poor broken bodies and hear the cries of their tormented souls. No, I write in the hope that in some way I might find relief for I can never tell these things to another and, like an inmate of Salpêtrière, I am trapped with them forever.

It finished. One of them went up close to the girl and plunged a dagger into her and then they dragged her, and she was still alive, back into the building, six or seven of them, and the door slammed shut. What then took place in there must have even shamed those accursed walls.

We outside were quiet then. Those inside were not of our kind. We felt only despair. Whatever we had tried to do, and there had been good and honourable wishes with generosity in our hearts, had been snatched from us and cruelly twisted to a form so grotesque that it came from the darkest recess of the human soul.

The next day we were all to be assembled again for the so called "trial" and Giraud and his friends stood there, pride of place, arms crossed and heads in the air, like the new nobility. They had had their will with the mad women the night before, poor wild creatures that no one would miss. Now they were the judge, the jury and to their pleasure, the executioners of the women held as criminals. All was a mockery. Many women were pulled before them. There are hundreds of women gaoled in Salpêtrière—for what? Some are women who work the streets and give their services to the very men who condemn them. There were some, and their names and charges were read out, though little else was said, whose crimes had been so small that if it were your own child a cuff around the ears would be punishment enough. And how many could they try anyway? They went on for as long as their need to kill, and indeed there were more than thirty poor souls who were condemned that day and passed on to the mob, and I will never call these men sans-culottes; they were like wolves in a pack that tear apart their prey. There were to be no easy deaths, no dignity, no prayers, only jeers as the last sounds heard in a life.

There were women that were freed. Over a hundred. What made them different to the ones who were condemned is unknown to me. One thing I do know is that none of them, dead or alive, had the strength in a single finger to endanger France. Some of those freed ones wept whilst some raged at the walls that had enclosed them. They had few clothes and belongings, but the day was fine and many vanished as soon as they were touched by that clean warm air. Others, the bolder and the more brazen, stayed outside joking and laughing, some of them flicking their hair at their saviours, and they were greatly pleased to partake of the flagons that were handed around. And then, to their terrible shame, there were even those who now looked on and gave vent to their pleasure in the massacre.

I walked home and away from that accursed scene and there were companions with me, men that I trust, but it brought no comfort. No words were said. We were citizens, soldiers of freedom, but no longer with pride. Our great aims now lay in ruins, bleeding amongst the bodies that were piled like mangled sacks in the courtyard of the hospital of the Salpêtrière.

So now, cursed by the visions of these last two days, I write. My only hope is that in years to come, as I remember this woeful time, it may be that instead of the torture of its memory I will have sadness instead, as heavy as it need be, for I would rather live with grief than with the horror that besets me now.

Jacques Bignan
5th September 1792

I too live with your horror. There are those who maintain that evil will always be the companion of good—that each exists only through its relation to the other. This is useless. Evil is its own entity. As the greatest love is pure and unadulterated, so is the greatest evil. It resides now and again gathers strength in our city.

Lambert (Chaplain and Archivist) January 1885

CHAPTER TWO

The patient Madeleine Seguin

Notes on the case of Mademoiselle Madeleine Seguin

Joseph Babinski
Chef de clinique
Hospital of the Salpêtrière
Paris

June 6th 1885

The patient Madeleine Seguin, now twenty years old, was first admitted to Salpêtrière on 18th August 1881, aged seventeen. The girl had been brought to the hospital by an elderly lady who identified herself as an aunt and whose exit was so rapid that one can only say that Madeleine was practically left on the doorstep. On the departure of the aunt the poor girl collapsed upon the floor. She had with her the clothes that she was dressed in and a valise that contained apparel for one more change, along with some items for personal toilet use. Charles Féré, the intern who received her, was intrigued by the fact that, though there was an apparent austerity about the look of the girl—the clothes being mainly grey and dark blue, with her long hair tied up in a most utilitarian and indecorous fashion, and no jewellery whatsoever—the material of her clothing was of an excellent quality; so too apparently the quality of her toilet items. I believe the handle of her hairbrush was made of pure ivory and the main body of silver. Whether such a valuable item has survived the clutches of some of the more deviant amongst her fellow patients, I cannot say.

Mademoiselle Seguin's appearance is now much as it was then. She is of slender build, of medium height, and I suppose one could say that there is congruence to the observations made concerning her original clothing in that there is no physical adornment. Everything is kept plain; the hair is still long, though it is now allowed to fall around her shoulders. The skin is pale with no addition of cosmetic colouring, yet the natural bone structure of her face is very fine and the general proportions of the body, as far as I can see from the contours that do manage to manifest through the plain lines of her dresses, are also of a fine, though slim, structure. This is endorsed by a simple economy of grace in her general movements when she is well.

There was a substantial amount of money left by the aunt at the time of the patient's admission and I am aware that regular amounts are still paid to the hospital for her treatment and continued board with us. The fact that the payments are made a year in advance has struck me as particularly pessimistic on the part of her providers, as if they have few expectations of a cure, and since she receives no visits or correspondence from friends or family, I can only surmise that they have washed their hands of her. I do wonder whether to some extent this has influenced Professor Charcot's treatment of her as she seems to have become an ongoing, resident feature of the Salpêtrière Hospital and its programme of lectures and demonstrations.

Apart from the financial gains, there were certainly substantial clinical grounds for accepting her admission when she was first brought here. At the time Féré listed the symptomatology thus:

Occasional blindness and deafness.

Perpetual muteness.

Extreme somnambulistic activity (which still to this day can necessitate either her restriction to a small room with locked door at night, or some kind of mechanical restraint to prevent her leaving her bed if in an open ward).

After these original and rather cursory observations the list of symptoms has grown to include:

Phases of extreme paralysis accompanied by anaesthesia where, in their most acute states, there is no discernible movement made except for the occasional flicking of an eyelid and very slight and sporadic respiratory movements. (As this symptom has continued it has on more than one occasion caused a nurse, new to her job and the department, to go rushing to the nearest physician proclaiming her patient dead. This paralysis is of a kind that shows a complete lack of any motor activity as if the brain has simply switched off the body.)

There have also been several recorded periods of muscular spasm that have caused the alternative form of paralysis, that of utmost rigidity (and of course Professor Charcot has induced this aspect of an otherwise spontaneous symptom during his public demonstrations with this patient). In its most dramatic manifestation the patient straightens, stiffens, and then arches backwards to such an extreme as to practically join head to feet with her face and the whole front of her body facing outwards and forming a contortion that we have come to name the "arc de cercle".

My colleague Paul Richer has also observed Mlle Seguin in a state of paralytic spasm in which each of her limbs became rigidly extended and projected outwards, the arms at right angles to the shoulders and the legs also rigid, pointing down and close together, so that Richer with dark humour dubbed the patient the "Vitruvian Woman" alluding to Leonardo's drawing of the ideally proportioned man, limbs outstretched and perfectly contained within the circumference of a circle. I was unable to fully endorse his joke as I am too aware that such criteria of beauty and perfection have no issue within the corridors and wards of Salpêtrière. We still have nuns working in our wards and they apparently had their own reaction and took this contortion as a semblance of the crucifixion and were rather in awe. I suppose that they are always looking for miracles and saints, especially in young women. Some of the other serving staff were less enthusiastic seeing it as macabre and devilish, the very opposite of holy. So there we are—religious fervour on one hand and superstitious fear on the other. To my mind there is little to separate them. No doubt both parties made much of the patient's frequent hallucinations, the contents of which were always a mystery as she remained mute, though clearly she was seeing things, as her eyes moved as rapidly and distinctly as those of an infant in its first throes of taking in the world.

There was a time when due to the severity of her symptoms this girl might well have been referred to the alienists, dispatched to the hall of the insane and left to languish there, but Professor Charcot had no hesitation in directing her admittance to the department of hystero-epilepsy, and we now regard her as a classical case of neurosis and "la grande hystérie".

There have of course been a range of treatments that have been applied since the patient's first admittance, notably hydrotherapy, electrotherapy, and massage, but the use of these has diminished during her years at the hospital and the Professor himself has now advised against them, believing hypnosis and contact with her physicians to be the most effective ways forward and I am in full agreement with this. Indeed that process in hydrotherapy which involves the forceful direction of a current of water upon the genital area would seem to me to be less an attempt at cure than an assault upon one so young.

The initial examination on admittance had shown her hymen to be intact so there can be no excess of sexual practice as a factor in the development of her illness, and anyway there is a demure element in her deportment and character that would belie such a notion. As then to the actual precipitating features in this case of hysteria, we have little notion and can have no knowledge of hereditary disposition. However it is my view that the traumatic element that the Professor has recently been describing as pathogenic in this disease must surely be a factor. The very nature of her abandonment at the hospital and the continuity of this tragic state with no contact from any family member show that the most shocking and painful events must have preceded her admittance.

Madeleine's progress of recovery has been remarkable in the past year. Really this is during the period in which she has been a subject of the Professor's demonstrations both at his Tuesday clinical sessions and his Friday public lectures. I believe that electric faradic stimulation to the muscles and the various massage techniques may have helped with the paralysis, but it occurs to me that the intense presence of Professor Charcot's attention and the remarkable calm confidence that marks his relations to his patients may well be the crucial ingredients in her improvement.

I continue to find Mademoiselle Seguin clinically a most interesting patient and as her personality emerges, to be a most likeable and intelligent young woman. It is also of interest that, as one reviews her history at Salpêtrière, it is clear that even in her most ill and unavailable states she has in mysterious fashion managed to elicit remarkably strong and subjective engagements from those around her, both amongst the patients and the hospital staff.

Joseph Babinski
June 6th 1885

CHAPTER THREE

The artist

Letter to:
Marcel Dupont, Marmande, Lot-et-Garonne département, SW France

From:
Louis Martens, rue Lamarck, Paris, France

Dated 13th November 1885

My dear Marcel,

Where does one find inspiration? Should one search in the city or wander through the countryside? In your choice, the countryside, the hand of God is evident. I would not deny it and maybe it is to that influence that an artist should open his mind—my goodness, not only the mind, the heart, the stomach, the genitals! The countryside is as physical and sensual as the body of one's most wondrous lover, and I believe that God would be happy with such a comparison. Good luck to you, Marcel, with your bright and undulating landscapes. I love your work; you know that.

For me though it is where I am now, the city. I seem unable to escape it and since I find no pleasure in the appearance of houses and factories and municipal buildings, and since I am little impressed by the mutations to sunlight that occur when it must struggle through smoke and fog, I increasingly am needing to look within for the images that inspire. And maybe that, in truth, is why I am here. My inner world must compensate for the privation caused by my surroundings. I am forced to imagine. It has become a discipline.

And of course also there is the company. "Our" company I suppose I could say. We are the dreamers, the mystical painters, and so there is a sense of belonging to a group. It has been suggested that we are tainted with decadence. Does a decadent group still have ideals? Yes, quite clearly so, and as I think of it now, I do feel a pleasure at the "belonging". I hold my council though, and my ground. There are some strong and forceful personalities and it seems to me that it is the strongest personalities that have the most fantastical ideas. Do you believe in the séance? The occult is of course dearly beloved to some of my colleagues and I have attended three séances now, two of which left me feeling that I was not so much travelling to wondrous new dimensions as attending a party with peculiar people who prefer to spend an evening sitting in the dark. I made the most of it and spent a fruitful time imagining a new painting.

As for real thrills, city life is profligate in its offerings, with all the fantastic juxtaposition of its people and their dramas. And I have indeed been seeking these out. So where does one hunt for these thrills? Well, I have visited the circus; you saw two of my drawings of that series. I have been to freak shows; fascinating, though they leave me feeling sad and shaken and I shall not go again; there is nothing there that moves me in any direction except away from art. And an awful thrill, I saw an execution, and felt that I was amongst an audience of perverts. One woman was clearly masturbating, another fed her baby from her breast throughout (what milk!), and one man saw fit to free his member from his trousers and let loose a stream of urine just as the blade fell and cut the head from the shoulders. No one seemed to be shocked, not at these actions or at the execution itself. This is what amazed, the assimilation of the horrific into a thing of entertainment and sexual thrill (there is in Paris at present an artist called Rops who makes such a combination his stock in trade).

With both fascination and repulsion I have allowed my imagination to roam these scenes, but they have provided little source for a picture. Something though has worked and I am going to tell you about it now. You must write back, Marcel, to tell me what you think.

My employer, the Professor Charcot, is a generous man. He is a patron of the arts and I am a struggling young artist, and though I do not really feel he sees my work as I do, and I am therefore bound to consider his view somewhat lacking, I am pleased that he believes that I have some talent. Anyway, I am an artist and he a patron, and my decorative attempts to enliven and beautify the interior walls of the garden summer house of his Paris home seem to have been received well enough. Indeed he is paying me generously over the agreed amount and as an additional bonus, he is a man of some pride I think, I was also invited to see him perform. The learned Professor perform? Indeed yes, it is certainly the word to use. Perform like the star of a grand circus; no, not the star, I will come on to the star in a moment, the grand ring-master is the better title for the Professor. I mean him no ill in saying this. Indeed I feel affection and respect for him and by all accounts his is one of the greatest intellects in Paris. But there is no doubt that the man is also a magnificent performer. And I would suggest that he knows it, hence the twinkle in his eye when, as the extra reward for my artistic endeavours, he invited me to one of his Salpêtrière demonstrations. The Professor certainly knew that I would not be attending with an academic's note book and pencil, but with an artist's pencil and sketchbook and with a view to catching a scene. The man knows the power of the visual. He told me that if I so wished I should feel free to draw throughout the session. I believe that he wanted a portrait of himself in the midst of his circus!

The lecture room at the Salpêtrière Hospital was absolutely packed. Squeezed in together were the grand and stuffy and the grand and glamorous. Yes, I did feel rather shabby, but in there too were some impecunious young science students and their presence helped me to feel not quite such an oddity.

The Professor was to display to us two cases that he described as "grand hysteria". The man is a marvel of presentation. Firstly he described some of his views about hysteria. He drew and wrote upon a blackboard (I could see the latent artist there), so that already we had the visual as well as the verbal.

But this was nothing compared to the theatre that was about to follow. First we had the "supporting artist". This was a young man whom Charcot introduced to us by giving a history of his hysteria, how and why he had come to the hospital and the current manifestations of his illness, though given the man's very normal appearance, these were at the time in abeyance. He was then taken out by Charcot's assistant, hypnotised (I was rather sorry that this happened outside and we were not able to see how such a thing is done) and then returned to the stage, to be commanded into all kind of weird physical contortions—the manifestations of hysteria—by the Professor, now no longer just the ring master, but the magician as well.

Eventually the demonstration was completed; it seemed to me that the man's exposure and indignity could be no further accessed, and he was released back to the wards to be calmed down.

The audience was undoubtedly impressed and I had managed some quick drawings, a couple of which I am still quite happy with, though I had a somewhat irritating and vocal critic of the arts peering over my shoulder and loudly comparing my version with the actual scene. Indeed I took the trouble to exchange my seat for an inferior one, but one that at least precluded my artistic advisor. It was whilst I was rather clumsily and noisily making the transition, that the next patient entered. I was just gathering myself together and finding a fresh page of my drawing book, when I heard the room go quiet and indeed sensed a considerable difference in the atmosphere. All very sudden of course and I looked up to see that Charcot's next patient was already in the room and was standing next to him, very close to him, he with his hand upon her arm in a rather fatherly, gentle, but perhaps possessive way. Seeing the response from the cognoscenti in the audience I understood at once that this was the star of the afternoon's performance. Then it was the girl's eyes that I noticed, and I think now that it was because of their vagueness. No, wrong word—their absence is a better word. Indeed a whole absence of something in the person, which yet brought me more profoundly to have a sense of her presence in the room. The eyes just looked through and past the audience, and my goodness Marcel, on to God knows where, maybe through to those mountains, forests and oceans that our romantic hero Friedrich has so often painted for us. Or maybe to where I am, where my art lives now, in the opposite direction, inwards to the very core. Wherever she was looking, whether it was into the distance or into a strange place deep within herself, it was indeed far removed from the room in which she stood before us.

Everything in this new demonstration was in reverse to the previous one. On the occasion of the male patient, we had been shown first of all a state of mind that was relatively normal. The man, at that particular time, was in no great state of suffering. It was after the hypnotic state had been induced that Charcot demonstrated to us, through his suggestions to the patient, the strange physical symptoms that the poor individual so often endures as part of his illness.

The young woman, now present before us, had already been mesmerised and was full of her hysterical symptoms. She stood, barefooted and in a plain smock, indifferent, quite removed from life as we know it. Then the Professor, the magician, proceeded to lead her through a repertoire of the most bizarre physical symptoms, like some slow, grotesque, metaphysical dance which culminated with him placing her upon a couch and inducing her to perform what I gather is called an "arc de cercle"; her whole body arched back so that her head literally touched her heels. For some reason, I suddenly thought of the execution that I was telling you about.

She too was led out of the lecture room and Charcot, having watched his assistant help and conduct her from the room, turned to us and now with a learned professorial manner, gave us a raft of theoretical details whilst the assembled crowd generally coughed, sneezed, shuffled their feet, and adjusted themselves to a relative state of normality.

And then the patient returned, but whilst away from our view, within another room of the hospital and under the auspices of Charcot's doctors, she had now been hypnotised *out* of her symptoms. The Professor greeted her warmly, again with an affectionate, protective, and to my mind even a rather proud demeanour. The girl was quite different now, and I saw her differently. There was no more drawing to do. I just looked at her and it was as if her double, her healthy twin had come in and they had left the mad girl back in her cell. The eyes now were completely aware of their surroundings but, and who can blame her, they were filled with astonishment and fear. Despite the Professor's voice softening as he spoke to the audience, a change which was surely made in deference to his patient's state, she stayed shocked. I watched her now in a different way, seeing a human being like the rest of us. I saw her human form, no longer a kind of wraith, but a slender and quite beautiful young woman, probably in her mid-twenties, long, soft brown hair, pale of complexion, and with distinctly grey eyes which now darted around, apprehending her surroundings and without that faraway gaze that before had protected her. And all of a sudden I saw a colour come into her cheeks. She blushed.

I am reminded of a painting. You may know it as engravings of it have been circulating. It has become a rather popular image. It is Gérôme's painting of Phryme. Do you remember it and its story? I will describe it anyway just in case. Phryme was the courtesan in Ancient Greece who utterly upset the status quo by being naive enough, though one also imagines enjoyably aware enough of her own beauty, to bathe naked in a place that was visible to a great gathering of pilgrims. They had gathered together for a religious festival that aspired to pay homage to the gods, particularly to the goddess of love and beauty, Aphrodite. Well this bathing was considered to be an affront to Aphrodite herself, as surely only Aphrodite could be thought of as the great beauty during her own festival. You know that these classical deities could be as jealous as children. So, for this great indiscretion Phryme was tried before a large tribunal of judges. Her advocate at the trial, a former lover I believe, decided on a rather unusual and risky mode of conducting her defence. Presenting her before the assembled judges (and remember our dear Professor now), he in a sudden act disrobed her, leaving her standing naked before the tribunal. So astounded were they by her beauty, that they ruled her innocent. What Aphrodite had to say about this is probably another story.

So to Gérôme's painting of this. It is a very horizontal picture, taking in the wide breadth of the tribunal chamber. To the far left stands Phryme's advocate and just to his right is Phryme. They both stand on a raised area of grey stone flooring, like a small stage that protrudes outwards amongst the gathered tribunal who spread themselves to the right and throughout the rest of the plain of the picture. This gathering of men, young and old, all sitting dressed in their red robes, stare and gasp and some raise their hands up in wonderment at this moment when the advocate, with a great fluent gesture, pulls away the large blue garment that has covered her. And this is what Gérôme does to the scene—in this moment of nakedness the girl feels such

21

shame at her exposure that with her hand and arms she hides, not her body but her face and her eyes. This of course leaves the full length of her body for all to see. Shame or the wish to expose? I have no doubt that the artist in so well describing the shame was also providing the exposure.

So this was what came to my mind very soon after the demonstration by the Professor. As I walked home I thought of his young patient's blush, and the painting of Phryme came straight into my thoughts.

So, dear Marcel, I come back to a place near the beginning of this rather long account I have sent you. Yes, I am most interested in the juxtapositions between people. And here in this story that I have just told you, to my own mind, the juxtaposition is about power.

I will be thinking more about this. Enough for now though. My next letter will be written to you—well, probably soon. I have to finish Charcot's summer house. Write back to me my friend and tell me what you think about all this. And enjoy your countryside.

Your friend, affectionately,
Louis

And I will dare to add a little extra, though I know, Marcel, how you will tease me. I was filled too with the conviction, accompanied by an increasingly warm glow, that Charcot's girl, just as she turned to exit, had met my own gaze with one of her own and for a wondrous moment we had remained just so, as in a strange and enticing recognition.

You will of course say that I am already asleep and dreaming!

L.

CHAPTER FOUR

From a student at the Salpêtrière

Letter to:
Madame Cécile Lamond, Amiens, Somme département, France

From:
Jacques Lamond, rue du Clos de Ganay, Paris, France

Dated 13th November 1885

My dear Mamma,

I have just returned from an experience of such excitement and here I am with no company other than a bottle of cognac to share it with. I know that you will understand my wish to describe my feelings and if I was at home with you and Amelie and Josephine we could talk happily of such things through-out the evening. Such good conversation I miss greatly, and yes, here in Paris I do have lonely times. But I can still write, and though in truth it will be some days before you read and know my thoughts, I can in the writing still imagine that I am conversing with the family that I miss so much.

I realise now how much I love to be inspired. I didn't know, but as I look back through my life, I see that such inspiration has at times happened before and that I have been lifted in its powerful grasp and even placed ahead of myself, though never have I felt it so much as today. Now I must catch up with myself; something that I believe may take some time, though I savour its prospect and wonder at its outcome. I start, dear Mamma, by writing to you now, by opening the conversation in this letter, which is of course also to my dear sisters whose brightness and laughter is so absent in these gloomy lodgings, and in doing this I can also begin the process of transforming the excitement of inspiration into learning and new understanding. As you know, it is most important for me that such understanding should be sound and should survive honest enquiry. I am after all a young scientist and a student of neurology, and if our theories are celebrated as discoveries and are yet, in reality, mere conjectures, then we are nothing other than the cohorts of the emperor with no clothes. Pride can energise us in our research, but should never be allowed to distort the outcome. So, in our work we measure, we try to weigh the evidence, we do this with great care; our aim is to show proof. I have today been "shown proof", though in a way that I had never expected. The laboratory played no part in this and no instruments of scientific enquiry were involved. These I would previously have assumed to be indispensable, but it is in the essence of these new revelations that the proof is, so to speak, in the pudding. I refer here to the expositions of my learned teacher the Professor Charcot who is now demonstrating, on a regular basis, and on occasions to the most eclectic of audiences, that when we are studying the aberrations and disorders of the human brain, we must encounter and include phenomena that are beyond traditional chemical and neurological analysis. I have seen an aspect of science today that convinces me that we can no longer be solely searching for our answers on the dissecting table; that to delve into the mysteries of the human mind may require a completely new means of observation, and that observation itself will supply the tools that we need.

24

I was already full of gratitude for my stay here in Paris. I am fortunate I know, to have a position in this massive institution, a hospital and a home for women, some neurologically ill and many insane. It is probably one of the greatest collections of madness in our civilised world. I feel like a diver in a deep sea who suddenly is swimming amongst the most bizarre, grotesquely fascinating finned creatures. There can be beauty in this too; perhaps there are even mermaids in the Salpêtrière! It is a new thought—strange creatures cut off from their true element. After today there is nothing that strikes me as too strange.

Each day, as you know, we learn more here; from the lectures, the ward rounds, from the lively discussions between students and doctors, and I have now been allowed no fewer than five times to act as a practitioner myself, interviewing and as well as I could, trying my hand as a diagnostician, maybe even providing some help to the patient! Three patients I have seen and two of them I have interviewed twice. These poor souls, I am sure, suffer greatly, though in some ways they would try to tell one otherwise. How closely and cleverly the mad will protect their madness. If one believes oneself to be communing with God and his angels, it may seem madness itself to allow a doctor to force a descent to the grey superficialities of a mundane life! Of course, some of the inmates are not communing with angels, but fleeing in terror from the devils that pursue them; worse, much worse, the devil that inexorably exists within them. Such is madness, to be trapped within the wildest creations of one's own mind with catatonia the only place of escape. There are some who might say that "the devil" with his vile persecuting hoard was there inside to begin with, a universal inheritance for humanity, but one harsher and more malevolently crushing for these tormented few. The superstitious believe that evil gets inside, forces its way in. They call it "possession". The devil invades the soul of a poor victim—a sinner is a suitable candidate, or maybe someone who has been cursed. They then become his evil thing. He gloats at the acquisition of a human soul, his triumph in this, his theft from Christ. Then what happens? There has to be an exorcism and a certain priest, an expert in the field, will perform this. An epic battle with the demonic powers takes place and as to its result, who can be sure? Only the years will truly tell, and surely once devilry has been there and left its dreaded calling card a further visit will come.

But I err. I find myself given to expression that is non-scientific and I am not to be numbered amongst the superstitious; and indeed yes Mamma, to your constant and loving regret, not even inclined towards religion. The devil can reside inside the human soul, but to me only as a metaphor, a symbol of torment and this because, and only because, that soul is filled with anguish. What goes on in our minds? We know so little. We plod on with our data and our microscopic lenses, scanning the dissected brain, tracing through the myriad strands of the nervous system. To study the human mind is like looking out and up to the night sky on the clearest of nights, away from the city, and marvelling at the multitude of stars and where they are and how they may be in relation to each other, and just how many more there may be because we have no idea of the extent of the universe, and for all we know it could even go on forever! So much is beyond us and out of sight. This I feel too when we search into and probe the physical human brain. There is so much to just wonder at. And my experience today has of course confirmed the wonder.

Now I wonder about the imagination. It is something that is assuredly to do with our minds and our brains, but how on earth can we physically locate and measure that? Yet don't we somehow need to find a way, since clearly, if one is not a Christian exorcist at war with actual demons, the devil inside our mad, tormented patients can only be a product of the imagination. I am left reaching towards a troubled, yet growing idea that there can be such accumulation of anguish from

26

the experiences of a human life, such a historical sequence of pained misfortune, that all such recollections must be thrust to the very back of the mind, into its dark and dusty vaults—they are too terrible to remember—they would blind with pain. It is like storing and hiding away letters of rejection from loved ones who have left us; we cannot destroy them, but nor can we bear to read them. Or, for some, the photo of a loved one lost brings too much pain in a world of living creatures that can be seen, touched and savoured. Lock the photo away! This I think is what happens to our patients. But anything resigned to the archives must be filed, buried away in its own dark cellar, and the cellar door marked with a name. We try to have a name for everything. For argument, file it under "the devil", or place it in the "museum of madness". It is our work and research here at the hospital to shine a scientific light into these dark and forbidding places. They seem as if they exist within another world, unlike ours, and it is this that needs our intrepid exploration!

Now there are those, and I have seen this, who can move between worlds. At times they are lucid, quite sane and in the light, but at other times completely strange, lost in the darkness. It is my fascination to observe these two worlds and to wonder where they may meet and interact. My own nearest experience is when I am falling asleep and can actually feel with some conscious part of my mind, still just remaining, that yes, I am also having a dream. Or when I awake from a dream and gradually shake off a delightful imaginary world, still just there, or sometimes wrestle with the clinging tangle of a nightmare that will not depart.

We have much to learn and much to wonder about. Today I saw the two worlds and a transport between them which seemed as sudden and complete as the opening and shutting of a door.

It is Friday today and you know that this is the day that our renowned Professor makes his spectacular appearance to the intelligentsia of Paris. My word—of Paris I say! Not at all. There were clearly visitors from all over Europe and I have no doubt, judging from the deference that was paid to some who were present from those sitting near to them, that we had amongst us dignitaries of a high order. One could tell from the clothes too and the general bearing. I have to admit that I felt rather shabby and overawed by the assembled presence. I wish Mamma that dear Papa was still with us and could have accompanied me as one of those guests; I know that I would have drawn confidence from that look of dignity that always graced his presence. However there were some there whom I knew, students from abroad, studying with the Professor like myself, and I stayed close to such a one, a young neurologist from Vienna whom I have already come to rather like, though I know him barely as yet.

The event is held in the major lecture room of the hospital. The room is large enough for four hundred people, but it felt as if we had at least half a thousand inside. This of course added to the excited feelings of expectation. There was much animated conversation, a general untidy jostling for the best seats and loud voices grandly hailing each other across the amphitheatre. Gradually the assembly settled as the time came for the "master" to emerge. Shabby and rather inconsequential as I felt, my new friend and I did nevertheless have a seat; we had come early enough for that, whereas two or three dignified fellows were compelled to stand at the back and one of them for sure was looking most agitated to be in such a position, the status of it, I suspect, as much as any physical discomfort. Anyway, all such considerations soon became insignificant. Powerfully, at the head of his entourage, his special assistants and staff of the Salpêtrière, our Professor made his entrance.

Professor Charcot is a man whose presence immediately demands the attention of the whole room. Indeed all rise when he enters. My belief is that he is one of those who immediately is at home in such a setting. The whole hospital is of course his domain and here in this principal lecture theatre on a Friday afternoon he holds court to visiting academics and also to the well-informed public. He realises there are many who come purposely to be impressed. He knows too that there are those who are present as inquisitors of scientific heresy and they will correspond vindictively and publish their criticisms and for some, their outrage. But on a Friday afternoon they must just watch and listen and whatever their immediate professional and scientific objections to the drama, or their doubts later when the thrill has worn away, they at least surely feel that they are observing something they have rarely seen before.

I think I should say a few words now that may be necessary. You have known me to refer to a certain term on several occasions, and the degree to which you have required any special knowledge as to its fuller meaning has been small. It has, Mamma, just been a vaguely descriptive word between us. However, I find increasingly that the term can evoke such strong and contradictory emotional reactions that I have come to be concerned that mentioning it is equivalent to tossing someone a hot coal. The instinctive response to such an object so delivered is to catch it and then of course violently fling it away. If found to be not quite so burningly dangerous there are some who might quickly pass it between their hands as it cools. But the heat felt from this particular smouldering object is entirely dependent on the mind and thoughtfulness of its recipient. And so to others, it may be purely an object of interest to be held up and examined with no ill effect. I am already reminded, as I write this, of a certain category of Indian holy man, popularly known as a "fakir", who proves the resilience of his mind over the bare matter of his body by grossly testing his ability to ignore, indeed to be immune from, pain. One such test of this is to be exposed to terrible physical danger by walking on burning hot coals. They can do this and remain after their enterprise completely unscathed, without the slightest physical damage. There are also tribal people from Africa

29

and from other exotic countries in which similar feats of endurance and immunity are ceremoniously celebrated as part of their culture. To we feeble, city-dwelling Europeans it is all amazing, like magic or superhuman powers. In fact the ancient texts of the Hindus often refer to those who are superhuman. They are mentioned as a matter of course and the yogic traditions still practiced in India today have as their central tenet the cultivation of a remarkable ascendancy over the mortal coil. Yet to the yogi it is simply a matter of training and an aspect of their science, the living proof that the mind can be controlled and trained to focus itself so intently that the material physical body becomes an irrelevance. In fact, to the advanced yogi the public exhibition of such powers by the fakir is an unnecessary vulgar sideshow. There are always those of course, who need to perform.

But I hold you overlong in anticipation of the explanation that I promised. The method of the yogi is founded upon the power that comes from the concentration of the mind and to such an extent that a single point of thought is fixed upon, and all else, all extraneous and mundane thought, all sensations and emotions, disappear, just as the sun and a fresh breeze will gently disperse the mist hovering over a lake in the pale early hours of a dawn.

Some would call this state self-hypnosis, and so, now, I have managed to arrive at the word. It is "hypnosis", and a fascinating hot coal indeed. Burning and dangerous to many because they fear it as a terrible manipulation, or worse, an evil art conducted through magical powers; the mesmerist is like the sorcerer. It is the horrific fate of being controlled by another, of being possessed by their will. This is of course a universal fear. It is true that the subject of a hypnotic trance has for a time given up the control of his mind to another, but some fear that this state of acute disempowerment will continue on and that they will forever be subject to the commands of their hypnotist. Just now we are hearing much of this. There have been stories in the newspapers about appalling criminal events in Paris and the perpetrators, when apprehended, have claimed in their defence that they had been induced into a hypnotic trance and were carrying out the commands of an evil manipulator. Indeed, very recently there was a public execution (how barbarous our society can still be!) of a sadistic murderer who did not deny his responsibility for physically carrying out the act, but declared himself to be absolutely innocent of any intent as he had been placed in a hypnotic trance during a satanic ritual. I am doubtful, but as the physician of the mind that I wish to be, I keep an open mind.

The power of suggestion is enormous and it undoubtedly can be a component in the hysterical states that affect so many of the patients here at the hospital. Let me give you an example. This is a gruesome but true story told to us in one of our lectures to illustrate the hysterical transmission of an idea within a gathering of people. Of course if those people happen to be a collection of certified hysterical women living together in a crowded hospital this can happen with the speed and thoroughness of a forest fire. But first I must set the scene. I believe you will know that there have been events of infamy, and periods of tragic cruelty during the long history of the Salpêtrière. At first the building was a gunpowder factory. From the 1650s it was given over to the incarceration of Parisian flotsam and jetsam that offended the refined tastes of the higher establishment and ruined the omniscient aesthetic of the culture of Louis the "Sun King". Louis himself signed the Royal edict. All beggars, vagrants, mad people, and par excellence prostitutes were rounded up and placed in confinement there. True, some of these were criminals but many, in your estimation and in mine, would be seen as unfortunate innocents, destitute through no real fault of their own. Very bad things happened. The insane suffered particularly and were treated as such worthless creatures that, for the convenience of any so-called physicians and their staff, they were left chained to the walls. It is reported that the screams of these inmates as they were bitten by rats could be heard by those unfortunate enough to be walking past the building. I pause Mamma, because I know that I have already gone too far here. Indeed I am myself shocked that I have written such words to you. Should I tear up this letter and begin again? You are a woman of such fine sensibility and I know that you will quake to think of such cruelties enacted between human beings. But I know too your strength and that you understand that it is the remnants of these persecutions that I so much wish to confront and do battle with as a physician. I will continue, though please forgive me as I fear that there is worse to come.

We have at the hospital, the Chapelle Saint-Louis de la Salpêtrière. More than a chapel, it is the size of a church, much the size of our Sainte Jeanne d'Arc where as a family we attended, much to yours and Papa's insistence! You know too well that I am no longer one of those who would make regular attendance to such a place of Christian worship, but I believe that here at the Salpêtrière the church does have its value. It offers moments of peace to our patients and to some of our staff and provides that reassurance of certainty that is so enviably utilised by those who actually believe. Of course, as science blows away these sticky Christian cobwebs, "the flock" are to my mind an increasingly diminishing number, yet at the hospital the Sunday services are well attended and the most raucous singing can be heard without as one passes by. Surely this must be a help to those whose existence is reduced within the wards of a heavily-walled institution. They also benefit from the exhortations of one who, for a change, is not a medical practitioner. This will of course be severely couched within biblical references, but I believe that the resident priest, Father Pierre Lambert, is a good man at heart, though he is unnervingly intense about religious matters and quite strangely obsessed with the history of the chapel and of the hospital.

It was Lambert's pre-occupation with such matters that caused him to make what turned out to be a gross error, and one that I believe any competent doctor could have warned him against. Being the very beginning of September it was the occasion of an anniversary in the troubled history of the institution; an event that happened at the Salpêtrière but, to our everlasting shame, one of many that were occurring in Paris during that terrible late Summer of 1792. It had happened almost a hundred years previously, but clearly in the turbulent thinking of Father Lambert, as good as yesterday.

He was conducting a service at the Chapel at its usual Sunday time. He had in his mind the September Massacres, and especially the one perpetrated right here at the hospital, the night of September 3rd and the following day of that year, and he could not help himself but make the terrors of that awful time the subject of his sermon. I think you know the background history to this, Mamma. It was three years on from the beginning of the Revolution and the Prussians were threatening to invade France and to overturn the Assembly and the Paris Commune and restore what remained of the monarchy. All of this became the subject of mass anxiety and in the streets the stories of impending doom became increasingly virulent as they spread from one mindless individual to another. The response of the mob was to commence a killing spree against all who might be considered counter to the revolution. Rudimentary courts were set up which were utterly ramshackle and were little more than meagre tokens. On September 2nd a large number of priests were murdered and prisons were stormed in order for the mob to lay their bloody hands on those deemed a threat to the movement. Easy pickings indeed. The next day the Princesse de Lamballe, a close friend of the royal family who had been imprisoned, was sadistically murdered and her head paraded on a pike, a grim pointer to what was soon to follow for the aristocrats. And then the same night an alcohol-sodden crowd from the nearby area of Faubourg Saint-Marcel marched on the Salpêtrière. Some thought their initial purpose was to free from imprisonment the many women of the street who had been removed there. A number of them were freed, but there were others in the mob who strangely held that in amongst the Salpêtrière prisoners were those who were a threat to the Revolution and to France. The next day they held mock trials and killed over thirty of them. But of course the Salpêtrière was an institution that housed all types whose presence offended the dilettanti wealthy Parisian aesthetic, and this included the insane. According to Father Lambert, on the previous night these self-appointed guardians of the revolution with their pikes and clubs, first dragged four of the mad women outside, their chains of captivity still attached, and slaughtered them. Why? How could such a thing happen? Deep in the recesses of the human mind, in those places in which the most primitive instincts reside, there can be terrible savagery against the strange and abnormal. Such effects have the mad upon the populace. The unpredictability of their bizarre behaviour, their distress that so obviously cannot be calmed by mere words, the weird manifestations of their imaginations, all these cause the "sane" men to at best shun them, and at the very worst to carry out the actions that ensued on this night in 1792. For these poor victims an agonising end to lives filled with agony.

It was agony too for Father Lambert: an event from the previous century, but one that occurred right in his own parish and just yards away from the doors of his church. I can only imagine that to this profoundly righteous man the massacre of the Salpêtrière was absolute evil made manifest, and as he had inherited the Chapel of Saint Louis he had also inherited the sins of those who, within its precinct, had carried out the heinous crimes. He therefore made it the subject of one of his sermons and in so doing offered to the substantial number of hysterical patients who were in his congregation, that element of suggestion that can lead to the utmost panic.

34

Later that night, the nurses reported that there was a noticeable atmosphere of unease in the wards. They felt that this was growing worse. Some of the women were so restless that they had to be constrained in their beds. One even tried to flee screaming from the main building and was forcibly brought back by the nurses and locked into a single room of confinement where she could do no harm to herself and could no longer contribute to what was by now a distinctly escalating situation. A physician was called. This luckless person, who by his very presence and status was meant to bring calm, came too late. The general hysteria had advanced to a level that was beyond his capacity as a doctor and as a man. In one of the wards there was a particularly chronic patient, I will call her Marthe, a woman of middle age whose unpredictable and sometimes violent actions had, on several occasions over the years, marked her out as a potential danger to both the staff and her fellow patients. She had though developed a particularly warm affection for another patient, a very quiet young girl who shared her ward. Marthe, in her strange and deeply disturbed state, a state we must assume much heightened earlier in the day by Father Lambert's sermon, was convinced that her young friend was in danger. The misfortune for the attending physician, who by now was visiting all the wards in his attempt to induce a degree of calm, was that Marthe experienced the absolute spontaneous conviction that it was he who was the danger and that he had come to kill her young friend. Using her bed as a spring board she leaped at him, biting, hitting, and tearing at his flesh with her fingernails. Two more of the patients joined in whilst the others wailed piteously or screamed out their fear and excitement. The nurses rushed in and were just in time to save the physician from death. He had an eye almost gouged out and an enormous clump of hair torn out at the roots. The sheer physical power of several nurses eventually restored a vestige of calm. Marthe was of course placed in confinement and has for evermore been severely restricted. Interestingly her young friend, whom in her deluded state she was protecting, looked on at all this with a somewhat disconcerting quietude.

Such is the power of suggestion. All this came from the priest's sermon as he recounted to his flock, in far too much detail, the events at the Salpêtrière almost a hundred years before. In fact I give you two examples of such collective hysteria because it is also in those events of 1792 that we see the same transmission of an idea and an emotion spreading through a crowd as the wind will bend each and every reed as it sweeps along a river. There were evil men there that night, but there were also the others who joined in and who must, throughout their remaining lives, have rued that day.

It is this same power of suggestion that we see in hypnosis and it was so fascinatingly demonstrated today in the lecture by the Professor. He used two subjects, a man and a woman. The man, a fairly recent admission to the men's section of the hospital, had been enjoying in the preceding days a relatively symptom-free period. Through hypnosis Charcot brought about the re-occurrence of the man's previous physical hysterical symptoms, and quite possibly one or two extras to boot. He was led away to be relieved of these (so I am assured) by two of the Professor's colleagues waiting in the wings. The second subject, a young woman, had been placed in a hypnotic trance that intensified the symptoms of her own hysterical afflictions, and which allowed Charcot to floridly demonstrate these to the audience. As well as her looking completely dazed and vacant of thought, they included a paralysis of one side of her body with anaesthesia in one arm and then a remarkable "arc de cercle" from head to toe. It ended with her collapsing into the arms of an assistant in a complete faint. The girl was then carried from the amphitheatre and the Professor commenced a long and most fascinating review of the history of her illness.

It was a remarkable moment when on finishing his theoretical exposition he dramatically walked to the side of the platform to welcome back his subject who now returned in a completely different state. Whilst he had been addressing the audience his assistants, still utilising the hypnotic trance, had now *relieved* her of her symptoms. He spoke quietly in to the girl's ear and led her to the front of the stage. It was as if she had woken from a long and troubled sleep. She looked dazed but completely well.

Mamma, my excitement at this is that we had seen firstly the physical manifestations of hysteria induced in a patient who was in a relatively healthy state and then, with the girl who was clearly acutely suffering from such symptoms, those symptoms completely relieved. Such relief will only be temporary, but it has been brought about by hypnosis. What does this mean? It means that hysteria cannot be just a physical disease. How can it be caused by abnormality of the brain, or damage to the neural system, if its very symptoms can be either brought about or relieved by suggestion, indeed from a personal interaction between the doctor and his patient? So the roots of hysteria are surely found, not in the body or the physical brain, but in the mind with its memories and imagination.

I will quite soon have an opportunity to discuss these great advances with the Professor himself. I cannot wait! Sadly the new friend that I mentioned, a man called Freud, will be travelling home to Vienna in the new year, but I know that he too was greatly impressed and I hope that we will correspond. By the way, an interesting thing, I am told that the girl in the demonstration is the very same patient whom the ferocious Marthe was trying to defend. There is something rather appealing and different about her.

Dear Mamma, I have now shared with you my news. It was not my intention when I began this letter, but I know that I have written of some things that are almost too awful to contemplate. I trust that their effect is lessened by your knowledge that I am devoted to that spirit of enquiry that will surely in time shine light and I hope, give remedy to such dark areas of the human spirit. The candle flickers; it is, I think, time for bed.

I miss you.

Your loving son,
Jacques

CHAPTER FIVE

Dinner at Charcot's

Letter to:
Marcel Dupont, Marmande, Lot-et-Garonne département, SW France

From:
Louis Martens, rue Lamarck, Paris, France

Dated 20th April 1886

My dear Marcel,

I have sneered at the bourgeoisie haven't I? Yes, I have even written an article or two. I have proclaimed my views out loud and have argued them, admittedly to others who hold the same, at our favourite cafés. Though I have sold my art to my bourgeois customers, I have merely deigned to do so. And I insist that nothing changes, our art must challenge superficial realities, must confront the bourgeoisie with the dreams that they wilfully cast aside and forget as they wake to each new dreary day. These principles I hold to, but why should I not lapse occasionally? Should I become as fixed in my ideas as those whom I criticise? Of course not, and this anyway is an exceptional exception! I refer to my invitation to dinner at Charcot's.

My dear employer must like an element of difference now and again; someone dissimilar to his usual house guests. Not that his usual guests would be necessarily uninteresting. He entertains great scientific minds, aristocrats, political figures of our day, but I think rarely an impecunious young Belgian artist, with paint in his hair and under his fingernails, and without a smart jacket to his name (I was lent one for the occasion by the butler). I have my theories of course. Charcot is himself an artist, but only when taking a break from being the leader of the Salpêtrière and the grandest Professor of Neurology. Perhaps sometimes he longs to just dabble in paint.

For me it was a very different arrival that evening than for the other guests, all of whom were to arrive by carriage. I was already ensconced at the rear of the house where I had spent the day working on my mural (a good day's work on this occasion and now perhaps nearing completion). The doorbell rang first at around seven o'clock and after hearing it for the second time I thought that I would feel safe enough to start mingling with the other guests. The funny thing was that though I dreaded appearing early and also feared arriving late, I found it difficult to lay down my brushes and put my painting out of mind.

True, that day the work had flowed well and I certainly would have been happy to continue even in an artificial light, but I think that really it was nerves that held me back. Charcot has been kind to me, but he is my current employer and I always feel a little nervous with him anyway—the dark piercing eyes perhaps. But also I had heard from dear Agnès, the maid, as she swept around and indeed over my feet with her broom, that there would be a count and even an Indian prince there. So I had to be up to scratch and ready not to make a fool of myself—said she to me! Unfortunately I agreed and yes I did feel nervous and therefore tried to concentrate very hard on it being a bourgeois occasion and therefore only worthy of my tolerance, though now I had heard about the Count and the Prince it was feeling less easy to designate in that way.

40

Nevertheless, when the doorbell rang once more, I knew that it was time to move and confront my anxiety. As promised, a suitable jacket and necktie had been laid out for me in the housekeeper's little parlour area and dear Agnès had also found me a carnation for my buttonhole. I think she likes me—I wonder whether she might pose? She does have a certain willingness about her as well as a full and enticing shape. As I think about it now, perhaps she is waiting to be asked?

I tried the jacket on; a little tight under the arms, but it would suffice. It buttoned up just fine until the last button, which was missing. And the buttonhole, to be worn at an evening dinner? Fine for an artist. I placed it in and had a reassuring thought about the possibilities with Agnès.

The Charcot residence is massive, and I have not seen that much of it, but I knew the way well enough from my workstation at the rear, through to the front vestibule with its main entrance. But unfortunately I had not thought through the movements that would be required on arriving there. I had to be announced, decorum would not allow otherwise, and as they were occupied within there was no butler or maid waiting by the door. It felt ridiculous for me to open the front door from the inside, step outside, close it and then ring the bell for entrance. So I stood there in something of a state of paralysis (I suppose in a way, Charcot induced!) and just watched the hands of the big old grandfather clock reproach me with the fact that I was now three minutes late and, in my frozen state, getting later. Deep inside the house I could hear sounds of formal greetings and the clinking of glass upon bottle. One loud guffaw of laughter came through which increased my misery no end, but then I was suddenly expelled from emotional torpor by a shock of electrifying intensity as the vestibule bell rang out, louder from my present proximity than I would have thought possible. This did now bring the presence of the butler and as he strode past me towards the front door he gave me not the slightest encouragement. He gripped the door handles, and standing slightly to one side as he carried out the action, drew the doors towards him open wide, so that the door step and its incumbent were exposed to grand view.

It was in fact the ornate carriage that I saw first, a beautiful, shining black affair with a team of four dark horses, plus a driver and footman who paused for the safe entrance of their master before departing. He, who was indeed their lord and master, then came into focus, immaculately dressed of course with white satin waistcoat and a pristine top hat that seemed to glow as splendidly as his carriage and horses.

He was medium height and thick set, with hair as black as the brim of the hat under which it curled. His beard and moustache mingled together in an exuberance of rich rococo growth upon a colour and complexion of skin that could only belong to a native of Asia. He looked immensely comfortable in his own substantial frame and his "good evening", notwithstanding a marked foreign accent, resonated easily from within his chest. Clearly no identification was needed, or more to the point, was seen as appropriate. He gave me a brief look, raised his heavy eyebrows, and I do believe that there was a sparkle of humour in his eyes.

And so he and I together, almost side by side, were ushered through the long corridor to the main reception room where we were loudly announced to the assembled guests:

"His Highness Maharaja Jaswant Singh, the Maharaja of Jodhpur, and Monsieur Louis Martens, resident artist."

Since there were large double doors to the reception room I was able to make my grand entrance almost abreast of the aforementioned prince. Did I hold back a little? Well Marcel, you will know me as someone who embraces the unusual, welcomes the bizarre, favours the unexpected; qualities which also reign supreme in my art. I will push myself forward in these situations, but just here, on this evening, I again felt a certain inhibition. So, as we crossed the threshold, I duly allowed the Maharaja a few inches lead.

42

Of course one cannot help but instantaneously make an assessment of the waiting group's reaction to one's arrival. It happens in a flash: the reading of the eyes, the calculation of the direction of the looks; to the Maharaja, to me, to the butler. Inside the room was a gathering of seven people, including the Professor and Madame Charcot.

There was a middle-aged couple holding glasses and standing close to the Charcots, with whom they had clearly been in conversation. The man had spectacles, a light-coloured beard, a large sculptured moustache, and was almost bald. There was the suggestion of past adolescent acne upon his cheeks and his expression was bland, difficult to assess. His female companion was tall and slim with dark hair that curled around an attractive face. She had that enticing but perplexing physicality that leaves one unsure as to whether one beholds a body that is attuned to its sensuality or, quite to the contrary, is unconscious, even fearful of it.

Two of the guests were seated. One of these was elderly, a stout man with huge grey beard and wearing pince-nez upon a large and rather bulbous nose. Next to him sat a lady whom I assumed, though she was younger, to be his wife. The man's walking stick with ornate silver handle, rested against the sofa's arm. I found myself thinking of all the unsuccessful portraits one sees of successful men. They are passed by in a moment and without reflection. As an artist it rankles. Could I paint his wife though? Yes, indeed I could. I was immediately interested in her aesthetically. Quite large, she would have made a superb nude subject for Rubens. (The female subjects favoured by my associates in Paris do tend to be rather thin don't they? Here I find myself ruing the fact and even for a moment thinking of paying a visit to the other side, to Auguste Renoir—what a haven of lovely flesh and gorgeous artefacts his studio must be. I suppose in our group we do have Fantin-Latour placing his most sensually-proportioned ladies in his magnificent Wagnerian works, so maybe there is some hope, but this only, alas, when he is not painting flowers!) But I digress—the facial features of the lady were also striking. The nose was strong but not overly prominent; her mouth was large with the bottom lip full and the top lip curling up towards the centre. Her skin was pale as was the blue of her eyes and, in contrast to the pronounced mature sensuality of her features, there was the hint of freckles above her nose. A chandelier that hung near to her gave her light brown hair a distinct golden lustre.

The remaining figure was the first to approach us—I say "us"—you see the Indian Prince and I had already become a couple! A tall, thin, earnest-looking man in his thirties, who unsmilingly, but with a degree of care I think, ushered us further into the room and then gestured to a table on which were glasses of wine and offered to pour. Clearly he was a guest, but it would seem at the same time he assumed a certain role of service.

Charcot and his wife were centre stage. Charcot, the only clean-shaven man in the room, was looking very handsome; perhaps not as tall as the others, but he and the Maharaja shared the strongest features, and of course with those dark eyes which create such a powerful effect. The grey hair, still streaked with black, was brushed severely back above his ears to rest upon the collar of his jacket. And then, dear Madame Charcot; I have become fond of her. She is warm, she has character, and she is nice to me! She is a bustling small lady with powdered hair and is quite rotund in the most cosy of ways. I can well imagine how she has the affection and the intelligent attention to run the family and their magnificent house in such a way that the scientific personage is free in turn to manage his great hospital.

"Welcome Your Highness, and welcome Louis," said Charcot. "We are indeed honoured," and I think there was the slightest suggestion of a knowing wink as he looked warmly at me. "Let me introduce you to your fellow guests for tonight."

And first of all gesturing to the couple standing next to him, "This is Monsieur and Madame Dubois."

The bland Monsieur Dubois made a cursory bow towards the ample and relaxed presence of the Indian Prince and then offered a stiff handshake to me. Madame Dubois followed in suit with a slight curtsey to the Prince and then a hand proffered to me that I can only describe as disappointingly cold and limp, thus leaving the impression that of the two alternatives that I had earlier considered it was the latter—a body as yet unrealised, that was the case.

Next Charcot turned to the couple upon the couch.

"We are most fortunate to receive in our home once again our dear friends the Count and the Countess of Bolvoir." The Count muttered something into his huge beard and received the compliment as due course. The Countess was far more responsive, stretching her hand out to the Professor who warmly responded by leaning forward to take it and to brush it with his lips. I was struck by the elegance of the Countess in this. Whilst her arm with the proffered hand seemed to traverse some distance towards the Professor, her head, shoulders and body remained perfectly poised, still and relaxed amongst the cushions of the couch.

Lastly Charcot turned towards the tall thin man who had so earnestly attended to our drinks.

"And may I introduce you to Jacques Lamond, a member of my staff at the hospital and one who I am delighted to say has recently become a House Officer." And then turning to the Prince and I, he raised his voice as this was for the whole room,

"The Maharaja has come all the way from Rajputana in India to stay a few weeks in Paris, and Louis Martens here is a most excellent artist, indeed later this evening we may even go and see something of his work since he is decorating our garden summer house with some wonderful murals," and then with a

45

smile, "That is if you allow us to at this stage Louis, I know that it can be a sensitive thing when a work is not yet completed."

I could see that Charcot was warming up. Now, standing in its centre, with the guests all assembled, he could make the room his stage, even though the audience was a small one, and indeed it was to this point that he then referred.

"Madame Charcot and I are so pleased that you have agreed to come to such a small event as this, our simple dinner party. I hope that those of you who are more used to being here 'en masse' at our soirées will not find an evening of this kind uninteresting in comparison. The truth is that it is a pleasure for us to at times be able to speak at greater depth and in a more relaxed fashion to our guests, and of course we do consider you to be special guests."

Here, Marcel, there was a flash of the ringmaster and it took me back to that amazing display five months ago at the Salpêtrière lecture. It had been so extraordinary and I was of course hoping that something related to that subject would surface during the evening's conversation; I was certainly not to be disappointed in this wish.

The Maharaja took a seat, as did I, and it was from there that I saw a little Corot landscape upon the wall and a nice one too. More to your liking than to mine, Marcel, though what a talent—a realist but a poet nevertheless. And then quite close to it, though not at first so noticeable because of the monochrome, I espied no less than Goya's "Sleep of Reason". Well of course this was to be a great conversation piece. Marcel, I think you have heard of the series of etchings by Goya that he called "Los Caprichos". What a feat to produce eighty different images, and what a challenge he made to Spanish society—"Los Caprichos"—those caprices of his day, and his vision of them as sharp and cutting as the etching needle with which he made them and cutting enough to the power of the church, and the control of the establishment for the prints to be banned. What an appalling disgrace of censorship. And this one here on our host's wall, perhaps the best of them all, "The Sleep of Reason". I was so taken at seeing it there that I jumped from my seat and got close enough to mist its glass with my excited breath.

The centrepiece is the figure of a man, I like to think that it is Goya himself, and he has fallen asleep at his desk, so he has slumped over it, his face hidden in his arms, his long hair askew and abandoned paper and pens to his side, and then gathering all around him, with more flying towards him from the distance flapping their ghastly wings, are the creatures of his nightmare. There are owls and bats and they have horrid little beaks and sitting on the floor with squinting eyes is a sinister cat and right behind the sleeping figure, from out of the dark shadows, the silhouette of another cat or owl or bat—they all have ears! And it glares straight at us from the only brightness within its dark features, its piercing eyes.

And inscribed on the side of the desk the full title: "The Sleep of Reason Produces Monsters".

Charcot was clearly delighted to see the notice that I was taking in his acquisition.

"My dear Louis, you are looking at my etching by Goya. Very well, tell me as an artist what you think and then I, as a physician and collector will tell you what I think, and will it be possible I wonder for us to have the same view?"

"Professor," said I, not to be too automatic or dull in my response, "A physician you may be, but as I have been informed, you are also an artist, at least when time allows you to enjoy such occupation. So, with respect, I believe that you speak not just as a simple appreciator of art. I also know that it is the case that you are not just a collector of pictures, but one who is respected for the very able choices that you make. And so, given these factors, one might well expect you to own a Goya. And 'Los Caprichos' is a series that many cognoscenti are wishing to collect. Am I right in thinking that this one is from Goya's own first edition?"

"Wonderful Louis," laughed Charcot, "indeed it is. This picture gives me special pleasure for it contains the absolute essence of our work. Our poor hysterics suffer all those nightmares and delusions that the great Goya portrays with his terrifying winged creatures. For some we may say that the imagery is symbolic but for others, in their agony of fear, the visions are reality. They have lost 'their reason', but in our school of the Salpêtrière we must never succumb to any sleep of our powers of reason, our science must always be awake to the nightmares of ignorant superstition, and thus we are joined with Goya in his great cause."

Marcel, I now dared to interject in a way that to most in my position would have been unthinkable, but as you know of your friend, I cannot resist the impulse to show off!

"Though also, we know the words with which the artist himself described his theme: 'Imagination abandoned by reason produces impossible monsters; united with her, she is the mother of the arts and the source of their wonders'. So Monsieur, imagination abandoned by reason is no more a tragedy than if reason should abandon imagination."

So fast works a mind when alert to its own creation of danger. Had I usurped the Professor's position, his pleasure in the possession and knowledge of his acquisition—one that he found so meaningful? Yet surely Charcot is no cold scientist living only in the rational mind. A home crammed full of an immense variety of art, his own love of drawing, a wife who could also call herself an artist, his use of the visual in all his demonstrations, the hundreds of drawings he has used to display his theory, the theatre of his demonstrations. This is a man of the visual, a scientist and an artist as well.

"If I may further venture my view Monsieur, this etching of Goya and the sentiments that it expresses, though now some sixty years old, could indeed have been commissioned this day by the Salpêtrière to express that very union of science and artistic expression that you have developed and which makes visible to all, doctors and laymen alike, the hidden experience of hysteria, 'the great neurosis'."

And there was the sound of light clapping from the elegant white hands of the Countess. She smiled and called gently across the room,

"Monsieur Martens, we will think that such a consummately pleasing answer to our host must mean that you have been suitably hypnotised by his assistants before your entry."

All laughed merrily at this and there was some relief I think at us experiencing the leg of our esteemed and so often powerfully intense host being gently pulled.

"But we do hear rumoured that perhaps more goes on between your assistants and your hysterics, in the wings so to speak, preparing for the performance, than your audience may realise." This was from the Count who spoke in a relaxed, but gruff fashion that clearly showed the confidence of his own senior position in society.

Charcot here ceased to smile. His hands were clasped behind his back, his large head tilted forward. Those dark eyes, a moment ago sparkling with pleasure, seemed fixed upon the pattern of an oriental rug that filled the central space of the room and on which he stood. The focus was though, upon his own thoughts.

"It is true," he said, as someone who is considering and working through a problem as he speaks it. "It is true that I have assistants. One who may well soon join their ranks is with us tonight," and he gestured to the tall thin and serious Jacques Lamond. "Indeed my expectation of this and my pleasure in his work have prompted my invitation to him."

The soon-to-be-promoted young physician bent his gaunt figure slightly forward to acknowledge the compliment.

"My assistants are most loyal and trustworthy. In any scientific laboratory, and in a sense our whole hospital is such a place, there will be assistants to the principal scientist. And in any hospital, whatever its size, and our Salpêtrière is

49

enormous, there will be staff, other doctors, nurses; we even have priests!"

Here I noticed that he cast a quick glance at Madame Dubois.

"It is true that I have assistants and some of them may see far more of my patients than I. My position as Hospital Director takes up a substantial amount of my time as too, the writing of scientific books and papers. Much of our day to day clinical work is carried out by my staff, and the best of them keep me well-informed. But I know to what you refer Monsieur."

No gesture or look to the Count seemed needed here and indeed Charcot's gaze became even more directed towards the carpet and his face increasingly expressed the concentration in his thought. The hands were still clasped tightly behind his back. The head and shoulders moved a little further forward. The feet remained set firmly in the middle of the rug.

"Let me tell you something here about the hysteric. The hysteric is trying to tell us something, but the thing about that ..." he paused, "though trying is not the right word. We are normally aware of trying to do something. I may have a physical condition that causes me to have difficulty in breathing. So I will struggle to breathe; it is hard, but I certainly know that I am trying to breath. Or, perhaps more to the point, I may wish to tell you something important, but have an impairment of speech, a pathological condition affecting my voice, so I cannot tell you what I wish to. But nevertheless I will struggle to do so and I know that I am trying. The hysteric has a story that needs telling, but she, unlike my examples, cannot try to tell me the story, as she is not aware she needs to tell it in the first place! The need is there but not in consciousness. It exists in some other locked-away part of the mind.

"It is a remarkable thing and one of great fascination to me," and here Charcot's countenance changed; he looked up to share his pleasure with us, "a remarkable thing that this story that is locked away, that cannot be thought about or understood

50

by the patient, still gets told. Oh yes! In a most distorted way, and only discernible to the acutely watching eye"—the dark eyes flashed at us here—"and to the mind that wants that eye to see." The shoulders dropped a little, the whole demeanour relaxed.

"The hysteric, my friends, is a mime artist who mimes her own traumas, but realises not the dramas that she enacts. Real events from life, difficult unthinkable ones, have been converted into theatre."

Charcot's concentration was now relaxed. He was at ease in the room again and he seemed to have thought himself through to a place of increased certainty.

"Now, as I say Monsieur, I know the topic to which you refer. Some state, 'Charcot, he is only a performer and people come from far and wide just to see him perform.'" And there was a spontaneous but gracious gesture towards the Maharaja, who graciously inclined his head in acknowledgement.

"'Many of them', people say, 'come just for the entertainment, the sensation; they are not even themselves scientists or physicians. Can that Charcot even call *himself* a scientist! He gathers together hysterics and lucky assistants who will all do his bidding. The patients are first prepared in the wings so they will perform to Charcot's script. His conniving long-term patients even become familiar with the script and are only too happy to be hypnotised, or to pretend to be hypnotised and to do his bidding and manifest their weird symptoms before a mesmerized audience.'

"So my friends I am seen as the writer of the play. Well, I know something of myself. Charcot is a good lecturer!" And with a smile to the carpet, "He also hosts splendid soirées. Yes all of this I do indeed enjoy—this entertaining—otherwise it would not happen. But Charcot also works with his patients. He thinks, he tests, he spends many hours carefully observing and writing about his discoveries. And I feel affection for many of these poor creatures who inhabit our hospital, perhaps

51

indeed especially for those women whose suffering is that of the grand hysteric."

Again the posture changed to that of concentration, the eyes on the carpet, but the attention inwards.

"And I can say, yes I know with sincerity, that however much in his poor vanity Charcot may need to be a performer, such performance is irrelevant compared to that of his patients who perform, not as manipulated puppets, but as hysterics in a hospital expressing their agony in the only way they can—in the theatre of hysteria!

"Then is it such a surprise, amongst so much drama, that I as their principal physician should be pulled into the ring, included in the proceedings and accused of being the great self-serving impresario of the Salpêtrière?"

The Professor was done. Certainly to his own mind he had carried his argument to a place of unassailable resolution and it was clear that no one else present was at all minded, or critically enthused enough to attempt to undermine the intensity and surety of his retort. The Maharaja, apart from his brief nod to Charcot, had maintained an expressionless demeanour, though the black eyebrows had perhaps twitched momentarily as Charcot reached his climax. He sat firm and square onto the room without any self-consciousness, a man of royalty and, at this stage of the evening, yet to declare himself as anything less.

The Count of Bolvoir, whose remark had so initiated the oratorical defence from our host, was still seated on the large sofa, now with a hint of discomfort showing in the drumming of one finger upon the silver handle of his walking stick. The Countess, seated next to him, had a smile that played lightly upon her lips and clearly remained consummately relaxed. She would of course have known many important and self-important men, the Count being amongst the former if not the latter. He had become oblivious of his glass while she now sipped at hers.

Madame Dubois, who with her husband was still standing quite close to the Professor, seemed thoughtful and about to be the first to break the silence. It was though her husband who interjected.

"Monsieur Professeur, when people make analogies with the theatre, you are surely understandably concerned and due your defence. As a lawyer I would say that you have just exercised that admirably and at the same time you gave me insight into the behaviour and sufferings of these poor creatures and indeed presented a defence and a plea for clemency on their behalf. I thank you for it Monsieur and feel pleased and honoured to hear you speak on such matters so personally.

"It also seems to me, and I do wonder whether this may have occurred to you, that if we are considering how the expressions of the internal tribulations of mankind can manifest as theatre we should also include within this grand theatre, and indeed sometimes I would say—circus, the elaborate and ridiculous rigmaroles of the Catholic Church?"

Charcot's eyes went resolutely back to the carpet whilst the hands remained firmly clasped behind. He was of course a host, and a host must look after all his guests and hope to encompass and contain the differences of opinion that may divide them. And here there seemed to be an area that required an unaccustomed reticence.

This was emphasised by the sudden movement of Madame Dubois as she turned towards her husband and by the sharpness of her disapproving tone. "Georges, where is your respect?"

To whom the respect should be given was not clear. We all were aware I think that Charcot is much more a scientist than a man of religion, so no harm there. The Indian Prince was most unlikely to be a follower of Rome. I, a young artist, was unlikely to be a candidate for offence though she did not know me. Madame Charcot I have seen on her way to church, but am not aware that she has any special inclination. Then there was Charcot's thin student. Somehow there was not the

53

air of a churchgoer about this gentleman, earnest though he seemed. Lastly, there were the Count and the Countess and the aristocracy is of course at least historically entwined with the church. My view though was that Madame Dubois had chided her husband principally on behalf of herself and of God.

Monsieur Dubois, whom I now knew to be a lawyer, and his wife whom I now knew to be of religion, had clearly entered upon a subject that divided them not just in Charcot's drawing room but at their own home, their bedroom, and in their lives. We all sat silently in icy fascination and then I heard the clink of a ring upon a glass and the rustle of a richly-embroidered sleeve and looked and saw the Countess lift her glass to her lips and saw upon them and in her eyes a smile of amused disdain. In a deep, quiet, but very clear voice she addressed the lawyer, though I believe she was speaking more generally to the room and indeed to herself.

"Bravo Dubois, for your courage. A vacuous business is religion and needs to be turned quite on its head."

Her husband the Count shifted in his seat next to her, gruffly cleared his throat, but said nothing. I instantly imagined that if those two had their own deep disagreements it would be of little consequence since the Countess in her elegant self-assurance seemed impermeable to challenge. She also clearly had no concern for the religious sensibilities of Madame Dubois.

Madame Charcot of course intervened.

"Georges," she said to the lawyer, "you are like my dear husband; you are men for whom reason and intellect have been great assets in your success and indeed our France must be thanked for its championing of all who like yourselves bring sense and justice to our lives. But I do believe that we must spare a little room, a piece of our thinking, for those things in life of which we do not already have knowledge, indeed those things which can be so hard to readily understand." And then touching Charcot affectionately and pulling him gently by the sleeve towards one of the exits of the room, "As indeed does my husband for his hysterics."

And so with the mysteries of religion and of hysteria so closely juxtaposed we were led by the Professor and his wife out of the drawing room, across the antechamber and into the exquisite dining room where the table was perfectly laid and a servant stood quietly against the dark, richly-patterned wall waiting to serve us.

The patterns that had formed in our conversations proved not to be set. In the midst of the wonderful food and the full glasses of an excellent wine there was now a greater ease and lack of consequence to our discourse and it pleased me greatly that my opinions on art were sought and appreciated. Both the Charcots and the Countess were particularly interested and I would readily grant, showed much knowledge of their own. My dear Marcel, there is more that I wish to share with you, and there were some intriguing matters which arose later that evening for which your considered thoughts would, as always, be of great value to me. But I shall rest it there for now. The candle burns low, the night is cool and I look forward to the warmth of the blankets.

Sleep well dear friend.
Louis

CHAPTER SIX

Charcot's study

Letter to:
Marcel Dupont, Marmande, Lot-et-Garonne département, SW France

From:
Louis Martens, rue Lamarck, Paris, France

Dated 21st April 1886

So, my dear Marcel,

Last night on my return I wrote to you about the dinner at Charcot's. It was too much for my remaining energy to describe as well the events that immediately followed. Now I shall attempt to continue and to give as clear an account as I possibly can.

I was completely surprised when, having risen from my chair to join the other guests in the ritual of departure, I felt a firm hand on my shoulder and a deep voice in my ear that said,

"Do stay awhile Louis." At which I sat down again, in some confusion I must say, and watched the Charcots bid adieu to the other guests. The spindly physician, perhaps because he saw me still seated, seemed unsure whether to take his leave at that moment, but a formal nod from the Professor was clear evidence that his departure time had arrived. For the others there was no hesitancy, they were clearly ready to go. The Count, so much older than his wife, located his stick, raised himself from his chair and then coughed throatily into his handkerchief. He received no assistance from the Countess who is clearly a very independent woman with an air of authority in her own right. She had already thanked Madame Charcot and moved on rapidly to the Professor whom she apparently viewed as more worthy of her gratitude than his wife. He formally and most graciously thanked her for coming and looked forward to her next attendance at one of his lectures. She would seem to be a regular at these; my guess is that she would not be accompanied by her husband.

Meanwhile the Indian Prince remained solidly and quietly seated, waiting to be the last to leave; a natural expression of his status which, I expect to him at least, exceeds that of a French Count. There also seemed to be a particular intimacy between him and Charcot that was not shared with the others. At the time this puzzled me though I was to understand it more later that night. With a grace of movement that belied his large size he too eventually departed.

Madame Charcot had already left the room with the Dubois couple but now returned and whilst smiling affectionately at her husband kindly but firmly said to me that I should not keep him up for too long. A kiss upon his cheek and she was gone.

Professor Charcot is the most formal of men and it is daunting, but it can be daunting too when such a personage suddenly abandons the usual austerity of their presence to become, quite suddenly, remarkably lighter and more jovial. One is thrown off balance. Does one remain attentively respectful or be ready to share a joke? There is a balancing of qualities that must carefully be maintained. One must juxtapose the intimate position of being an invited guest with the formality of it being an invitation from one's employer and indeed from one of the most celebrated and respected men in France. And how does one live up to expectations when such an individual slips out of his jacket and proceeds to tell a risqué joke?

"There is a king who is travelling through his kingdom and he suddenly sees, amongst the crowd thronging around him, a man whose appearance is remarkably similar to his own. He summons the man to come over to him and addresses him with the question, 'Did your mother at one time serve in the palace?' 'No, Your Highness', came the reply, 'but my father did'."

Fortunately I found this joke to be very funny. So perhaps the dramatic change in Charcot did bring about a corresponding change in my own inner state. I felt a warmth between us and a surge of free expression. "A good joke Louis, yes? Told to me by young Freud from Vienna who was studying with me. He is going to translate my lectures. Come now, we will go to my study," and the Professor led me through to his domain, one that is the setting for some of the most inspired medical and scientific thinking of our time.

I should pause for a moment here. I am amazed at how early I have woken and how quickly I have set pen to paper—most unlike your good friend! There are two reasons. One is that my sleep was restless and there were dreams, unclear to my memory now, that left me disturbed. Perhaps it was the food, far richer than I am used to. Charcot had also given me a huge cigar to smoke that, delicious as it was, certainly set my pulse racing. And then there was our conversation, still reverberating in my mind as I lay in bed. And this is the other reason that I sit at my writing table now—I wish to remember the discourse in as much detail as possible.

The Charcot residence, the Hôtel de Varengeville, is fantastically grand. Within Faubourg Saint-Germain and on the Boulevard Saint Germain. They have only recently purchased it and moved in and much work has been carried out to fit it to their requirements. They have done away with much of the original decor and the style is now of the neo-renaissance. Madame Charcot, I have to say, is an artist. As you know, I have little affection or respect for those "artists" who emerge on the occasions when they can free themselves from their dull office or shop employment. They set up their easels on the bridges of Paris and often enough the results are sickly renditions of the Seine drearily dappled by sunlight. And I have even less respect for those wives who have servants to look after their every need and who have the temerity to consider as proper art their dribbly watercolours of flowers in vases.

Though my temptation is to reduce the extremely affluent and servant-endowed Madame Charcot to this latter group of mere hobbyists, I am unable to do so. The lady has talent. But above all she is favoured with, and I believe also driven by, an enormous capacity to create. The evidence is there in this huge mansion which despite its size is filled with her products. She turns her hand to everything: ceramics, and the place abounds with her hand-painted plates; actual paintings, not to my taste but adequately executed; decorated and coloured glass which is something that the Charcots have really gone in for throughout the house; etchings, enamelled works, her range knows no bounds. It has of course been a source of some conversation between us as I have carried out my commission in the summer house and I believe that a degree of friendliness has formed that would not otherwise have existed. It is a constant surprise to me, one that I am of course glad to experience, that it is not she that is painting the murals. However, I believe that it is explained by the subject matter. Charcot's love of Shakespeare has led him to strongly desire a theme of scenes from his favourite plays and I can only imagine that the two of them had decided that in this case the project was outside even her expansive repertoire.

They have added two new wings to the existing building. One side includes Madame's studio in which Charcot too occasionally indulges his own artistic inclinations, and then on the other side is his remarkable study, which we were now approaching. In fact the study is also a library and a most impressive room that has been designed specifically for the Professor's needs. Everything is in character with the learned scientist and the physician. A magnificent desk, the large leather chairs and the rows upon rows of books that line the walls right up to the ceiling, which is such a height that stairs have been built leading to a narrow gallery half way up.

I believe the Professor not to be a drinking man, but there was brandy ready for us and he poured me a liberal quantity and himself somewhat less. I was feeling increasingly relaxed and welcome and began to look around the room. Some good art on the walls, not to my taste of course, Flemish genre stuff mainly. I know he has a Franz Hals somewhere.

I was studying as well as possible, from my chair and in the muted lamplight, one such oil painting, when everything suddenly changed and I was on the edge of my seat and in shock. As Charcot's heavy form leant towards me passing me the glass, there was a sudden and pronounced movement which caused the glass to slip from my fingers. A shadowy and diabolical shape flew through the air and attached itself to the Professor's shoulder. The shape had a face and the face had eyes that glittered at me and sharp teeth that were bared. It was the sight of a demon.

Paris we know has become a city where the black magicians practise their arts. Had this learned man of science summoned up a diabolical creature? And he treated this apparition now, not with horror but with affection. He tickled the little devil under its chin.

"Ah, my little Rosalie."

The lights were low in the room, the shadows extensive, but with my eyes now adjusted (the shock had indeed hastened this process), I saw perched on the professor's shoulder, a small monkey that now raised its head and, looking upwards emitted a piercing high-pitched chattering. At which the usually severe commander of the Sâlpetrière Hospital and indeed of the world of neurology laughed indulgently and tickled the creature's tummy.

"My dear Louis, you look a little surprised, and what a waste of good brandy." He produced a large handkerchief with which he dabbed at the spillage on the ornate rug.

"Let me refill your glass anyway, and perhaps no more surprises?" This was intoned more as a question. "I am sorry for your shock. Rosalie should never be allowed into my study. I believe that one of the children may have been mischievous. Nevertheless, as she is here we will let her remain." And then with a sly smile, "Unless of course you object—I do have a great affection for animals, and what a change from humans with all their hysterical mysteries!"

Charcot placed the monkey upon his fine antique desk and from his waistcoat pocket produced some item of monkey food that was snatched by the creature in its little hand with a disconcertingly human movement. As it gobbled down the morsel the Professor returned to his chair.

"Ah yes, and just so—it is one of those hysterical mysteries that I will speak to you about, but that in a moment. Firstly, what did you think of your fellow guests tonight?"

Once again, I was disorientated by the sudden and unexpected intimacy. He must have seen this because I gulped a couple of times and swallowed too much of my brandy for comfort so that I feared another spillage. Was I to be openly discussing with the "Napoleon of the Sâlpetrière" his very guests who, like him, were from the upper echelons of society? And I, Louis Martens, the poor artist (not yet as famous as I am undoubtedly destined to be).

Charcot now used his intuition—perhaps it is a quality that has helped him in his great career. I have heard that on Tuesday mornings at the hospital he runs a clinic which is open to outpatients and held in front of students, colleagues, and visiting dignitaries and having keenly examined a new patient, he astounds everyone with an on the spot, yet profound diagnosis of the patient's ailment. It is a little miracle. He had certainly diagnosed my state and the prescription and treatment was to be even greater openness.

"My dear Louis, Charcot is feared by nearly everyone he treats and works with. And this Charcot—should he be feared? Why not? I work harder; I see more; I gain more respect and fame for my opinions than any of my contemporaries, Pasteur excepted perhaps, but I hold no grudge there. I take my authority for granted. I believe it to be deserved and to be necessary; I have a hospital to run and a place in the world of medical science to preserve. There are daggers you know."

He then most impressively and no doubt exactly quoted Shakespeare—a line about plucking feathers from Caesar's wing to lower his soaring flight.

"My status keeps me safe from such strikes though in other ways of course it is an allure that draws the envy of my more rivalrous colleagues. Some would topple Charcot if they could. You heard a bit of this through the mouth of the Count this evening. He means no malice, but he is a crotchety old man and he has picked up what some say. The use of hypnotism that has been such a help to us in our research into hysteria, that has caused such interest within medicine and wonderment in the press is now being turned against me." The usually deep and resonant voice was becoming harsher. "I isolate and demonstrate the processes of la grande hystérie, I show the components, there they are, the four stages for all to see! True, my hysterics are prone to suggestion, it is part of their state and as such, with the use of hypnotism, I have a route through to their strange neurology. Thus, in front of my learned and not so learned audiences, I bring about the four manifestations: the seizures, the contortions, those attitudes passionnelles, and finally the delirium. The people think Charcot is wonderful for this and they thank him and then, as if to feel guilty about their pleasure and their praise, they turn against him. Do they feel they have seen too much, been too much the voyeurs? So Charcot then becomes just a showman. A man dominating and exhibiting helpless young women for his own ends! It is, at best, that I rely on the hysterics' great talent for mimicry and at worst my compulsion to exhibit and bully pretty young girls in a lecture hall—as if I don't now show the men too! One critic likened it to Gérôme's painting of Phryne naked before the Roman judges!" Here Charcot softened for a moment. Clearly the affront of the comparison was mingled with some irony. "Not that I object to the choice of such a fine artist, indeed a gentleman Madame and I are pleased to have on our guest list."

Here, Marcel, I must pause. You will remember that I myself likened my experience of the lecture that I attended to that very same painting. So, had Charcot seen my letter to you? Had I left it lying open in the Summer House before I sent it? Or maybe this was purely a consequence of fine minds think-ing alike! Once again though I was uneasy; the Professor was becoming angry and I feared that I may become his next target. But of course, intuiting my previous confusion he had wished, at least initially, to set me at ease. Unfortunately the attempt to protect me from his status had culminated in the two of us becoming more nervous through his need to defend it. I though was certainly no threat, indeed as an artist I was from another universe. So, remembering his initial intention, he shrugged his shoulders and allowed them to drop. He sipped at his drink, glanced at the monkey that was now examining some of the paperwork on his desk, and continued in a measured tone.

"I have all this status Louis, but I can ask you here to talk because you are an artist and sometimes, when I can—so am I. It is a great pleasure for me to draw those scenes that please me when we holiday, or to capture the essence of a person in a little drawing—how pleasing that is too. Once I did the Count."

Here Charcot strode across to an ornate mahogany chest of draws. He pulled open the bottom drawer and I could see that it was filled with drawings. After leafing through he returned with a conspiratorial smile. It was indeed a drawing of the Count of Bolvoir, a caricature of some skill. Not that I can really grant that such work is proper art, but this would certainly have qualified for the newspapers. I held it, turned it over and saw that it was drawn on the back of a theatre programme.

"It was Zola's *Thérèse Raquin*, a particularly boring production that my wife insisted on seeing and we were sitting close enough to the Count and Countess, a couple whom we had not previously met, for me to be able to relieve the monotony by drawing him. I finished it, thought no more of it and placed it in my pocket. The Count was of course oblivious, but the Countess misses nothing and with a friendly challenge to me in the vestibule afterwards, asked to see it. It was a friendly challenge, so I showed her. She was greatly amused and introduced herself. We had both made sure that the drawing was back in my coat pocket before she also introduced me to her husband. She clearly already knew who I was. Now they visit our home as our guests and we to theirs. She also is a regular attendant at my Friday lectures and occasionally I have invited her to the Tuesday clinic which she comes to with interest. So Louis, I think we are now back to discussing the evening's guests."

Charcot was obviously pleased at having completed the circle. "And as you will see later, all have a little something in common. So I return to my first question, what did you think of our little gathering tonight? There is only Rosalie to overhear us."

Rosalie had by now dismembered the neat pile of papers on the desk and, finding nothing else of interest there, had returned to her master. With rapid movements of her head she was looking at us, from one to the other.

"Perhaps it would help if you speak first as an artist Louis." This was a help because my answer could be immediate and unequivocal.

"As an artist, without a doubt, my interest would be in the Countess. Such a striking presence and a strong personality and so stylishly dressed. The jewels alone would be a most satisfying challenge for a painter. Perhaps the skill of a Van der Weyden to pick up those little details and present them with a calm clarity. I noticed a wisp of hair that had separated from her immaculate coiffure. How lovingly he would have captured that small detail."

Here Charcot interjected a deep "Bravo", and clapped his hands.

"But there," I continued, "the comparison with Van der Weyden must end. The Countess is not a Renaissance Virgin."

I know that I blushed at my own statement. Whether it was evident in the low light of the study I cannot say, but the sensation was evidence enough to me. Had I clumsily lurched into forbidden territory in a way that could only be seen by my host as grossly impertinent—the physicality of the Countess! But having gone so far I could only plunge ahead. I had been invited to speak as the artist and artists deal in what they see. So having alluded to my distinct impression that the Countess was no "Virgin", I went the full distance and summoned up Rubens.

I did at least have the reassurance of knowing that Rubens was greatly admired by the Professor. How interesting it is, the way that art allows for such expression that would otherwise be quite taboo. Perhaps even both I and my learned host were now picturing a voluptuous Countess bursting free of her satins and silks and nakedly frolicking amongst the pagan gods.

If that were the case it was beyond any fantasy that Charcot was prepared to share with me, or perhaps even with himself. His look was now inexpressive, but there was no reproach.

"It is indeed true that in her youth the Countess of Bolvoir, then Marguerite Lapierre, was one of the most admired of society beauties and now in her middle age is still considered by many to be a woman of fine appearance and grace."

Not the pure grace of a Van der Weyden Madonna I thought, but the rococo elegance and erotic refinement of a François Boucher and now with the added flesh of a Rubens Venus.

"A strange couple," mused Charcot, thinking now also of the Count. "She did not need the money. She comes from a very wealthy family and it's difficult to see what she wished for in a man so much older. Perhaps the title. They have no children though there was a rumour, malicious I am sure, that Marguerite fell pregnant in her youth. There is no child to show as evidence for that. Things happen, wealthy families can cover them up. But such speculation can be a gratuitous wish to pull the highest down and stain them with the habits of the common people. Anyway, she shares your own inspirations in art and knows that poet fellow Mallarmé and goes to gatherings in his house. They are all inspired by Baudelaire's poetry and Delacroix's art. The latter I certainly concur with, but now they go into all these new areas of the imagination. Too often the painting becomes subservient to the subject matter and the subject matter subservient to the imagination, even the deranged dreams of the artist. It is of course here that your group of artists, Louis, become akin to my hysterics—you let your imaginations get the better of you!"

Charcot seemed very pleased with his own remark. I know from our conversations in front of my developing murals that he is no enthusiast for modern art and palpably detests Monet, Renoir, and the Impressionists. You, Marcel, would no doubt have much that you would wish to defend if you were ensconced with the Professor in his study. I believe though that he is a little less sure of what to make of the style of my own colleagues. If they are indeed "hysterics" he would have to take notice. He now though wished to push on with our reflections upon his guests.

"We did have an embarrassing moment with the Dubois couple. Georges Dubois is connected to us at the Sâlpetrière through his legal, financial, and accounting skills. We have private endowments and in-patients who receive private incomes and he is the overseer of such matters. Of course he has his own financial interests elsewhere too. Dubois is a successful lawyer and has become a wealthy man. He does his job for us well and I have entrusted him with a task which I will come to, Louis, before you leave, because it again involves you."

Clearly the Professor was making assumptions about my future involvement in something and in some circumstances I may well have objected or hastened some explanation. However I could see that he was settling into his more authoritative mode.

"Now, the subject of their little dispute. Such a lively issue for our times. Madame Dubois, I have no doubt, is a fine lady, but is I fear to say besotted with her religion and I must have some sympathy in this with her husband. My own wife brings our children up in the accepted Christian manner. We observe the religious customs of our society and I have no exception to the moral reinforcement that the priests can offer. The lower levels of our society can especially benefit from moral restraint. However, to have a wife who surrenders herself so consummately to the indoctrinations of the church must leave a husband feeling somewhat bereft. I do believe that the man is frustrated. Probably the wife too."

Charcot now sat silently, taken up by his own thoughts.

"Some of our hysterics show a religious passion that borders on the erotic. We had one that imagined she was carrying Christ's child. She suffered with a mixture of utter bliss and tortuous guilt; sometimes the two seemed strangely co-existent. I presented her case at one of my lectures and the Countess wrote to me afterwards with some well-observed comments. She was quite taken by the case. She has a remarkable knowledge of the history of the excesses of the church, particularly in its persecution of heresy and witchcraft. Of course many of those poor creatures who were tortured and killed as witches were no different to the poor deranged women in my acute

67

wards. I will be publishing a little book on this subject quite soon. One of my subordinates, Richer, is helping me with it. We have as much information as we need."

And here he waved an arm towards his huge collection of books. "But the Countess too has given some guidance—an unusual interest to find in a woman."

I had heard of Paul Richer who I knew to be one of the Professor's junior colleagues and also an artist whose drawings had chronicled some of their work at the hospital. The room seemed darker now. Perhaps it was the conversation's turn towards witchcraft. The lights were already very low and the smoke from my cigar circled close to the ground and then lifted rapidly towards the high ceiling causing a veil around us. I had instinctively followed the gesture of Charcot's arm toward the shelves with their darkly bound books rising towards the gloom above; a sombre mass of learning including, I had heard, many volumes on the occult. Then towards the top of a wall, to one side and through the murk, my vision was drawn towards a strange and repellent shape. It was the silhouette of a crucifix transfixed to a cluster of book spines. There was Charcot's monkey, arms stretched, clinging to the books with its sharp little fingers. Its back was to us though its head turned to look. The beady little eyes faintly glimmered.

Charcot had risen from his chair. The fire in the grate was low now. He poked at it without enthusiasm, his mind on other things. Outside it was pitch black. He went to one of the windows. The long lengths of thick dark velvet made no sound as he drew the curtains together. They touched and settled and he returned to the ailing fire. He stood there and the solid mass of his shadow was pitched across the floor with its great hunched shoulders. There was a chill in the air and his jacket was still in the dining room where he had discarded it. The mood had changed.

"They think differently to us in the East. They have religion too, but they have managed through a strange wisdom to protect their beliefs from the bigots and the sadists. They allow thought into their religion. Sometimes there can be little to separate their religious thought from philosophy or from science. In that I believe they share something with those who in our country follow the occult. Is it true science? I would say no, not at all. But what am I to do when confronted by a man such as the Maharaja who tells me that it is? A man of exceptional intellect and a man who has his religious science, but who also practices the science of the laboratory—our science. True, for him that is just a hobby, something to entertain and satisfy a fine mind, but he has my latest papers sent to his home in India; he reads them, and then he corresponds with me with the most acute observations. Everything of course graciously and respectfully couched in the language of one who wishes to learn."

Charcot walked slowly back to his chair and his shadow was gone. The monkey had disappeared, perhaps climbed even higher. He eased himself into his chair. Now that his thinking had turned towards the Maharaja his mood had again eased.

"He is an honoured guest here tonight; a man whom I thoroughly trust. He has been here now for a month to attend the lectures and visit the clinic and he has sat just where you are now Louis and we have talked until the early hours of the morning, once indeed until daybreak."

Here I could only feel inadequate comparing myself to an oriental ruler, a man of wealth, scientific knowledge, spiritual refinement, and intellectual brilliance. If he was so highly esteemed by the Professor he had to be something special. Would I be able to keep my host occupied and entertained in conversation until daybreak? Would I want to? However he had enough of his own thoughts to nourish him.

"He informs me that there are holy men in India who train themselves to resist pain. You will realise that I as a neurologist find this of some interest."

We were now again in the presence of the learned professor and the tone of his delivery changed, became more formal.

"There are cases, he tells me, of not just a resistance to pain, but of the ability to influence, through the mind, the autonomous functions of the body, those functions that act independently of conscious thought. The heart beat can be slowed. The temperature of the body reduced or raised; that an Indian sage can sit naked high up in the Himalayan snow in freezing cold and feel no discomfort, only the blissful contact with his own soul, and that the very essence of those mountains, the sky above them and the plains below is contained within that soul. You see Louis, the Christian priests would never let you get away with that—for them a soul belongs not to the individual, but only to God! So can these strange aberrations the Maharaja tells me of be true? In my wards I have patients who have anaesthesia in one or more parts of their anatomy. Stick in a pin, they feel nothing. I have them hypnotised, I tell them in their trance that they will feel pain—and they do. I hypnotise them again and tell them that they won't, and they don't. But before I get to them they have done the job for themselves. How can they have done this? Is there some switch in the brain that gets turned on or off? Prince Jaswant Singh would say yes, and he would describe his science as one that shows how to find and use that switch. What a boon to mankind such a thing would be. I cannot argue with him about his holy men in India. I believe them not to be hysterics and would not wish to offend him by calling them such. For them the mind can dictate to the autonomous functions as part of a conscious discipline. For my patients the mind also dictates, but in helplessness and as an unconscious symptom. Of course we look for that weakness or damage to their neurological systems that must surely underlie their illness. That aspect of the science though seems of less interest to the Prince. My experiments with hypnosis fascinate him, but he is by no means a pathologist.

"And Louis, he too is part of my plan."

This last remark came as a surprise, bringing us so abruptly back to the issue, still unknown to me, one that had relevance for each of his guests and that would apparently require my involvement in the future. He glanced across to the ornate clock upon the mantel. A bronze gilt rococo affair with a small face that could only just be discerned and which sent out a light and speedy tick which I now noticed for the first time. He strained, but his eyes failed him in the dim light and instead he lifted his watch from a waistcoat pocket.

"It is very late and we will soon call a carriage for you."

I had been prepared to walk. The distance was not too great and I had much to think about, but the offer was generous and it seemed rude to decline. The watch slipped back into the pocket. The tone of voice and manner of the Professor changed again. He was now becoming tired and was ready to reach to the conclusion of his summary.

"So, lastly there is young Jacques Lamond. You probably found him quite still and uninteresting."

I could well have nodded with agreement, but again the onus of being a guest required a false politeness and I made the necessary facial contortions required to express protest. Charcot had anyway made his assumption and denial on my part was irrelevant.

"He is though a recently qualified physician whom I am taking great care over. He has strong potential, is loyal, and he has contributed to our scientific enquiries; he is a true, if fledgling, member of our Salpêtrière school. He has a fresh and enquiring mind and I have a task for him too."

We had now reached the climax of what had largely been a Charcot soliloquy. I sucked the glowing embers down into the stub of my cigar. It had reached the musty richness of the last few draws. Our glasses were empty. There was no more than an intermittent glimmer of light from the fire. The monkey had disappeared from sight.

"I will be putting a patient exclusively into Lamond's care. She is a young woman who has been with us for over four years. She was more or less left on our doorstep when she was

71

a girl—completely mysterious. Her upkeep and treatment are paid for through certain channels that keep their identity, and indeed hers, completely secret. Dubois, who was here tonight, handles all that side. He has always been perplexed by the arrangements but can find no financial or legal fault with them. When she came to us she was in another world. She seemed barely conscious, was deaf and mute and we had no proper communication with her for two years. Almost half her body was paralysed. She was brought in by an unidentified woman and then left. Charles Féré was the intern on duty and when he found her she was in a crumpled heap just inside the main doors. She had a letter of introduction and a small case with some belongings and clothes. Féré himself carried her to a ward. She has been with us ever since. Because of improvements already made I believe that she will continue to respond under Lamond and she also now needs to begin a life outside the hospital. Dubois is using the income provided for her to rent a little apartment near the Jardin des Plantes. It's near to the hospital, a pleasant and safe enough area for a young woman, and I have also asked the Countess of Bolvoir to provide some parental care. She was only too pleased to assist and maintain a watchful eye. I should say that it was the Maharaja, who has come to know the case quite well, who recommended this issue into the outside world as the next stage of her recovery. I do believe him, as is disconcertingly often the case, to be right.

"So Louis, where do you come into all of this? Mademoiselle Madeleine Seguin is the patient and she is going to need friends and what better than a fine young man like yourself, and indeed an artist, to be gentle and generous and to visit her and offer friendship. And yes, as a man—she has hardly ever met a man of her own age group. Whether or not the Countess feels that she must chaperone I will leave to yourselves. I'm sure that I can trust you Louis. It is a responsibility for you, but perhaps also a pleasure. We find now that conversation with her can sometimes be possible, and mute or otherwise she is a fascinating creature, indeed she has become quite well known amongst the intelligentsia of Paris. You have seen her of course. She has often been one of my subjects for demonstration at the lectures and was one such case when you attended and made those interesting little drawings."

The thought of that blissful apparition that Charcot had materialised upon the stage of the Salpêtrière amphitheatre in front of hundreds of fascinated viewers—Phrene indeed; the thought of those grey eyes which looked into eternity and which for a moment of sheer magic had focussed on me; the sense of that graceful pliant body underneath the white smock; the soft long brown hair. All these things rose into my consciousness with a convergence so warm and heartfelt that in any other surroundings I would have let out a cry of joy. Never before in my life have I felt myself the recipient of such amazingly good fortune.

I do not believe that for a moment Charcot expected me to decline his offer. Not because he knew of the ecstasy of expectation that now filled me, but because he assumed that the consequence of his good idea would be obediently carried out. The other players in the scenario had all accepted their roles and were ready to play their parts. And Marcel, who am I to impede the process of such a well thought out plan!

The Professor rang for a manservant to see me to the door. The idea of the carriage seemed now to have been forgotten, but it made little difference to me; I knew I would rejoice in the cool air, the breeze, the pleasure of my feet stepping upon the paving stones, all the way home. He shook my hand warmly. The great man, a personage of tremendous energy, had tiredness in his eyes, but perhaps too the satisfaction of arranging a new phase of life for a patient who seems also to have become his ward. But I may exaggerate. I understand that "Madeleine S." has become something of the star of his show. Perhaps the impresario is indebted to his main attraction.

There was no sign of the monkey as we left and Charcot seemed to have abandoned it for the night. He closed the study door behind him.

And now for me the day beckons!

Your affectionate friend,
Louis

CHAPTER SEVEN

A letter from the Countess of Bolvoir to Roberto V.

6th May 1886

Maître,

My most trusted servant Lucas will deliver this to you. I have instructed him to return with written confirmation that you are in safe receipt of this note. I apologise for my need to ask this of you, but it is no mere indulgence and you will understand the need for the greatest secrecy once you have read it.

I write with a proposal that I also hope you can receive as a gift. I offer something, Maître, that I believe will fill you with joy, and I hope in my meagre understanding of your deepest teachings that it will bring about a fulfilment, I think that is the right word, a fulfilment in action of the precious philosophical process that you have shared with us. But no, I wish to change the word—consummation is a better one.

It is the case, and it is an understanding I have received from you without reservation, that there can be no half measures when we worship at the alternative altar. When you thrashed me and put me through the most painful abuse I realised that this was an opening that you offered, a gateway through pain and humiliation, so that I have been reborn into a freedom that has changed my very existence, that has given me each day and night a resolute and profound sense of purpose. Not that my husband, family or friends have the slightest notion. This of course adds great savour to my pleasure. One or two artist lovers have been inquisitive and Félicien Rops I can speak to with relative ease. You know his work and approve of it. There is as well my beautiful Natalie, who offers me the occasional delectable diversions from the monotony of my husband's attentions. She senses something. I know that you think well of my dalliance with her and I have not forgotten your instruction that I should bring her to you. She will of course come to you in time. Just allow me that time to place in her mind the preliminaries. Then a visit to a service should be all that is needed.

My purpose now though is indeed to make a gift, an offering to your eminence, and one that surely cannot be bettered as an act of devotion to the path, or as a celebration of the distance travelled as I crawl in your footsteps. It is the proof that I have indeed thrown off those pathetic rules of conscience and morality that seek to make us such prisoners of life. I now offer you the means for that thing which you have told us is necessary and for an act which will reduce our usual rituals to pathetic trifles. I have now, through a rare social opportunity, access to a girl. She has been an inmate at Charcot's Salpêtrière. She has become quite famous as one of his prized hysterics and has performed magnificently at his lectures on several occasions. That is of no matter though. As a person she has no more significance to Charcot's audience than the lecture of the day and he now has little clinical involvement with her. That role has been given to one of his subordinates, a nonentity whom I met at a dinner party at his house the other day. The circumstances are that this girl has no family that anyone can locate, anywhere! She was dropped off at the hospital over four years ago, by an unknown person, as if at the steps of an orphanage. The girl has been so deranged that she has never been able to give an account of herself. No memory whatsoever. Some money is sent anonymously towards her upkeep, but nothing else. No visits, no letters, not even an attempt to communicate with the physicians. My husband, who of course knows of such things, thinks the payments must be made through a trust fund and the originators of the fund could well be dead by now. So, she will not be missed. Really she is one of hundreds of mad girls who can have no life of their own and frankly would be better off dead. Let her do some service to a greater power.

Now arises our splendid opportunity. I have become the benefactor and patron for this poor unwanted creature. Charcot has, as one might say, handed her to me on a plate. She is now discharged from the hospital and resides in her own little apartment under my watchful and protective eye. But who can constantly watch over a poor mad girl or prevent her from disappearing into the bowels of a cruel and greedy city?

Need I add, as it is essential for your purpose, the girl, whose name is Madeleine, is undoubtedly a virgin.

I await your reply. I am ready to act at any time and could easily begin by introducing her to you at the current house. It would be a most pleasant day out in the country.

I am in your service and in His,
M.

CHAPTER EIGHT

A reply from Roberto V. to the Countess of Bolvoir

8th May 1886

My dear Marguerite,

It pleases me greatly to hear this news. All this is opportune indeed. We have fortune gracing our endeavours. The auspices are perfect. There would not be a better time for this should we wait for a hundred more years. So, we must begin. First I will meet the girl. Bring her to me in the country on Sunday the 16th. It can indeed be a day out for her.

I have the use of the house and the chapel until the autumn, but the matter now in hand should be completed during the month of June. It would then be wise for us to move on.

RV.

CHAPTER NINE

A further note from the Countess of Bolvoir to Roberto V.

18th May 1886

Maître,

I am so pleased that you approve of my choice. The girl seemed to enjoy her visit to a country house and even became quite talkative on our return to Paris. Of course her life is beginning to open. The young artist Martens visits her and tries to get her to read Baudelaire's poetry and even Mallarmé, something that at first I found quite absurd until she suddenly recited by heart a completely obscure verse by the latter and asked me what I thought! Now she has also met you, Maitre—a kind gentleman living in the country. So she will be ready to visit you again and I will have everything ready for that momentous night, and really not too soon as she continues to awake from the trance of her illness and is looking with a growing interest towards the world.

If only, Maître, you could have allowed my presence when you conversed with her. As you know, I wish to be ever-present in our endeavour, to not miss the slightest moment of such a magical work. But yours is the wisdom.

Marguerite

CHAPTER TEN

Madeleine is free and Louis visits the Countess

Letter to:
Marcel Dupont, Marmande, Lot-et-Garonne département, SW France

From:
Louis Martens, rue Lamarck, Paris, France

Dated 20th May 1886

My dear Marcel,

A splendid thing. After nearly five years Madeleine is now free from the asylum. What incredible days these have been! Most of these women seem to stay there forever, to veritably rot away within its walls. Is she cured? Well the physicians are prepared to let her go. All is as Charcot prescribed. Yes, she is still strange, sometimes quite mute, but Oh! She moves so beautifully. Already she is my inspiration. Through her my art will explode into new life. I will draw her and paint her. She will be my Aphrodite, my Minerva, my Proserpine. She is all the figures of transformation and of love, the embodiment of art itself, the queen of the "palace of beauty". But, again, I hear you say—is she cured? What would a cure be? Would she then lose that essence she offers to me and to my art and which may be her destiny to bestow upon the world? What better role for her than to serve art and what greater prospect for me than to accept the gift that she is now here in my life, waiting for my visits to her little room. She likes to read you know. I will get her the books that she wants and she can read them when I draw and paint her. She reads poets as well. Already I have brought her Baudelaire, Verlaine, and Mallarmé. Yes, I know, she may be a little shocked, but I have been entrusted with an honourable mission—to escort her to the outside world. I will let her know of the works that inspire me. She can read Baudelaire and I will paint her as his Francisca. How true to the cause is that!

I thank Charcot for bringing me into her life and for liberating her to become a priestess to art. As to her hospital treatment, I think the Professor's man Lamond is actually helping her with all his funny methods and ideas. He must have sat with her for many hours in silence. Now she visits the hospital for her sessions with him and apparently they talk. Charcot no longer calls upon her for the hypnotic performances at his lectures, where of course she first graced my eyes, and what a performance it was. You know Marcel, as I look back I have the feeling that somehow her trance was related to me and that in the midst of it there was a communication between us. I think now of a loss of consciousness through ecstasy. When she came round, when Charcot released her from the trance and her eyes began focussing into consciousness and those grey pupils seemed to open up wide to catch the light and then, oh that glorious moment when her eyes met mine. Am I raving Marcel? I think I am in love! But it is for the cause of art!

She has two small rooms near the Rue Berthollet. All nicely painted with bright floral curtains and the windows looking out onto a pretty street with trees. A table, some small comfy chairs and a bed with a pretty brass bedstead. There is a simple book case made of oak with a touch of carving for decoration and resting upon one of its shelves is her collection of five books! There will of course soon be more. The floor has stained bare floorboards with some gay oriental-style rugs, two in each room. It is all lovely and so fitting and bright a place for a young soul beginning a new life in the city. These furnishings are modest, but in no way cheap; so what has made this possible? I act as a friend, and as part of Charcot's grand design I am there to help her to meet others and become a social being after all the years interned within the hospital, and yes of course, there is also my own vision of her future. But there is also the patronage of the grand and wealthy Countess whom the Professor has designated as her temporary guardian and it is she who has found Madeleine this apartment and furnished it for her with such affection, indeed I might say, with love. The effect that this girl has upon others! Madeleine was surely a muse to the Professor's science and then in the amphitheatre he would display the stunning results to a crowd, many of whom would have fervently been hoping that it would be she upon the stage that day. I understand that the Countess, who was often present at these scenes, now sees her own role with Madeleine as a chance to do a little good in the world. She adds an extra sum to the existing allowance so that there is enough to pay for comfortable and easy living. Of course she and I, thanks to Charcot's planning, now share something in common which I could never in my wildest dreams have imagined. I believe it fitting to now describe the Countess Marguerite to you in much greater detail, especially since I have just had the occasion of a much closer contact and with the most surprising of results!

To start off I would estimate her age to be in the latter part of her fourth decade. She is of course as a wealthy and privileged woman likely to enjoy a conservation of physical appearance that would not be the preserve of a woman less fortunate and thus one might even consider her to have elegantly reached her fiftieth year. She is tall and undoubtedly still retains some beauty and if she is not with the slimness of waist that would have been her due in the summer of her womanhood, there is now in the autumnal years the recompense of grace and sophistication. I could continue in this way but in telling you of today's most interesting encounter it may be that I am able to bring her to life in a more vital and painterly fashion.

She has invited me to paint a portrait of her husband. It is to be a present for him on his seventieth birthday and will no doubt be a nice gift for him, but certainly no pleasure for me, though the fee of course I need. But to have to paint yet another boring picture of another dull old aristocrat sitting propped up in his chair—what one must do to survive! However as you will see, there is an addition to this matter and it has brought with it a distinct relief from the tedium that had set in at even the thought of such a commission. I shall explain.

A week ago I received by messenger the invitation to visit the Countess at her home in the faubourg Saint-Germain (I assume she would have obtained my address from Professor Charcot), and the time stipulated was to be at three pm on Thursday, that is yesterday. Of course I attended. As I have described to you Charcot's house is splendid, but this was certainly at least its match and with such a casual finesse and lack of artifice that to me it was the superior. Although there is clearly not the slightest need to impress, the Count and Countess do not stint on their use of servants. A butler brought me in and within minutes a servant had offered me refreshment including wine which I gratefully received. There was then a very long period of waiting and I fended off a developing agitation by studying my surroundings. I was seated in a fabulously ornate reception room. All rococo with pillars, a massive carved fireplace, oriental rugs, and amongst the many pictures a gorgeous Fragonard! A young lady exquisite in the most luxurious of apparel, her very clothes surrounding her like an exotic bouffant from which at one end there protruded slim and graceful white legs and from the other a delicate little breast with a pink nipple. Just like the icing with a cherry on a cake and delicious in every way. As I gazed at this picture the long wait for my

83

hostess no longer seemed so bad and indeed I felt rather inter-
rupted when Milady did eventually sweep in. I rather feel like
calling her by that name because there is something about her
that makes me think of Milady in the Dumas Three Musketeers
novel. You may have read it; it's rather good and really races
along. Apparently Dumas was a fencer himself. Of course in
the novel Milady is an arch-villainess whereas this one is being
so kind to my Madeleine. All the same, as you will see, there
may be grounds … Anyway, she enters, all cool elegance, and
then we go into another room even grander than the one before.
And guess what is there—Claude Lorraine! Marcel, you would
have died of happiness. Of course the work is completely without imagination, but what a wonder! A scene based on some
mythological subject, but with the characters so tiny in the
overall scale that they are just there to justify the title or maybe
to bring about some kind of evocative feel, and for sure they
must not get in the way of the landscape. A big picture; a pale
blue morning sky, a touch of mist in one part, absolute clarity
in another, the beginnings of the heat of the day and you can
feel it arriving, and at the same time a touch of coolness from
the remains of the night before; all the elements floating in
crystal clear magical light, the distant mountains, calm water, a
classical ruin, a world of serene beauty.

We were just quiet for a while in front of the picture and then
we spoke a little; her husband "collects", and yes it must surely
be an honour for me that I should be "accepted by such a con-
noisseur" to be the painter of his portrait. We went over the
details of that; the days when he will be available for sitting, the
proposed completion date which is one that gives me plenty of
time as I have until the beginning of January, the month of his
birthday, and then of course we came to the fee. Dear Marcel,
your impecunious friend is beginning to feel rather well off—for
the next few months anyway. I know it is yet one more portrait
and will give me no chance to creatively surprise myself, but
for a while I will be dining well and frequenting the theatre and

at least I still have the last of Charcot's Shakespearean scenes to give my imagination some licence to roam.

After our negotiations the Countess rose from her chair and snapped shut the book in which she had been recording the dates and details of the commission. Sighing, she placed it along with her elegant pen upon a nearby table and the whole action was as dismissive of the subject that had just been our main focus as were my own thoughts about the matter. She smoothed down the layers of silk and satin at the front of her dress, a confection of pink, emerald green and cream, and raised herself to her full height. The dress rustled and seemed so luxuriously full of her that it was ready to overflow. I caught in myself that special sensation, one that comes as a surprise because it is independent and free of the mind; a wave of erotic impulse that has no source in social interaction but is the simple essence of desire.

I think that it was the mutuality felt in the dismissal of the portrait details; her sudden contempt for the matter that matched so well my own feelings and which showed a wider dislike for procedures and formalities and a preference for the spontaneous, for more selfish pleasures. But this was merely an indication of what was to come.

"I know, Louis, for I have heard it from several sources including our good Professor, that your preference is for the art of those that love the poetry of Baudelaire and Gautier and the images of Moreau and Redon. You no doubt therefore visit their studios and others of those that we are so fortunate to host in our city. I expect that I am correct."

I was unclear whether this last remark was a question or a statement, but in any case she waved away the beginnings of my answer as an irrelevance.

"You will of course be having a wonderful time in Paris, but do not abandon your native Brussels, there are some fine exhibitions there and Redon himself has sent work to their Salon of the XX—an interesting group. I know of a young artist there

85

called Fernand Khnopff who is looking most promising. And will you, Louis, exhibit in our own Salons des Indépendants?"

You will know Marcel that the Salon des Indépendants is a complete Godsend, a tremendous gesture against the old art aristocracy. Anyone can exhibit and new ideas and visions abound. No longer must we be controlled, hidebound and rejected by the official Salon. So I was delighted to tell her that I had indeed exhibited in its first exhibition and most certainly planned to do so again in the summer.

"I saw the last one" she said. "I do not remember any works by you, but of course I did not then know the name of Louis Martens. Perhaps I might recognise the paintings if I saw them again. But you know, Louis, do you really think it good that just anyone can exhibit? Surely it lessens the achievement." I have to say, Marcel, that this was a thought that had already made an unwelcome raid upon my more liberal ideals and somewhat won the skirmish, but I felt that to admit this to the Countess would be a second defeat. I therefore protested. However she had already relegated the subject in preference for another one.

"And do you know Péladan?"

Of course by now my expression was genuinely showing surprise at her knowledge of the unconventional in art, and her knowing smile showed that this was in line with her expectations.

"I have conversed with Péladan," she continued, "and I find him rather a fool." She looked for my surprise. "However he understands something about magic and the mystical and he does well to promote art that is moved by these things. And you, Louis, are you such a one?"

I am glad that I answered as I did, as it probably served as the "password" to allow our move to yet another room and this one like the veritable treasure cave of a more fictional Count—that of Monte Cristo!

"Yes, I have an interest in matters of the occult," though as you know, Marcel, in truth I find this preoccupation shared by many of my fellows in Paris of no more than passing interest. But to my mind Joséphin Péladan is no fool, strange though he may be in appearance and character. I first met him in a Montmartre café where he was more or less holding court. I admit that though I was somewhat on the prowl for contacts of influence and Péladan is certainly such a one, I balked when I saw him there and but for a mutual friend who called me over I would have slipped away. It is the look of him I suppose—really quite alarming—tall and heavily bearded and he insists on wearing robes, and on laying eyes upon him my first reaction was that I would be getting into a conversation with a mad monk. He also has upon his head a great pile of black hair accompanied by bushy black eyebrows and dark staring eyes so that the whole visual package exudes an intense weirdness, which was not mitigated when our mutual friend gave an introduction which was as grand as Charcot's butler for the Indian Maharajah.

"Louis, how nice to see you and what a pleasure for me to introduce you to Sâr Mérodack Péladan." Well, Marcel, you are a most level-headed person, what would you have done at being introduced to a "Sâr"? I really could not tell whether the mutual friend was amusing himself at my expense, but I think not as the "Sâr" listened and looked on with complete seriousness and clearly expected to be introduced in that way. The title is an Assyrian term for a king and I have learned since that Mérodack was a Babylonian king from the Old Testament. It was too late for me to escape from this exotic regal personage, but much to my surprise, two hours later I was feeling very pleased to have made his acquaintance. Péladan is a man of considerable energy, a great idealist who champions those in whom he can see something of his own vision. As well as his art criticisms he has written a novel called *Le Vice Suprême* and this I had come across—it has a lurid frontispiece by the artist Félicien Rops, and it took Paris by storm. Much of it is about magic and the occult and this was the area in which the Countess clearly had an interest—one which she wished me to share.

She gestured me to follow her. We left the reception room and the bright purity of Claude Lorraine was exchanged for a dark corridor scarcely lit by the lamp that burned upon an oriental table half way along. We reached its end and to a door that she pushed open to show, through a similarly sombre light, a very different kind of room. There were huge windows but the heavy red velvet curtains were closed and the sunlight which must have been strong and full against that wall of the house, was constricted to shoot only sharp knife edges of brilliance across the darkly-patterned carpet. We walked in and all felt strangely soft underfoot and the room was so large that in the dimness of the light the walls, the furniture, the objects around us seemed like those strange changing shapes one might see through a mist at sea.

In that moment my very presence there seemed to me a mystery. A strange and disturbing incongruity, for as the shapes began to evolve into recognisable forms I realised that I was in this illustrious and increasingly surprising lady's bedroom. The very invitation into the stateliness of such an aristocratic home had been daunting, but after an hour or so to find myself standing with the Countess in her private chamber and within sight of her bed was a cause for real embarrassment. On reflection, Marcel, it strikes me that embarrassment and excitement can be rather close together in the spectrum of emotions. Both are accompanied by a warm flush, pleasurable for the one, sometimes excruciating for the other, but is the reddening of embarrassment the signal of an excitement denied? I had already once that afternoon felt the thrill of Milady's unconformity and now it was to move me again.

But this chamber was not simply a bedroom. The bed with its canopy was at one end, but there was all the paraphernalia of a room of work, of study and research, with many books upon the shelves and some stacked upon the floor. On an ornate rococo writing desk there rested paper, ink and a variety of pens. Two large armchairs and a settee formed soft dark masses in the gloom.

The Countess, choosing against daylight, ignored the curtains and lit two large lamps and a number of candles, spaced around the room. She gestured to the settee for me to sit and walked softly across the thickly piled carpet to a large mahogany chest. This was a moment for me to move my attention from the interior features of the room, the large objects and the furniture, to its perimeter, the walls, and of course the pictures, and here were the treasures. Against a heavy flock paper of a deep shade of purple, there hung a number of works, small in themselves, but mainly in heavy and ornate frames. They were indeed by artists that I know and admire. The largest of the pictures was one that looked like a Moreau watercolour, a mythological scene with an enchanting beauty dressed in ornamental robes. How splendid those watercolours are, so light and spontaneous, brilliant things which sadly always have to play second fiddle to his finely finished oils. More simply framed and of a very different nature were a group of black and white prints, quite small, but with the intrinsic forms of the imagery emitting an enticingly sinister quality. A severed head upon a plate, a disgusting-looking spider, a horrifying head with one great central eye—of course the work of Odilon Redon.

The Countess returned from the chest with papers in her hand and approvingly noted my scrutiny of the walls.

"You have seen some of my husband's collection, and now you are seeing my own."

She sat next to me, close enough to hold the papers for us both to view. I felt the warmth of her body and the rare smell of her perfume and there flashed into my mind the image of the exotic and bejewelled creature in the Moreau watercolour. She moved her arms to arrange the sheets of paper so that there was a slight stirring of the air and for a moment I had the strangest of feelings that I was outside in the garden and sitting under the sun. She was so close to me on the settee that

I dared not look at her though I sensed that she was looking at me and was smiling and I felt very weak and unable to speak. She was holding a number of drawings and she moved as if to show me the first of these, but then held back. She dropped the papers onto her lap and lightly moved her hands across them. For a moment her ring caught the candlelight, a most beautiful turquoise stone with serpentine coils of silver and gold. The serpent had eyes, of diamonds perhaps, which glittered.

"I am going to speak to you now, Louis, as … shall I say …" and the voice, throaty in tone and usually so direct in delivery, paused for a moment, "as a fellow traveller. This world can be such a dull place. Here we are in this mansion, a palace of art, full of beautiful things; exquisite objects created by the most skilled of artists and craftsmen. I have the resources to demand and to receive whatever I want from the material world. But of course, and you will know this, it is not enough."

The hands gently, gracefully moved so that the palms were raised upwards, and then softly dropped back to her lap.

"One wants more, and then one realises that to really make the difference the search has to be made in the places that ordinary creatures cannot even begin to imagine, places that are known only to a few, to those who are not deterred by fear of the consequences of what they will find. After, our lives can never be the same. Fear will always interweave with our pleasures, but the pleasures still lead us on. I speak of course of ecstasy and I speak of this to you, because amongst your brothers in art there are those who most certainly have known its taste and who will never cease in their search for more. It comes with abandonment of wretched familiarities and monotonous reassurances and it feeds on the triumph over these of the imagination and of dream, and it is imagination in excess that truly delivers. This is why I like the art of your friends … even perhaps your own art, Louis."

My hot and nervous discomfort was now profoundly intensified as in the midst of her last statement she lifted her hand close to my ear and with two fingers fondled a lock of my hair. I felt the plaything, the object of a game, but a game with inevitable sensual overtones and indeed undertones and I have to say that I, a man who considers himself to be more than adept in the company of attractive women, began to tremble quite uncontrollably. So of course she laughed, and after a sharp tug, released my hair and dropped her hand once more into her lap, where still lay the drawings. Her manner now changed and once again she became the formal Countess.

"You came here today to discuss and accept my commission for the portrait of my husband, but I have another project for you which will not be a present for my husband and will certainly be of a different nature."

She paused for a moment and I sensed that we had come to the main point of my summons to her house, one that had been deftly camouflaged within the portrait commission but that now, after some preliminary testing on her part, was deemed almost ready for discussion. She had one more question.

"Have I been speaking to you, Louis, in a language you understand?"

Dear Marcel, this was said to me calmly, though the tone was dry, and it quite left me with a chill and I felt concerned that anything less than a response of complete affirmation would mark me out as foe rather than friend and lead to my immediate dismissal. I therefore nodded with an enthusiasm that had little basis in reality. The truth, as you well know, is that I have little regard for the more sinister outreaches of our imaginative art. My dreams are not nightmares, but visions of beauty and my inspirations are the Arcadian lakeside scenes of Puvis de Chavannes rather than the murky puddles of Félicien Rops. However, I was beginning to realise that the classical and the Arcadian would have a sweetness and romance to their nature that would offer little satisfaction to the more rarefied and sharper tastes of Milady. And indeed the next half hour bore this out as she shared with me the more secret part of her

91

collection. All unframed, on paper, either drawings or etchings, delivered to me straight from her lap, one after the other and each increasingly debauched and accompanied by piercing looks as she scrutinised my reactions. We went through a number of prints by Rops. By all accounts he is a splendid and likeable fellow and carries a tremendous seal of approval as he had been close to Baudelaire, but his imagination so often runs into the very gutters of city life and I am unable to comprehend why anyone would wish to make drawings of ruined syphilitic prostitutes. However Milady's pictures were not by Rops in his Parisian underworld mode, but in his glorification of the satanic rites and these always involve ecstatic naked females as either the corrupting instruments of Satan or his very partners in the acts of copulation. She paused at one such image; a voluptuous young woman lying in absolute abandonment on a sacrificial alter, her hair cascading over its edge, whilst a most vile horned figure floats above and dangles below a phallus so enormous that it snakes down to penetrate her. As we viewed this aberration the Countess sighed and as if to herself, softly spoke the most remarkable words.

"Ah, my dear Félicien—I think that as a draughtsman he is a little overvalued, but not at all as a lover."

She sighed again and then moved on to the next picture, and I felt that her eyes were once more upon me. I was being looked at whilst I looked, and when we came to a picture which was an immensely detailed black ink drawing of an orgy presided over by a figure that looked like Beelzebub himself, I became quite frozen. She must though have considered this to be my fascination with the scene as she gave a little laugh of pleasure.

The viewing was complete. She rose, walked back to the huge chest of drawers with its intricate carvings, these themselves now seeming monstrous to me, and deposited the papers in its dark recess. She did not return to my side but looked at me across the room. For a moment she was quiet and thoughtful and then—

"You understand Louis that I trust you. There are few who have seen these works. It is not their detail that I require from you, or their content, but just something of their spirit. Are you game?"

The truth is that I was not game even to following in the spirit, but I confess that I also heard the question as "Are you man enough?" There was something of that in her manner of asking so that it called for a bravado in my response. I know that I also felt a duty not to let down the artistic cause, even though her predilection for imaginative art arose from different stimuli to my own. I know too that I experienced fear, as if in a strange way it would be dangerous to turn her down, to give suggestion that our tastes so differed. Such fear is irrational I know, but in any case I have agreed. I am still to be told the content of the commission. By then she had had enough of me, or done enough with me, and her hand disappeared amongst the folds of one of the huge curtains to reach what must have been a bell pull to the servants' quarters. I left her chamber and progressed alone through the faintly lit corridor and at the end there was a servant waiting to escort me to the main doors of the house. Though I had increasingly met more light on my way to the exit, the blaze of the sun outside quite blinded me and I was left blinking at the top of the steps and surprised at how quite suddenly summer was fully upon us with real warmth in the sunshine. As I walked away I thought of both the heat and the chill of my encounter with the Countess and how much the temperature within those rooms had depended, not upon the air around us, but upon her whim. And then the opening lines from an English poem by Swinburne came into my mind and remained throughout my journey home:

Cold eyelids that hide like a jewel

Hard eyes that grow soft for an hour.

As ever,
Your dear friend, Louis

CHAPTER ELEVEN

The Countess of Bolvoir confirms. A letter to Louis Martens

To be delivered by hand to Monsieur Louis Martens

24th May 1886

Dear Louis,

How pleasant it was to receive you last week. I am so glad that we have made our arrangements for my husband's portrait. I can assure you that the Count looks forward to a first sitting and suggests that the work should begin in early September when he returns to Paris. I am sure that you will find him a satisfactory subject; such strong features, rendered more striking of course through age. He is likely to be dressed in either grey or black, but no doubt you can find occasion for at least a little splash of colour as he is bound to wear some of his many decorations, perhaps even a sash! He will want to read during the sitting; it would not occur to him that it might cause any difficulty for you. Of course we do not want him to be reading in the portrait—not so much a picture of a Renaissance man but of a statesman and an aristocrat. I expect that he assumes that you will portray him gazing steadfastly over your shoulder at some noble endeavour or ideal. Anyway, if he reads it will do you some service as it will keep him still and spare you from having to converse.

I know perfectly well, Louis, that this is a chore for you. Do not think for a moment that I am taken in by your polite enthusiasm for the task. But I feel no remorse for condemning you to this commission. The payment is, I imagine, tremendous for you and there is of course the other commission that we discussed and that will be much more to your liking.

It is about the Charcot girl. I think when I call her that you know who I mean. Madeleine Seguin, the star of Charcot's shows, so pretty, so mad, so innocent; so dreamy and easily hypnotised. She was surely in all our minds that evening at Charcot's residence, including that funny thin man who is now treating her as an outpatient, though I intend to put a stop to that. As you know, I have taken the girl under my wing. It is high time that I reach into the material fortune that I have enjoyed and from it find some excess, unneeded by me, but of great value to one less blessed. Who could be a better recipient then than a lone young woman, with apparently no family, no friends and certainly for at least five years, very little sanity? Charcot has decreed that she is now ready to begin a life in the world outside those oppressive walls of his hospital. Perhaps he and the skinny doctor have done some good after all. You, Louis, I understand, have also been recruited as a friend nearer to her in age. Make sure you behave yourself when you visit her. Anyway, I guess that Charcot has tired of her and has another rising star to perform for him. A thought—could these girls represent an element of the esteemed Professor's own being? Could it in fact be Charcot himself dancing for the crowd at the show? So little is as it seems in our manifest world; behind it all there lie such different ambitions. What more can we wish to seek than the truth, and to reach the truth we must allow for all that is forbidden, all that we glimpse in our dreams and nightmares and hastily put away, to be known to us. Thus we can realise the true darkness that resides in the soul, and if it is the truth, then it must come out. I believe that Charcot understands this which is why we are friends, and you in your manner of art will understand this, Louis, and so I can speak to you from that, "vast desert, where luminous liberty lies in her abduction".

Art can do justice to these matters and I believe as well that science will one day follow. How many of that mass of tortured womankind in Charcot's hospital might take up their beds and walk if they could only truly allow the excitement of their own darkest imaginings? I look to see who is happy in this world. Is it the priest or the sinner, the good citizen or the debauched villain? I see no bonus of happiness awarded to the moral for their goodness. Not at all; the pleasure so often accrues to the other side. The guardians of society are threatened by their deep envy of the freedom of the villainous; they put away "the bad" to protect their sanctimonious structures, their fantasies of benevolence.

Perhaps I shock even you with these thoughts, Louis, and I mean no criticism to Charcot. I know too that he has been a generous and encouraging patron to you as he has been a friend to me. I have learned much from him.

Now—to the business of this letter. I want you to paint the girl for me. She is very pretty, so that already makes it something of a relief from the forthcoming travails of painting my husband. I also want her in a special setting and to be playing a role, so you will not be able to carry this out in her home. For this role and for the setting I will now share with you the inspiration for my vision.

The concept of sacrifice is one we all honour—do we not? You make a sacrifice when payment for your art is hard to find and no doubt there have been winters without coal for your fire and when hunger has been an ache in your belly. You have sacrificed the comforts of life for your art. You may well scorn me for such remarks. Who am I, a wealthy aristocrat, to speak of hunger and cold? True, I have all the comforts but all this is relative, and believe me, Louis, I have known the challenges of sacrifice and met them and refused the seductions of convention.

I know where my path is leading and I am prepared to pay any price to protect my goal. Even with my life? Well there is a thing—because of course in myth and religion we know of the sacrifices that are made that require the life of a living creature and even that such a one may be human. And why should this happen? Well obviously it is the greatest gift that mankind can offer to a Supreme Power. Our little lives mean next to nothing to such a One, yet for us life is to be clung to whatever the cost. We cannot allow ourselves to die and all our instincts fight to preserve us. Or do they? Perhaps things are not all that they may seem. We have this instinct to live and it is one that is beyond any power of reason, completely independent of the will. Any danger and there is the absolute reflex that is there, quicker than thought, to escape and to survive. We are governed by this, our need to stay alive. But then why do we die? How can this all-consuming instinct to live eventually give in to death? My view young Louis, is that there must surely also be an instinct to die. And if there is to be a contest between these two, between life and death, which is the winner? Well, really there is no contest is there? Death wins every time. So I must say that our instinct to die is the more powerful and is indeed supreme. So here we have another reason for the sanctity of the human sacrifice, it honours death and if the dedication is to a Supreme Force that relishes our progress towards death, then we show that we are truly committed to our belief. Goodness of course is always equated with life and with its glory and preservation, and evil always dressed in the dark costume of death. Love, without reservation and without thought, is assigned to life, and hatred and damage, equally without thought, are of the family of death. Jesus conquered death, was resurrected and lives forever radiant in the heavens. Satan, it is true, also lives forever, but his very kingdom is buried, deep down below. How unfair. And when men and women come together in ecstasy, can this not also be in cruelty? Can there not be in the dominance of one over another, in the infliction or receipt of pain, a new freedom, a spirituality and a realisation of truths denied. Such submission may even reach to the doors of death and then, the ultimate sacrifice to its supremacy, the climax can be death itself.

I hope, Louis, that these thoughts of mine do not disturb you too much. It is rare for me to be able to converse with one whom I believe has some sympathy for my ideas. Rops of course is another rare example, but I sometimes find him rather conflicted, despite the content of his art. There are others who have travelled through death's empire, some just dabbling, but also those who observe more deeply: Hieronymus Bosch, Goya, Delacroix, and I know that from your group we will have much more of this. Your mentors Moreau and Redon have shown the way and the sacrifice of the head of John the Baptist has moved Moreau in many of his works. This is welcome.

So the sacrifice can indeed be a most worthy happening—on any level. But the sacrifice of a human is the expression of that instinct for death, pure and undiluted, as close as we can be to the most powerful force in our lives, as its agent or as its subject.

So my commission for you is for a painting, something in oils, quite magnificent, and depicting this greatest of ceremonies. I do believe that we are being remarkably daring in this, but I am relying on you, Louis, to be a man of bravado and to not disappoint me. The finished picture will be for my own pleasure and for some of my friends, one in particular.

Every artist needs a model, even for his works of imagination, and I wish you to use the girl Madeleine as the model. I just think that she would suit the painting well and it will be a novel experience for her too. You will paint her as the sacrificial subject as she enters the place of ceremony, standing close to the altar. I will be supplying her with a suitable costume to wear and I expect that she will enjoy dressing up. I will be taking her to visit a country house that I know, one that she has visited once before and which she may have mentioned to you. She thoroughly enjoyed her outing and wishes to go again. It will be a good place for you to make the preparatory drawing. There is also a chapel attached and you can make a drawing of its altar area that can serve as the setting for the scene. This will be on a date in June, so make sure that you have no firm commitments for that month. I will inform you of the exact date soon and of course will arrange for your travel.

Our thanks should really be with the Professor whose plans for all have brought us to such an interesting place. But we will not concern him with this little venture. He believes that to make a life for herself the girl needs a complete break from his influence and I expect that he too has cleared his mind for other things.

So, Louis, please be ready for a trip to the country.

With cordial greetings,
Marguerite Bolvoir

CHAPTER TWELVE

The Mardiste

Letter to:
Marcel Dupont, Marmande, Lot-et-Garonne département, SW France

From:
Louis Martens, rue Lamarck, Paris, France

Dated 26th May 1886

My dear Marcel,

You receive this celebratory letter from one who can now say that he has truly made the grade. I have received the literary and artistic keys to the city. Now, with intimacy, I can mingle with those who are at the very source of creative thought, for whom the "idea" is the brightest star to seek out and follow. I have become a Mardiste!

"A Mardiste is what?" you will say. A Mardiste, Marcel, is one who on a Tuesday evening makes his way to an address along the Rue de Rome and who ascends four floors to a tiny apartment whose door swings open to soft light, the curling of tobacco smoke, the warm sound of laughter and the friendliest of banter, and then, having entered the little dining room is welcomed by one who, sitting in the midst of those who celebrate thought, will give succour and inspiration to all around him. I speak of our host, Stéphane Mallarmé.

To reach such a pinnacle? Well, I have sat in the right chairs in the cafés of Saint Germain and Montmartre, and I have grabbed at the epaulettes of their famous patrons; have insisted that they speak, not just to their friends, but also to me, Louis Martens. I have cherished the slightest response, whether in utterance or in that connectedness which, if only for the most fleeting of moments, is confirmed by the mutual focus of two pairs of eyes. I have made myself known to Henri Rivière and Jules Lévi at Le Chat Noir. With seeming nonchalance, I have drawn my chair to a table where sat Verlaine and Jean Moréas or Paul Gauguin with his friend Schuffenecker, and have not left my seat until my own voice has registered within the mêlée of debate and until with pride and self-enhancement I can rise and bid my adieus and "look forward to the pleasure of their company should I be fortunate to meet them again"—which of course I will because I know very well where everyone meets and when! I particularly succeeded in my meeting with a gentleman, Edouard Dujardin, and I believe that this can be readily explained. I felt a spontaneous and real warmth between us and though I had set out that morning with a repertoire suitably prepared and rehearsed, I was immediately relieved as I sensed my script being abandoned to the wind and my artifice to the pleasures of a natural intimacy with one who clearly felt as I did.

I had never met Dujardin before, or even heard of him, but there he was with two friends at a table in the Bords du Rhin and speaking with such passion for the operas of Wagner that it was not just I who turned towards their group, but others who were ceasing their own conversations in deference to his. But it was I who was most ready to interject and this with a vigour that was greatly strengthened when I heard him make an astounding reference to Stéphane Mallarmé. He, this young fellow at the next table, was celebrating with his friends the fact that the great poet was contributing to a new magazine on Wagner that he, Dujardin had just created. Now, it was not difficult for me to interpose since, as you know, I have a great liking for the music of this composer. Unlike many others in Paris, I have no problem with whatever is German (indeed the Bords du Rhin celebrates the beers and repasts of the Alsace) and if Wagner exudes Germanic grandeur in his operas and expresses his delicacies without our own Gallic frills we are still treated to an unprecedented range of emotion. Of course the medium is the opera and it is this that Wagner used to his great advantage. He turned musical theatre completely on its head—the unity of sound and vision, music and poetry—all coalescing in the senses and welling up as pure emotion. And then he built his own theatre, specific to all his needs, and could perform his operas in the most ideal fashion. No concessions, no compromise. Such a man is an artist indeed. It is incredible. And of course he suffered. Such achievement rarely comes without much pain and sacrifice—as too, for Stéphane Mallarmé himself—I will come to this.

So, it was easy for me.

"Monsieur, forgive me, but I overheard your conversation about the great composer and could not believe my ears that you are the editor of a journal devoted solely to this great artist."

"Monsieur," said my new acquaintance, "if you should overhear my remarks, which I should say were made only to those who share my table, and if on listening you should feel moved to contribute to our discussion, my only response can be to offer you a seat at our table and let us profitably turn three into four, an altogether more wholesome number anyway. And if it is our talk of Wagner that draws you to us then how can I, surely now with my magazine one of his principal promoters, make any complaint since your enthusiasm, Monsieur, would otherwise only have reached me through the dry columns of our correspondence page."

And so, the flourish of our opening remarks completed, I drew a chair to the table of my three new companions, and those sitting around us, having quietly been attentive to our exchange, took this as the indication that all was now as before and resumed their attention to their own food, drinks and companions. As I have stated, Marcel, there was no difficulty here. Introductions were made and I had an immediate ease, especially with Dujardin. Of his two friends, one was a musician, a fellow ex-student from the Conservatory of Music, and the other a journalist striving to reach success as a theatre critic. We spoke enjoyably and all found absolute union in decrying the manner in which Wagner had at first been received in our city; a disgraceful occasion when his Tannhauser had been practically booed off the stage. Apart from his nationality as a German, there had been an utter consternation, one that developed into gross hostility, because Wagner had the temerity to insert a sequence of ballet at the beginning of Act 1 instead of the customary Act 2. The troublemakers were aristocrats from the Jockey Club who preferred to have their dinner during Act 1, turn up for the ballet in Act 2 and then hang on to the end of the opera when they could make their play for the female dancers. But Wagner did not concede. His vision was not to be undermined by wealthy ruffians. And how advanced this vision was! The ambition in his operas to include all the arts, to make the correspondences. And there are others dear to me who have also sought this in art and literature, and it was now my great pleasure to find that I had new companions just as excited as I about the changes that must come. And, of course, they were thrilled to know that I am a painter; one touched by the romance of Delacroix, the dream of Moreau, and the strangeness of Redon. But it was in speaking of Böcklin that our enthusiasm reached its heights, for who else in the visual arts could be Wagner's true companion. Marcel, you know of Fantin-Latour, a great romantic and painter of beauty and an artist deeply inspired by music. You like his work I know.

He has made fine paintings and lithographs of the operas, but it is Böcklin who shares the spirit of Wagner. With a vision of his own he has summoned the spirits of the undergrowth, rock and sea, evoked the gods that lurk deep and forgotten in our minds and has called upon those powers that some of our comrades can only find in the methods of the darker kinds of magic.

There are those artists who say that they are the modern ones and so they paint and write of the ordinary life. But I, and those like my new friends, love the extraordinary. We say that to be modern is to find the ancient meaning and then the method that will give it life, today.

And so it was through the generosity of my new friend, Edouard Dujardin, that I was formally invited by the great Stéphane Mallarmé to attend one of his celebrated Tuesday evenings, "the Mardis". I was asked to arrive early—most guests arrive between nine pm and ten pm—and really I believe I was given a gentle interview. Clearly I did not overly dismay our host as I was allowed to stay! Dujardin came with me and I am sure that his introduction counted greatly as Mallarmé is quite fatherly towards him and clearly thinks very well of him. By ten pm all had assembled, and the room that we were in, small when just containing the slight figure of Monsieur Mallarmé, was now defying physical logic by seating eleven and still allowing at least some space for arms to gesture and legs to be crossed. Physically I was comfortable enough and well placed to be able to look around me. My anxiety though was whether I could possibly be clever enough to warrant my place there at all. My consoling thought was that if I were to show too great a ponderousness of wit I would quickly be excluded from the intellectual contest and could at least then sit back and observe. It was therefore such a relief to find that I was able to account for myself rather well (an excellent wine provided some help with this) and one remark that I made stopped everyone in their tracks and was rewarded by a thoughtful silence that must have lasted a full thirty seconds! And in truth my expectation that it would be an evening of pure intellectual combat was quite unfounded and our host, though known for the sharp irony of his wit, never ceased to be a warm and encouraging presence. The malice that did surface came from an altogether different and very surprising source.

But first let me tell you who was there. There was of course Dujardin, such a lively and energetic presence. He had come with me for my introduction and had settled in for the remainder of the evening. There were three other young men, one of whom was a poet, one a journalist and critic of the arts, and the third another writer whose oeuvre remained unclear to me but was distinguished, apart from his considerable good looks, by arriving in the company of no less than the author Joris-Karl Huysmans. Well Huysmans, Marcel, I must tell you about, because it may well be the case that out there in Marmande he is little known. Or perhaps, through his associations with Zola, some of his early works have come to light for you. But that is all gone now. Huysmans, far from plodding through the dull naturalism of earthbound lives, has just written a novel, *À Rebours*, about a man who, through the most exquisite of sensualities, bends the forces of nature to his own will. This character, called Duc Jean Floressas des Esseintes, exists purely for art and a defiant refinement of the senses. In a perfumed cloister of a home he brews, like an alchemist, concoctions of the imagination that willingly pervert the laws of life that most hold dear. He has become the personification of "the decadence". This is a character, so perverse and disgusted with nature and the ordinary, that he painstakingly creates real orchids that will be mistaken as artificial. His favourite artists are Moreau and Redon and he adores the poetry of—Mallarmé. It is no surprise that this fictional Des Esseintes (Huysmans himself of course) should do so, since Mallarmé, par excellence, subverts all the accepted forms of literature. And Mallarmé has already returned the compliment with a piece published in *La Revue Indépendante* that is dedicated to Huysmans' fictional character.

There is in fact a degree of warmth that passes between these two writers that shows that a genuine friendship has formed.

There was also, in the room, another most clearly affectionate relationship. Mademoiselle Geneviève, Mallarmé's daughter graced us all with her presence and showed a most touching attention to her father's needs. I understand too that it is often the case that Madame Mallarmé attends the Mardis, but not on this occasion.

Three of us were artists. Besides myself there was an elderly man, I can only remember him as Alphonse, whose face was so covered from above by a mass of grey curls and from below by an enormous beard, that his true features were utterly obscured. One thinks of one of those dogs covered in great shaggy coats that if clipped short reveal the most alarmingly unexpected skinny bodies. And then there was Félicien Rops—I have mentioned him in my letters to you, indeed he was alarmingly evident in that collection of works shown me by the Countess. We have met briefly before. You might say that in our interest in the idea of a picture we are part of a like-minded group. But visual ideas can be expressed in vastly different ways and Rops, as you now know, has a vision dark enough to send one running to the Impressionists to beg for an antidote of light and colour. He has become infamous for his increasingly erotic subject matter, which is now also entwined with his fascination for devil worship. Indeed "entwined" is the word since his nudes do exactly that, curling themselves round his various renditions of the devil. He is off on his own wild canter into excess and really seems to imagine the devil as a rampant malevolent phallus. Goodness knows how such a man can be famed for being so desirable to women, for that is indeed his reputation. Anyway, these days he is more an illustrator than a painter. I have no prejudice against the artist as illustrator, but it can surely not be the case that one who is commissioned to create imagery with pen and ink or the paraphernalia of the etching process, can match the sheer endeavour of the painter.

I should return now to the final guest, the other of the two women present, and one who I was astounded to see there. Taking her place in a central position, indeed I might say, pride of place, was the Countess of Bolvoir. Of course we needed no introduction. Marcel, can I possibly convey to you the strangeness of the shifting and contrasting settings for my meetings with the Countess? At our last encounter, just days before, she showed me her private collection of art in the sumptuous gloom of her bedchamber, and before that our introduction at a gathering that had all the formality and pomp of dinner at the home of my esteemed patron the Professor Jean-Martin Charcot. Indeed, a dinner that included as guests the Countess's husband who is a senior figure in the government of the nation, and also an Indian prince! And also dear Madame Charcot who, like her husband, in fact more so, indulges in the arts, but in subject matter that is as dissimilar to Félicien Rops as a girl at her first confirmation is to a diseased prostitute plying her trade in Montmartre. The breadth of Parisian society! Rops of course loves such difference. And now to my initial surprise, but then with the glimmer of a fascinated awareness, I sensed that between Rops and the Countess there was a chemistry that could only suggest previous encounters. They eyed each other with a calculated and combative familiarity, at first rarely addressing each other, yet clearly sharing a vicarious rapport.

The Countess was dressed less formally than at Charcot's, though still with great style and elegance, and she smoked. Indeed, sitting next to Mallarmé, it was our venerable host who rolled the cigarettes for her. Rops too has an elegance about him, enhanced by the ease of his being. He must be fifty, his dark curls now streaked with grey, and a splendid moustache that curls triumphantly upwards at the tips. A fine-looking man it must be said and clearly one whose dark twinkling eyes can reflect a sparkle in the cool gaze of the Countess.

At first all who were present, except for the artist Alphonse who seemed quite elsewhere and only interjected the occasional grunt that bore no bearing to the conversation, engaged in a discussion about the current state of the Parisian theatre. Mallarmé and Huysmans became animated on the subject, as did Dujardin, and it led to a most wistful and eloquent soliloquy from Mallarmé concerning his ambition to create what he clearly envisages as a master work. It may be that he will produce it as a play, but in whatever medium it will transform the art of literature. How can I describe this? The best I can understand is that it will supplant the singular use of language and its formal and literal meaning of words. It will present words and phrases as symbols, as agents of association and in their juxtaposition, their sounds, express their very colour and musicality.

There was much laughter here as Mallarmé was gently teased by Huysmans as to the eventual date on which this great work will be offered to his friends, then sent to his publisher, and eventually reach the wider world. I understand that its gestation has been exceedingly prolonged. I expect too, Marcel, that when the wider world does receive this, it will be completely and utterly baffled, as Monsieur Mallarmé's poetry can test the most sophisticated and willing of intellects, and to the ordinary mortal is usually incomprehensible.

A lively conversation then returned to the subject of the theatre, with the views of our host particularly dominant. It was though Rops, whilst clearly being on less familiar terms with Mallarmé than some others present, but in no way unnerved by his reputation, who spoke as articulately and confidently as if the proceedings were taking place in his own home. For a while these two dominated the conversation, discussing with vigour current productions, until Rops, suddenly as if on a whim and giving a nonchalant flick to his moustache and a flash of a glance towards the Countess, propelled the conversation into a new, and for me, more familiar area.

"And have you attended the theatre at the hospital of the Salpêtrière?"

Here there was a stirring of fresh interest in the gathering. Mallarmé tapped the ash from his cigar, raised his thick dark eyebrows, an impressive sight as they are already prominently high, and looked with quizzical interest at the questioner, this in turn being taken as licence by the younger guests to speak. The young poet, with great enthusiasm responded:

"Ah! The impresario Jean-Martin Charcot and his cast of beautiful madwomen—and who has been to see the show?"

Rops of course, being a master of the erotic arts, would well have discerned the element of excitement that marked this young poet's enthusiasm and clearly felt like amusing himself with the subject and its increasing titillation.

"Just a flick of his fingers and they are in a veritable swoon."

There was laughter here, and with a particularly excited harshness from the younger men. As the subject matter is much more familiar to me, I felt more in a position to observe than to partake of the jollity, and it provided as well an opportune moment to study the others in the room.

Mallarmé, who had not laughed, remained a central figure, leaning back in his chair, his legs crossed, his cigar gently sending its curls of smoke to circulate in and around the tassels of a pale green lampshade. He was perhaps aloof, certainly thoughtful, any expression on his lips hidden within the heavy moustache. Huysmans, fully bearded with wiry hair, was bright-eyed and one could sense a restless, nervous energy. He was sitting on Mallarmé's left and seemed affable towards Rops and ready to be entertained by this new and surprising topic. He looked on warmly. Then there was the young poet and also the journalist (indeed Marcel, they are almost my own age—I sound increasingly elderly in my description of the "younger" men) and the sense of these as aspirants sitting at the feet of the master was palpable. Huysman's guest, of a similar age, was generally quiet, perhaps content to rest within the security of his remarkable good looks. He was not sitting with Huysmans but in one corner where also sat Mademoiselle Geneviève who had shown a considerable knowledge of the theatre which she had expressed with wit and charm. How fortunate for a great writer to have such a calm and beautiful daughter to support him. Dujardin was sitting next to me and I had felt his friendly reassurance throughout the evening. Such an enthusiastic man and with a confident and refined knowledge of the theatre especially when it involved the operas of his beloved composer. The elderly artist Alphonse seemed to have increasingly and contentedly withdrawn into his huge beard and was now barely endeavouring to open his eyes. The lids occasionally fluttered beneath the massive eye brows as if with the last residues of consciousness.

And then there was the Countess. Sitting to the right of Mallarmé, always articulate and utterly poised, I wondered whether anything or anyone could unsettle her, though this was quickly followed by the idea that if it were anyone it would be the one sitting opposite her—Félicien Rops.

He, with the smoothest expression, now continued his topic of the hypnotic magician drawing beautiful hysterics into the absolute compliance of the trance. When for a brief moment he paused, and I could tell that such a pause offered the rarest of opportunities for response, the cool and clear voice of the Countess, with that absolute distinction of pitch that can mark the confident female voice from the male, and with no condescension and indeed, no feminine warmth, brought his monologue to an abrupt end.

"My dear Félicien, for one who has as yet to actually attend the Professor Charcot's learned lectures, you seem to have a remarkable grasp of their content. I can see that I no longer need to observe the Professor at his work but simply from time to time consult with Monsieur Rops."

For a moment I felt, as I am sure did others, the threat of a disquieting animosity. The room that had been filled with a friendly and good-natured discourse was now utterly silent. I noticed Mallarmé glance toward his more trusted and

110

predictable friend Huysmans who briefly returned his glance before staring at the wall. More silence. Geneviève Mallarmé moved uncomfortably in her upright chair, stroked hard at her dress downwards over her knees and seemed about to speak when gradually there began the soft sound of a laughter, one that increased in strength, louder and louder until it resounded in the room. Rops, apparently both humiliated and reprimanded, was finding this interaction with the Countess a matter of joyful delight.

"My dear Countess, my dear Marguerite, I feel like a naughty boy full of stories who has received a good and hard spanking."

The young poet, who had been so stimulated by the earlier innuendos in Rops' account of helpless Salpêtrière women, seemed unable to extend his engagement to the sadomasochistic enactment now being displayed before him. He blushed crimson. The others in the room took the laughter of Monsieur Rops as a sign that, if not quite as before, the discussions in the room could resume on a more equal basis. It was Mallarmé who took up the subject of the Salpêtrière, but in a way that made it his own and of an easier, though surprising content.

"I am told that Professor Charcot has brought much understanding to the malady of the hysteric and the neurasthenic. Indeed it has even occurred to me that I might consult with him myself."

Here one of the other young writers, perhaps with a sense that the interaction between Rops and the Countess was still in need of remedy, interjected far too quickly with a bungled reference to the delay in the production of the "great work".

"Do you feel that it might reduce the block to your writing?"

Mallarmé was kind in his response.

"My dear young friend, it is indeed a most hard thing that we must endure as writers—when it feels that the words we need

111

are not available to us and indeed, in the direst of cases, when it feels that language itself is not fit for our purpose. But then, as well, what a challenge it is, to wring out from that which nature and civilisation have left us, a new meaning, a new joy in life. Indeed this is my great challenge and this is what in time I will produce. But first I must outlive the obstacles which too often seem to have a very life of their own."

For a moment he paused and looked down at the smouldering tip of his cigar, poised between the two fingers of his hand resting upon the arm of his chair. He looked up and addressed the young writer directly.

"And also I must earn money. On each day it is my duty to go and teach young students who share little of my own views on art and literature and who simply need to pass exams in subjects that to myself are of little consequence except for the gross impact of boredom that they impose on me. If you should have a family—and mine is dear to me," he now gently gestured with the same hand towards his daughter, "you will wish only and dearly to provide for them. But, you may well find, at night by candlelight, in the quiet apartment with your family sleeping, and with your mind and body beseeching you to give it its own rest, that the poetic muse is visiting elsewhere and that the page waiting before you remains dreadfully empty.

"Such moments will visit every writer. But when to these are added the torture of night upon night without the capacity to close my eyes and be rested by the grace of sleep, and when as I lie upon my bed I feel the pains in my body that for so long have cruelly accompanied me in my life, then I think—Oh for a hypnotist! One who may just command me not to suffer. But also for a great physician who might say, 'Mallarmé, why do you suffer? Are these maladies of the nerves really incurable? Come and visit me in my clinic—we will find a way!'"

Our host had now for sure resumed his rightful position at the centre of his gathering of Mardistes. He turned towards his friend Huysmans.

"Your character Des Esseintes in *À Rebours*, the great aesthete, turned such maladies into an art form. Such is the way of the most refined decadence, but sadly it is not my own. Despite you having your 'hero' declare that I, Mallarmé, am a poet of the greatest distinction, Mallarmé himself struggles to find the strength, let alone the time, to write a few lines worthy of his great French forebears."

"Ah!" said Rops, with all the energy of an opportunity seized and still completely unruffled by the contemptuous remark of the Countess, and in no way sharing the subservience of some of the younger Mardistes, "You will of course, be referring to Baudelaire—I know—a great hero of yours, and, I am so privileged to say, a man whom I was able to count as a friend. You will know that Baudelaire himself was not well. Those who reach into their very souls for their art must make a sacrifice unknown to the ordinary man. For most, a dream is a strange event dissolved through the mundane processes of the day. It is one that memory might just grasp and hold as a fleeting image or uncanny feeling, but still it remains an item of life not to be included in the agenda of living. But this the artist and the poet cannot accept! No, the passionate need is ever present to grasp the elemental, the element of the dream, to struggle with the unknown. Our dear mentor Baudelaire was our vanguard in the battle. What a struggle! We search deep inside our very beings and who do we find? We find our furious selves barring the way, with fists and teeth clenched and eyes sullen and horrible. Then starts the torment, the definitive struggle, and then seeps the pain through the nerves, the insomnia, the ghastly melancholia!"

Marcel, I try hard to quote Félicien Rops as carefully and as true to his own words as memory can allow. It is the case that it is made easier for me as I share both his excitement and his dismay, so that I hung upon every one of his words, words which were delivered with great passion as well as a supreme elegance.

But sadly, though the young poet looked on enthusiastically, as indeed did Geneviève Mallarmé, aided I think by the fact that Rops increasingly focused his dark and glistening eyes upon her as he spoke, the older members of the gathering seemed quite unimpressed. The Countess had the suggestion of a smile about her lips, no longer contemptuous but somewhat condescending, while Mallarmé was staring across the room at the little portrait of himself, hanging in pride of place and which is so intimate and made by his great friend Manet. Perhaps he was thinking of the struggle that Manet had in his own life. Or perhaps he was just wishing that it was Manet sitting there, back from the grave, rather than Rops.

There is no doubting the truth of Rops' words, but I expect that it was the aplomb with which they were delivered that undermined their effect with the sophisticated of the gathering. Huysmans is a writer of novels who is known to have to finance himself by working in an office as a civil servant, and he must surely have his own experience of conflict and the general unhelpfulness of the requirements of living. However, though his demeanour remained friendly, he seemed for the moment uninvolved, just tapping a finger upon his knee. The elderly artist remained as unspoken in his somnolence as he had been all evening. Indeed there was then just silence. This lasted for several minutes and was uncomfortable and it was I, having now formed a surprisingly sympathetic attachment to Rops, who was most driven to break it. I could do this perfectly, for it was time that I spoke anyway, and Mallarmé's references to Professor Charcot provided me with the complete opportunity.

"Monsieur, it would be my honour to introduce you to the Professor who has himself honoured me with a commission, the painting of a mural in the summer house of his beautiful new home. However I know that Madame the Countess knows both his person and his work far better than I and her influence in this respect would be much greater than mine."

Mallarmé was warm and generous in his reply to me.

"Thank you, Martens, for your thoughts. It is no issue for us though. To be truthful I spoke of mere passing fancies, vague wishes, the palliative of imagination. And truly there is no saviour for me in this respect. My view is that those who are cured in such a way by this undoubtedly learned man are so in need of a figure that has all the power that a medicine man exerts over the primitive savage. It is in the mind, and the cure they receive thrives only in proportion to the esteem in which they hold the healer. I have some sympathy for this. There are elements there of that need for the imagination and the creative idea that drives all of us who are here. But in truth it needs as well, an innocence, a naiveté that is sadly long departed from my own life."

There was a true sensitivity to his words. His speech slowed and there was a melancholy to his tone, a mood that softened and saddened the fine features of his face and for a moment his eyes were no longer on the room. Huysmans, sitting next to him, affectionately touched his arm.

"But Stéphane, think what stuff for theatre these Charcot lectures must be." And then to me:

"Tell us more about these lectures. Have you been to one?"

"Indeed I have, Monsieur, and with an excellent seat. I was invited by the Professor who wished me to make some drawings. Very quick and elementary, but no less interesting for this."

"Ah, yes," said Huysmans. "One must only look at Moreau's watercolours to see how a speedy sketch can conjure a vitality to compete even with the sumptuous oil that follows. One day I may perhaps see your drawings, if you should care to show them."

This, Marcel, would be no bad thing for me. As well as being the author of novels Huysmans is a respected critic of the arts. I will certainly follow up his offer. I must concede though that it was the subject of the demonstrations at the Salpêtrière that was truly stirring the interest of the Mardistes and the sketch that was now needed was one that I should make in words. I also felt myself warming to the subject, one that as you know, was already substantiated for me and that was quickly developing for them.

There was the extra pleasure of building a scene which has as its centrepiece a creature of beauty and mystery, the source of an inspiration that still exists for me since that day six months before. The Professor is of course the author of it all, the great thinker, the man whose genius is celebrated at the lectures and who, I had no doubt, would be the greater interest to these older men present with their fine and developed intellects. I thus began with a full and powerful description of Charcot himself, such a darkly impressive and magnetic presence, and then I described with as much understanding as I was able, the details of the lecture with its scientific descriptions of the malady of hysteria.

I summoned up the lecture hall full to bursting with men, and a few female faces, but the men—some talking loudly as if for ascendancy, many coughing through their cigar smoke, some even dressed as for the opera; a great sea of black and white and grey, and hundreds of the finest beards and moustaches in Paris, their owners now craning towards the figure upon the platform as he progressed towards his first demonstration. And I paid due diligence to that first case, that of the male subject, without rushing and stumbling through to reach my true aim. The Mardistes listened silently and to my surprise without interruption. I could see that Dujardin was pleased with my progress and I expect, relieved, perhaps proud that one introduced by him was proving his worth. Mallarmé's eyes were half closed and his slight physical frame seemed as if curled up within his chair, like a cat, resting but with full attention. The amiable Huysmans still tapped with one finger of the hand closest to Mallarmé as it rested upon the arm of his chair. The others were also completely attentive to my account, though Marcel, as by now you will not be surprised to hear, I could rely less on receiving easy reassurance from the Countess.

I had reached the conclusion of my description of the hypnosis of the male patient and the way was now clear for the grand entrance of Madeleine. What of course the young poet had been waiting for, and I dare say, some of the others too. I was determined that they should not be disappointed.

I decided to give immediate emphasis to my personal imagery. Firstly I gave them Madeleine as the waif. Wearing just the pale smock, barely hiding the contours of her slight and slim figure, the long straight brown hair, the eyes down cast, the face without human expression—waiting indeed for the imaginative attention of the poet! The soft footfall—surely a soft footfall if sound were to be registered in the now silent amphitheatre. And then I described the way her eyes had been without focus and seemed to be gazing past the audience through the walls of the theatre and far beyond the confines of the city, but how at the end she had looked outwards, and the soft grey of her eyes and how just for a moment the eyes had focused on the multitude of eyes before her and how I had thought of Gérôme's painting of "Phryme" and her exposure and shame.

Here the young poet was unable to contain himself causing the sole interruption to my account, though one that purely served to spur me on.

"My God! My next poem will be a hymn to your Phryme whose image can surely rescue us from all our maladies!"

I did notice here that from within the shadowy recess of his armchair the face of Mallarmé, one who has suffered from so many maladies, and for his art, showed for an instant a rare look of irritation.

I described Charcot's demonstration—the hypnotic trance of the subject leading first to the accentuation and then to the relief of her symptoms—a transformation that was as if by magic. I could not complete my description without evoking the innocent grace of her movement as at the conclusion

117

she was gently led away and back to her ward. I did though, Marcel, omit the moment that I have so joyously shared with you, of the still grey eyes meeting with mine. I believe that if I had included that I would myself have felt the embarrassment of a Phryme and that the blushing was best left to the young poet.

The response from those gathered was most gratifying. Huysmans was clearly fascinated by the subject of hypnosis. Dujardin made reference to the heroines of Wagner and was rather excited in this by clearly his favourite, Brunhilde the Valkyrie who, he declared, had defied her father Wotan (an allusion no doubt to Charcot), and who would never allow herself to be hypnotised by anyone! Others of Wagner's heroines, it was generally agreed, had been somewhat more passive in their relations to their "heroes". Huysmans' young guest then referred rather acidly to Gérôme's propensity for not only painting Phryme but also an assortment of naked girls of distinctly European appearance being sold in Arab slave markets and how popular these have been with the bourgeoisie.

It was here that Mallarmé joined in the conversation and, as no doubt the norm, it was a cue for the hubbub of our debate to be stilled.

"I am troubled by all this my friends. We speak of heroes and of heroines, of magic and mystery, of trance and poetry, of inspiration and the muse. But is this not in truth a young woman who has suffered from an illness, a disease of the nervous system? Is this not, though we have heard some details of a male case, an affliction that is particularly borne by women and may this not be a sign that we men—and just listen to us here—in our scrutiny of women and their habits, in our requirements of them and our need to have them grace our miserable lives, place such conditions upon their own lives that they become ill with the sheer weight of it all?"

Leaning forward, he had abruptly emerged from the shadows of his armchair and had abandoned his still burning cigar as an encumbrance to the arm that now gestured to the room at large.

"Indeed might not the expectations of the audience at the Salpêtrière, mirrored I might say by an audience present tonight at the residence of the Mallarmés, place such requirements on the very existence of this girl as to cause her nervous disabilities to descend to an even greater disaster? For disaster—a historical fact in the long history of the Salpêtrière—has also laid its mark upon these poor ill women who now fill its wards."

The mood in the room was now very suddenly and emphatically changed. I must say that it was a disappointment to me that our host, the great poet and such a champion of the power of the imagination, should seem so disapproving of our use of the muse. I do believe, Marcel, that a true artist could never be a physician, as we live and champion an existence that must transcend the restrictions of a material life. We suffer the need to place our art above all considerations, to even face poverty and starvation. Mallarmé has though, I know, had tragedy in his life, the loss of a young son, and of course the daily struggle with a teaching job and sore limbs that he had so poignantly described. Perhaps it was from such a position that he curtailed our excitement and called for our sobriety. I certainly felt great discomfort. It had been I who had excited the interest and had felt myself to be a candidate for most favoured guest in doing so, but now I found myself, more or less, being ticked off.

It was a reflex reaction to this that brought about my next remark, accompanied by the desperate hope that it might remedy my position.

"But with respect Monsieur, this patient of the Salpêtrière has been cured. After many years of illness the Professor has released her from the hospital and placed her in the care of one who is even here with us tonight." And with a gesture, made with all the extravagance of one determined to move the attention from himself—"The Countess Marguerite!"

There was in the room—amazement! What a turn of events, what a sequel to the rendition of my own experience. And such an act of compassion by the Countess seemed to turn the tide of Mallarmé's opposition as his eyebrows did that raised up thing which suggests surprise and interest, quite opposite to the annoyance of the knitted brow.

"Marguerite," he said, "how remarkable. I would never have imagined you as the protector of a soul so vulnerable."

Mallarmé is of course famed for his irony, though the application of such towards the Countess seemed to belong far more within the province of Félicien Rops. But the irony was there, along with genuine surprise and approval, and it played around his lips and lightened his eyes.

It was though indeed Rops who diverted my attention from the reaction of our host by his undisguised expression of absolute fascination at this new scenario. His look of surprise, fast followed by mirth was spectacular. His laugh rang out so clearly that all turned towards him and it was only I, now in a moment of personal recuperation, who espied the momentary flashing of the eyes that betrayed both the rage of the Countess and remarkably for her, her embarrassment. Rops was now in full exuberance.

"My dear Marguerite." And at this some of the faces turned back towards hers which was now again, completely composed. "Such generosity, such kindness of spirit, such concern for another! Clearly the Professor Charcot is a man of great perception, to entrust into your care one of his vulnerable offspring."

He paused and lightly touched the curled tip of his moustache.

"And I know Madame that you are certainly not one to forgo the chance of sharing your humanity with another, even one of such lower status than yourself."

Rops was not to be deflected by the impact that the inherent ambiguity in this statement might have on those present.

"My request, Madame, is that I might in some way be of help to you in a task that will considerably require your time and energy. I expect that your husband the Count has little role to play in this and so the presence of a protective father may well be a welcome one for your young, and now cured, hysteric."

"Félicien," replied the Countess, and her tone was as sharp and clear as the cracking of ice, "I understand your wish to play mummies and daddies, but I dare say that the rules of your game would not be appropriate to the faith and expectation that it has pleased me to receive from the Professor. Indeed it was his stated wish that I protect a lone young girl from being sucked into those bowels of the city, from which you sir, find such inspiration."

The interaction had now passed far beyond the good-natured banter and disagreement that Mallarmé considered a creative part of his Tuesday evenings. His dissatisfaction was evident in the tone which he now used. Surprisingly, in his next comment there was the element of defence for Rops.

Turning to the Countess, "My understanding, Marguerite, is that our fellow guest here is an artist who, though he has often depicted those women who have most severely fallen into depravity and disease, has done so with a disdain for any society that can so easily accept such misfortune."

"You are generous Stéphane," replied Rops, addressing his host with familiarity for the first time, and then most solemnly, "It is true."

And to the Countess, still with absolute seriousness, "Marguerite, I do hope that you can find time to introduce me to the girl. It could be such a treat for her if we were to take her out to tea."

The evening was near its end. A strange shift had occurred in which the notorious Rops had asserted himself, aided by the remark of Mallarmé, into a position of dignity, even integrity, and the Countess, who had offered her help and support to a dependant young girl, seemed isolated within her own aura of contempt.

But then, Marcel, how often we find that all is not what it seems and indeed never can be, as nothing is ever but one thing and we can only ever be ready to be surprised.

I have risen early to write this account to you of my evening as a Mardiste and to remember as truly as I may the words that were spoken. Please keep this letter Marcel! One day I may need to refresh my memory of a remarkable evening. What surprises it has brought. I will now rest for a while and then will go out on a fresh hunt of the cafés of St Germain. I have heard of a soirée held on Wednesdays by an aristocrat, at which all the guests smoke hashish. I wonder whom I might find to introduce me.

As ever, your best friend,
Louis

CHAPTER THIRTEEN

The Countess writes to Félicien Rops

Letter to:
Monsieur Félicien Rops, 19, Rue Gramont, Paris

From:
Marguerite Countess of Bolvoir

Dated 27th May 1886

My dear Félicien,

What a pleasure to encounter you again at Mallarmé's and to find that you are both as charming and obnoxious as ever. I am sure that our names will never again appear together on a Mardiste guest list. What did you think of Huysmans? His book is remarkable and his corrupted hero Des Esseintes—such an interesting character—must surely be him! But would you know it? The man works as a clerk for the Sûreté Générale. It might even be part of my husband's domain. Ah well, you and I, Félicien, can enjoy a greater freedom, the bureaucratic life has no claim over us.

Despite the risk of pandering to your extreme arrogance I will also congratulate you on your suite of engravings, the "Sataniques"—the one entitled "The Sacrifice" is particularly striking. I see that you have been allowing your imagination free reign to source its considerable perverse depths. These subject matters are also, as you know, of some interest to me. My dealer, Géroux, acquired for me a set. How preferable if these works had come as a gift—to one who has so enthusiastically encouraged and supported you in your descent into this depravity that suits you so well. But I know better than to expect such a gift to come my way and know too well the consummate ease with which you can change from one object of desire to another and with what speed your passion can degrade to indifference. Just remember where some of your allegiance should still reside.

You have enjoyed Paris to the full and made our city your own. Your reputation as an artist, as a socialite, as a famed teller of delicious, exciting tales, and not least as a human encyclopaedia of facts—these qualities, Félicien Rops, will no doubt grant you your place in the history books. My dear, I know though that all is not as it may seem to others and that you are a man of great contradictions. At night you prowl the taverns and cheap theatres of Paris; you search for a raw experience of the feminine, for women to draw and to engrave their beauty, but also you declare your pity and despair for their sickness and depravity. You, who are such an adept in the voluptuous, corrupt, culture of the city, yearn also for the countryside, for your house in Bièvre, for the purity of your garden and your tender plants. You are not all you seem, Félicien, but then you are such a man of our time. To follow one route through a life, guided by reassuring signs—this is not for you. Nor for any of us who have become truly aware. Now uncertainty chills the air that we breathe, mingled with the scent of pleasures offered as never before. And with the pleasure we must take the pain. As an artist you have chronicled this—your reputation depends on it. Who else but you can paint the syphilitic suffering that women of the streets carry in their wombs and inflict on their stupid clients? A lifetime of disease for a flimsy, sordid fuck.

124

And I know Félicien that you too have suffered pain. You lost your child. Such tragedies are not just of our time. You see no children in my household. The Count and I are known to be childless; the Countess is thought to be barren. But I too have known the tearing away of a beloved, the loss of a child. You will be amazed no doubt. It is true. Perhaps it has left its mark—my dalliance with the cruelties of life was not there before. But, Félicien, will I now become a softer, kinder person? In my favour to Charcot I give my care to a girl, one whose age would match that of my own daughter. You find it absurd and laughable that I should watch over such a one and I too find it quite absurd, but here we are. I shall do my best and care for this young girl who for many years spoke to no one, but who now speaks as the whim takes her and sometimes in the strangest and most infectious way. Heedless of the normal process of conversation, she instead exchanges ideas. One might speak of a subject quite mundane, of the weather or of a shopping trip, and she either responds with silence, not an unpleasant one, or will interject something that to her, and sometimes to me, carries real meaning and requires thought. I amuse myself imagining her as the only one who could converse with Mallarmé in pure abstractions. Clearly she is very bright, though with no education in her latter years. But it was there when she was younger as she is a linguist and can speak good English as well as French and will express herself in either as it suits her mood.

I am making sure that I form absolutely no attachment to this girl. She is of interest to me in various ways, but no doubt she will eventually be subsumed by the city and will disappear. As to your suggestion at Mallarmé's that you and I take her out to tea, this I will decline. I think a three way conversation with the girl over tea and cake could become too complex, and anyway she might decide to speak in English or be mute. However I will introduce you to her in her little apartment and you may wish to arrange to make a sketch of her sometime

125

soon, before we lose her. I am sure you will find her very pretty and a suitable subject, and then you can make your drawing a present to me. And after the introduction you and I may find time for a supper in the Rue des Martyrs. I know of a splendid little place that has rooms—if we should need one—and really, Félicien, surely we should concentrate on the thing we do best together.

Cordially yours,
Marguerite

CHAPTER FOURTEEN

A short note from the Countess to Roberto V.

10th June 1886

Maître,

To record the girl on the eve of our ceremony I have chosen a young artist, Louis Martens. Félicien Rops really cannot be trusted with the task, notwithstanding his inquisitiveness in these matters. Despite the extremes of his imagery I do believe that deep down he still has enough of a Christian morality to be unable to commit to our purpose; he is not truly free. So I have kept him in ignorance. He has incidentally met the girl, as I offered her to him as a model to win myself a night with him. A bait that of course he was completely unable to refuse. I had my night and he had his drawing and I doubt that I will see him again for some time now as he is increasingly taking himself off to his house in the country. His drawing of the girl did necessitate his visit to her apartment at a time when I was unable to be present—the scene must have been bizarre as she has been in one of her mute states recently. Still, he made his sketch and I have seen it—an unusually gentle little rendering for a Rops work.

And you have decided the date—June 16th.

Marguerite

CHAPTER FIFTEEN

An exhibition

Letter to:
Marcel Dupont, Marmande, Lot-et-Garonne département, SW France

From:
Louis Martens, rue Lamarck, Paris, France

Dated 12th June 1886

My dear Marcel,

It is time again to exhibit and the show has commenced! It was with great haste that we placed our treasures upon the walls and of course there was some rivalry for the best places. Jean Melott, who is very taken with George Seurat's methods and who has become fanatical in applying thousands of coloured dots, arrived late and with more paintings than his reputation can justify and finding that there was only one gloomy corner left, threw his works back together—I could see the chips of wood flying off the frames—and departed in arrogant fury. I had little sympathy since I believe he has become more of a mathematician than a painter and anyway only paints the bourgeoisie lounging around. With such attention to the science of colour he belongs more in a laboratory than a studio. I wonder whether he counts the number of dots in each painting? His dramatic exit engendered much pleasure and many jokes amongst those of us who had already secured our spaces and there was a confidence in our own prospects which was now strengthened by his self-inflicted failure. We were also unexpectedly freed to express approval for each other's works.

We have the most remarkable venue for our exhibition. We are showing our paintings all around the walls of a little theatre in Montparnasse, near to la rue de la Gaîté. The owner, a gentleman of tremendous taste and profoundly well disposed towards the arts, is beset with uncertainty as to his future as theatrical impresario. While he considers his position he has no wish for his premises to become a barren space, thus we are invited to festoon his already decorous walls with our works. We are greatly indebted to him.

Ours is an exhibition of artists who are working in Paris (otherwise, Marcel, you know you would be there with us for sure) and it will be a showcase for our time, for our decade and for the city—a celebration as we edge towards the passing of a century. There will be Impressionists, though the creative wind begins to blow elsewhere and their sails are clearly drooping. I understand that the current Impressionist exhibition may be their last, though who can begrudge the success of Monsieurs Monet and Dégas which will surely continue. But our own Monsieur Redon has put it so well when he finds their "ceiling" too low for his own comfort. We hope that the master will visit us.

There will be those who follow the Parnassian poets, and I have some favour for their work; at least there is serenity and an ideal, qualities also to be found in my beloved Puvis de Chavannes, but the Parnassians dwell too much in the past. Most of all there will be the artists who are truly modern, painters of the idea and of dream and the imagination, not deceived or despoiled by doctrines of realism, but those who have taken the romantic vision, shaken it from its torpor, and shown that a dream is not simply an affect but a token of unrealised wisdom within the mind. In our attention to the mind we are truly modern and how well my patron the Professor has shown this through his own work, a great scientist but also a lover of art. It is a fact, Marcel, that Madame Charcot told me how her husband as a young man had to choose whether to train in art or in medicine.

What times we live in and how blessed to find new freedom. It opens gateways to the darkest of alleys or the murkiest backwaters, yet can clear the mists for a glimpse of heaven itself. And what a setting for such art, this little theatre with its dark reds everywhere—in the flock of its heavy wall coverings, its worn patterned carpets, the velvet curtains across the stage, almost purple, and everything changing with a light that flickers on the burnished wings of the plaster cherubs. And the light—I fear that the paintings need their own inner light to be seen! Perhaps this will mark the best of them. Of course there is little daylight so we have installed as much light as we can, though in truth I feel that too great a light would give this theatre, lying so sedately within its shadows for so long, the shock felt by one who on waking throws open the curtains to be dazed by the glare of the sun, or the mortal blow dealt to a vampire mistaking daybreak for nightfall.

And our little red theatre could well be home to a vampire. As in the folds of the heavy velvet curtains that enclose the stage there are crevices, secret places, dusky corners—behind the stage, under the stage, in the dank cellars. There are dark creaking corridors leading to dressing rooms, now neglected and empty, with only the remains of actors once alive to their performance, their photographs pinned to the wall, yellowed corners curling up to meet and hide the faces that once offered autographs.

We have joked and talked loudly, perhaps from our nerves, and jumped and bounced on the meaty wooden boards of the stage thinking how it is to stride across them and be watched, our every move and gesture, by an audience full to capacity. And then there is the fear in this. How much easier to stand a wary distance from one's painting, watching, listening, then choosing to claim authorship or slink off in silent betrayal.

But of course we are also performers of a kind, waiting to be seen through our art. We wish for our paintings to be viewed and adored, even to be seen and judged and there will indeed be the scrutiny of discerning eyes. So who will come? Well we have a splendid lithographic poster by Paul Legrand, who has also organised our exhibition, a fellow with great energy and many contacts, the most important of whom is our host at the theatre. The poster is very decorative with an enticing female figure and lots of swirls. Sadly the address contains an error, but the name of the theatre will be enough. If people wish to wander around Montparnasse hopelessly seeking us, then that is their choice. A simple request for directions from any local should suffice. So we will not worry, the dates at least are correct. I made contact with Dujardin and beseeched him to mention us in his next Revue Wagnérienne and promised art that would not disappoint and that would meet the vision of the great composer. I believe he will oblige. It is too late for the opening but it can help in September, our final month. Legrand hopes to get us a review in *L'Art Moderne*. We have also of course, and there are twelve of us exhibiting, sent out our own notices and I notably to Huysmans who gave me his card on my Mallarmé evening.

I have three paintings on display. I must admit a certain influence from England. Maybe it comes from my work in Charcot's Summer House and all the Shakespeare. The English like their narratives so much. I have seen Rossetti's works inspired by the writing of Danté and his beautiful little watercolours of the court of King Arthur, with its knights and maidens. And Edward Burne-Jones—surely his very life is in homage to the tales of courtliness, the grace of mediaeval love. When I see his paintings I hear the grand chorus of Tannhäuser,

131

the clear Christian voices of the boys and then the crescendos of the grown men on their holy trek to Rome. But fear not Marcel! I have not fallen into religion. With the young Rossetti I glory in his Arthurian ideal, but then the laudanum seeps into his consciousness, the vision darkens, clear Christian mornings change to richly-coloured bedrooms and the girl from Camelot has become heavy and voluptuous—no longer Danté's Beatrice but Venus, Proserpine and yes, there it is—Madeleine becomes the Countess.

So now I think of those two. Madeleine, pure, delicate, barefoot with eyes downcast in modesty and the Countess, voluptuous in green silk like Rossetti's Astarte and surveying the world as her domain. Could she be a vampire herself?

Enough! Daydreams. But these were my thoughts as I chose the subjects for my paintings. If I were commissioned would I paint the Countess of Bolvoir? How could I refuse such a chance, but I only have the prospect of the portrait of her gruff old husband. A painting of the Countess cannot be, nor would I dare cast her without her approval—though parts she might play come vividly to mind. No, my main work is my Puvis painting, gentle, still and in absolute quiet and it is Madeleine, barefoot in classical robes and in contemplation by a lake. The breeze just strokes the surface smooth and all is serenity, the essence of poetry and calm philosophy, and the colours are the dusty blues of Puvis and his soft white and green and against the blue the mummy brown of Madeleine's hair, gathered gracefully upon her head. I worked intensely and have never made a painting with such speed, but then never before been so inspired!

My other two paintings have gestated for months. One, Marcel, you even saw on your visit a year ago. I've added a touch here, a touch there, but now my work for the Professor complete, I had no excuse but to finish it. It is the painting of music—you liked it a little—and it was the face of a girl from Brussels that I used. A good model though now of course it

132

would have been Madeleine—then like Burne-Jones or Rossetti people would say, "Ah! This is the face that he always paints." Too late for that. As music she is the spirit of that art that I most readily defer to. It is the most complete, but now no art exists alone and in the rhythms of my line, with the gentle harmonies of my colours, the subtle contrast of tones, I have done what I can to be the artist-composer. The spirit of music plays upon a lute and next to her, squeezed tight together, is an angelic choir and some of them have instruments, their arms flourishing their trumpets, and their bodies are in robes and so close as to make one great rhythmic swirl of cloth in white and gold, and out of this stretch slim pale arms and faces upturned, singing to heaven.

I have made this a small painting and crowded it, filled it to the brim, just like Rossetti in his little watercolours on paper. There is one I have seen where Sir Galahad receives the Grail. The holy cup is offered by a maiden, and in the background eight angels are lined across, shoulder to shoulder. The foreground is filled with three knights who stand in line, all in profile, with Sir Galahad at their fore and he bows before the maiden who holds the Grail and he reaches out to touch it and reaches behind to grasp the hand of his comrade whose own hand is upon the shoulder of the third knight, and the four figures are joined as if in a graceful dance across the plane of the picture with the angels as the chorus behind. Red alternates with green and there is some gold and just a touch of blue in the maiden's dress and throughout there is a rhythm of line and form and of colour and when I saw this picture I understood Baudelaire and his meaning of musicality in painting.

My third painting is completely of the narrative. To please Dujardin I have made it from Wagner and it is of Tannhäuser and Venus, Act 1 in the Venusberg. And did I say that I would not dare cast the Countess? Perhaps, without conscious intent I have. There lies Venus on her couch, with the young knight

Tannhäuser trapped in her sensual prison of desire, bereft of Christianity and denied salvation. A prison! My goodness could the great composer have struggled so hard with his own emotions? And am I just the same—transfixed by my sweet angel yet with an eye on the contours of the Countess?

It is no great painting, but it will suffice and is my offering to the Wagnerians. And so far, all has been well received and we have been remarkably well visited. The word has gone round and the strange, ornate, and mysterious nature of our venue may well have helped. People are inquisitive. Already my painting of "Music" is well on the way to being sold, which will cover all my expenses for the exhibition, though this has worried me less than usual as I am luxuriating in the proceeds of my commissions.

But now let me tell you of our visitors so far. You will see that though in this we have done well, I am left with a worry which lurks and springs upon me whenever I am alone and without distraction. Huysmans came. I had prayed for this and I felt that at Mallarmé's we had received each other well and that when he expressed an interest in my work he had meant it. Nevertheless, he has his office job and is a man who writes on many things and it is remarkable that he can accomplish so much. But there he was. He came on our first day, as did most of our important guests, two of whom besides Huysmans I will have need to mention.

But already I had managed the most remarkable thing. The previous morning, during a conversation of sorts with Madeleine, I had told her how pleasing it would be if, even for just an hour, she would accompany me to the exhibition. I suggested that she might help with the refreshments, a useful ruse I think as I know she likes helping the priest at the hospital chapel. I really expected this to be met with just vagueness and a temporary withdrawal, but to my surprise and delight she gave a little laugh and said yes. She is changing with such rapidity now that I sometimes have the weird sensation of being with a different woman, and that maybe there are two of her. Anyway, it was an affirmative, confident Madeleine and I could only hope that the mood would continue, so it was wonderful to find her the next day sitting by her open door, wearing a new and pretty blue frock and ready to depart.

So we did. A cab was necessary and we were soon heading for Montparnasse. What a wonderful feeling to be actually out with her. We have always met within the confines of her apartment and now I could have a new experience—the two of us together outside in the world. It was a physical sensation of pleasure, and it was almost fear, a new way of being with her and a different sense of her physical being, more palpable, tangible, nearer yet also more separate.

When we arrived the theatre was gradually filling. We had managed to clear some of the seats to create an open space, and as usual, many who had come to view the art were standing grouped together talking loudly with their backs resolutely turned to the paintings. No doubt most would give the exhibition at least a perfunctory tour before leaving. Madeleine's eyes were wide open and her gaze was full and with immediate response to the movements around her. I was delighted to see that she was the object of those sidelong looks that are given, whilst the viewer still purports to be attending to the face opposite them. She did not notice and was clearly enjoying the freedom of no longer being the main exhibit herself.

We reached the place of my own paintings and she gave a little gasp of pleasure as she recognised herself in my Puvis painting, barefoot and serene in the grace of the golden age. Of course she had never before seen the painting, only the drawing I made of her in her apartment, and she had no idea that she was to be the centrepiece of a picture in oils. And then I realised that her pale blue dress was in absolute harmony with the painting, so I asked her to stand just to the side of it and was marvelling at the tableau I had created when I was surprised by a voice that carried a hint of familiarity.

135

"Monsieur Martens, I have answered your summons." And there was J. K. Huysmans, looking tremendously compact and reassuring in a brown jacket, his thick hair jutting upwards and his face almost immersed in his beard. There was no overt friendliness, but I nevertheless felt the warmth of his interest and my gratitude at his presence must surely have been evident. As he looked at my paintings I looked at him—stared actually—it is a habit I have formed, understandable I think, but I know that I do it with an intensity that can be alarming for some. I have to see the reactions as they flit across the face. With Huysmans nothing flitted. He turned towards me and for a moment was silent and impassive. Then:

"Martens, I find your painting in the style of Puvis de Chavannes to be a fine work which certainly makes my visit here worthwhile. Your Venus and Tannhäuser I like too. But I wonder, Monsieur, how much you are a man of contrasts and perhaps contradictions and whether this may interfere with your success. Hanging beside the stillness and dignity of your Arcadian scene, you have the voluptuous goddess of sex, preening in her bower before the hopelessly tantalised knight. Both subjects are ones that I am ready to enjoy, but perhaps I should be more certain of what to expect when I view exhibits by Louis Martens. Is the gentleman of Paris who visits galleries and sometimes buys a painting, and who on one occasion will delight in the pure simplicity of a female in classical robes, and on another day and in a different mood be enthralled by an overpowering Venus or the malevolent seduction of a Salome—will this gentleman be pleased to be confronted by his opposing pleasures, thrust together before his eyes in adjacent works of art? It is just a thought, but I offer it for any use it may serve. Overall, Monsieur, I must say, well done."

And then turning towards Madeleine who was still standing exactly where I had placed her and who was eyeing him with curiosity:

"And am I to be introduced to Mademoiselle whom I see has at least granted that her resemblance may be used in your painting, and perhaps has also furnished the inspiration?"

Marcel, I was rather taken aback by Monsieur Huysmans' direct manner of speech, even more impressive in its accuracy of observation. I answered quickly:

"Forgive me, yes. It is my pleasure to introduce Mademoiselle Madeleine Seguin who was indeed an inspiration for my painting."

Huysmans is not a man who shows his emotions readily, though my sense of him in these short moments and my experience of his writing, particularly the novel *À Rebours*, show him to possess the most remarkable powers of observation and attention to detail. I was certainly prepared to receive his criticisms and make use of them. He was now looking at Madeleine with the same impassive expression, one that I understood masked a keen enquiry. She in turn just gazed back at him and said nothing. I felt obliged to speak for her, to apologise really, but then stopped abruptly and I am not really sure why except that as I think back, I believe that Huysmans gave a signal, perhaps the slightest and only just perceptible gesture, to silence me. The two seemed to stare at each other for an age and then Huysmans respectfully inclined his head and addressed her directly.

"It is a great pleasure to meet you, Mademoiselle."

At which Madeleine, as if recalling a more graceful life, one that had ended on the steps of the Salpêtrière, offered him her hand, which Huysmans took and courteously brushed with his lips.

Then to me, "Monsieur Martens, I believe that you have done well in this painting."

This was to be his parting remark, but his exit was prevented by a new arrival. First there loomed a huge shadow, both the product of the beams of our eccentric lighting system and the sizeable figure who now strode through them. In fact at first there was just a silhouette and if we were still to be thinking of vampires this would surely be such a one. The figure was made more massive by a cloak that swirled around the body and a profusion of hair that rose up high above the head; and then gradually materialising out of the darkness came the features of the face, strong and refined and in pale contrast to the blackness of the hair and the long byzantine beard. In response to this striking apparition and the dramatic nature of its appearance Huysmans was as impassive as ever. "It is the Sâr. How nice to see you." At which the self-declared personage of Sâr Joséphin Péladan nodded his head in acknowledgement and with indifference to any intended irony.

"Monsieur Huysmans, what a delightful surprise. A chance for me to say that I am overwhelmed by the magnificence of your *À Rebours*. A novel that turns the tide of literature! From your pages I breathe the heavy perfumes that your hero creates, and I see the visions of Gustave Moreau that he so adores and which radiate through the melancholic luxury of his home. Never has inverted sensibility been so exquisite and refined. It is, Monsieur, a tale that elevates art, and those artists whom you have allowed into the reveries of your hero draw from the life blood of the Renaissance masters and distil their essence for our modern sensibility. Such qualities I will continue to exhort and proclaim in my own writing, for through art we can shake mankind from his spiritual torpor."

Madeleine's stare was now upon the newcomer and was of the kind of a child's first viewing of some strange and fascinating object of nature.

Huysmans replied. "My thanks, Péladan. It is true that both I and my character Des Esseintes share a great liking for the works of Moreau. And if you will be proclaiming the virtues of such art then we can only applaud you for it. And you, Monsieur, have your own novel, your *Vice Suprème*, which has done splendidly, and with a frontispiece by Félicien Rops, another artist that Des Esseintes and I think well of."

"And now," added Péladan, "in its second edition with a frontispiece by Fernand Khnopff, a splendid new talent."

He stood tall and confident. Huysmans was standing in his shadow yet there was still a twinkle visible in the deep set eyes. Indeed I found myself, and perhaps the portraits I have painted have made it a habit, comparing the faces of the two men and particularly their eyes. In contrast to Huysmans, Péladan's were large and dark under thick black brows and seemed hooded, yet perhaps that was more from the expression they conveyed of one who, with a knowingness indicated if not declared, was scrutinising and collating every spoken word.

For a moment the eyes slid away from Huysmans and on to my Venus painting, though I believe that he saw nothing, but was considering his own thoughts. Then returning to focus on his fellow writer,

"We may both take pleasure in our success, but you will agree, Monsieur, that how one judges success is also relative to one's ideals and as to these we have far less in common."

If Huysmans wished to reply to Péladan's abrupt revision of his earlier compliments he was not to have the chance as we were now surprised by another new arrival. In this case it was the voice that reached us first, so loud and resonant that the conversations previously reaching us from the standing area were reduced to a mere background murmur.

"Huysmans and Péladan," boomed the voice. "What good fortune." And close behind it emerged the splendid figure of Jean Moréas.

Now Marcel, Jean Moréas you may not know. He is a writer and a poet and Mallarmé has spoken well of his work. I know him just a little—some brief café conversations with others present. Like Péladan he prefers to hold sway. In fact I can't really say that I conversed with him. I managed a few words perhaps and in that I did better than most who were present. He is a man most confident in his own views.

He was then upon us, greeting the two with elaborate bonhomie and a nod towards me—I fear that he did not recognise me at all, and no gesture whatsoever to Madeleine. He was immaculately dressed and he bears himself in a rather proud and military fashion, an impression that is emphasised by the most magnificent moustache that curls up almost to his ear lobes (one that puts Rops to shame) and all set off by a monocle that is grasped within the musculature of his right eye.

"Huysmans, you have cleaved yourself from the naturalists in the most ruthless fashion. À Rebours has trounced their self-righteous devotion to the mundane and left them sacrileged—and by one of their own! I hear that Zola has had apoplexy. We have made merry on this, Monsieur, and we congratulate you."

I noticed Madeleine at this point looking around her in a perplexed fashion as she could not fathom the nature of the "we".

"It has been coming," replied Huysmans, "but I feel no triumph in this. I have learned much from my realist friends and wish them well, though change has approached and I have welcomed her. And you Jean, you have no doubt been productive yourself."

Whether or not this was intended as a question, Moréas was clearly pleased to treat it as one.

"Thank you. I am preparing for an article, one that you will both find most relevant to your work. September should see it published in Paris Match. It is time now, my friends, to proclaim ourselves and our art and to do away with confusion. Too long we have been dismissed as Decadents. We must grant ourselves a title and a credo of our own. I will emphatically declare us as Symbolists and I will be proposing a Symbolist manifesto."

This of course, Marcel, as you may imagine, was announced with a considerable flourish and in a voice so resonant that even those absorbed in conversation or in examining the paintings were turning towards us. Madeleine, whose hospital environment had never been less than strange, was still not immune

140

to this completely new strain provided firstly by Péladan and now Moréas and was viewing them with a look best described as amazement.

"Ah, no longer the Decadents. How sad," said Huysmans with a hint of amusement.

"The title is inadequate and can no longer serve," declared Moréas. "We are Symbolists, Monsieur, and we owe you our gratitude. Your hero is decadent but your book is undoubtedly—Symbolist!"

The Sâr Péladan had been brooding over these matters whilst standing with a hand supporting one elbow so that the other could freely finger the long black beard. The brows were knitted and the dark eyes stared at the carpet, until in a startling fashion they were raised and directed straight at Huysmans.

"I think, Monsieur Huysmans, that given the nature of *À Rebours* you may not so easily enter the esteemed group heralded by our friend Moréas, but instead must linger in decadence. Your Des Esseintes celebrates art, but his pleasure is nothing but self-serving. To me, Monsieur, art is our means of transformation, a blessed gift to humanity. Through art we can commune with angels." And turning to Moréas, "I too will be making my views known."

I was certainly aware that angels were unlikely to play a part in Huysmans' thinking. He remained as stolid as ever: impassive, compact.

"Monsieur Péladan, we would seem to be in an age of declarations. You of course are a man with a mission for humanity and will certainly be a case for Moréas' Symbolism. Myself, I must undoubtedly decay—along with my Des Esseintes, in neurasthenic self-absorption. In fact I should probably be doing some of that right now."

And at this he pulled out a large watch from beneath his jacket, viewed the time, and then with decorum bid farewell to us all.

The three seemed propelled into their separate directions as when the polarities of a magnet are suddenly reversed.

141

Péladan headed for the clearance that still contained a number of conversing guests. Moréas moved briskly in the direction of the stage, keeping close to the walls with a brief examination as he passed each painting, and Huysmans headed towards the rear of the theatre and the exit.

But Huysmans moved more slowly than the other two and I realised that his intention was in fact to be free of them and that his interaction with me was not yet complete. He was clearly in deep thought and then he halted and walked back to where I and Madeleine still stood.

"Louis," and I was surprised and gladdened to hear him address me in so familiar a way. "I desire a brief word with you that should be in private. Mademoiselle Seguin, would it be an impoliteness to you if I should take your artist friend away for just a brief moment?" And again Madeleine, as if revisiting some earlier mode that had been cast off on her entry to the Salpêtrière, one that was now creeping back to surprise us all and that could be most readily elicited by Huysmans, gracefully concurred.

We walked just a few metres to the shadowy corner where Melott would have shown his pointillist paintings and, given my difficulty in making out the features of Huysmans' face from the mass of his beard, the artist had clearly made the right decision. However, from deep in the shadowy sockets the eyes still shone with intent.

"Listen, Martens. I realise now that this is the girl discussed with such fervour at Mallarmé's. There is something special about her, but that is by the by. Charcot has entrusted you to befriend her and as part of your friendship you must protect. He has also entrusted Marguerite Bolvoir with even greater patronage. This confuses me. Stéphane is friendly with her and he likes her mind and I think she excites him a little. He knows her better than I, but it is clear to me that the Countess is in no way a philanthropist. So why does Charcot have such faith in her? Perhaps she has excited him too."

This last was spoken more as a personal musing. He paused a little and then moved closer.

"I have begun to think of another novel. It may not be the next, but the ideas are coming. It will of course be different to *À Rebours*, but since I am such a cauldron of decadence I may as well dig deeper into the despair of our time. My Des Esseintes used a hyper-refinement of the senses to create a world in which to disappear. Others reject the ordinary life with even greater contempt. Their way is to study magic and to practice the darkest extremes of witchcraft. This will be the subject of my novel and my research has begun. There are those in Paris whose need for distortion takes them into areas of the greatest malevolence. I enquire, and then I hear amongst the whispers and allusions of those that may know but who fear knowing, the name of the Countess of Bolvoir."

He paused and looked down and then up in the direction of Madeleine. She remained in his vision as he finished.

"Be watchful, Martens."

And then, as if all else had become irrelevant, he turned and this time walking quickly, made his way up the incline to the exit and left the theatre.

To the pleasures of a successful and interesting day there had now been added the distinctly unpleasing feeling of a danger; one that could not be readily named but which added to the gathering disturbance that accompanied my growing involvement with the Countess. Marcel, I would be glad for your opinion on these matters. There can be no doubt that Marguerite Bolvoir is a most unusual woman who with relish disposes of the common niceties of social life. I have admired the aggressive independence of her stance, and even accepted her grim philosophy and the dark imagery that is her taste in art. But now Huysmans, clearly with concern for me and for Madeleine, has evoked a further and less manageable entity. The practice of magic is one that I have instinctively avoided and sense that it can engender the most damaging consequence.

143

The Countess has been a generous benefactor to Madeleine and is entrusted and respected by the Professor, admired by Mallarmé, married to a personage of the state—can it really be that in such a way she is a threat to her own ward?

And Huysmans is of course a novelist, a man of imagination, who dreams up stories. Perhaps I have become the victim of his latest imaginings. Yes, I suspect that that is the truth of it. I shall continue as before and the new pleasures in my life will not be spoiled by the fantasies of others.

There. Now I feel better.

Write to me, my friend. Will you still be exhibiting your own work in the autumn?

Let me know.

Your good friend,
Louis

CHAPTER SIXTEEN

A letter to the Archbishop of Paris
from his Vicar General

Letter to:
His Eminence Joseph-Hippolyte Cardinal Guibert, Archbishop of
Paris, Hôtel du Châtelet, rue de Grenelle

From:
Rt. Rev. Msgr. Jean Andrepont, Vicar General of the Archdiocese
of Paris

Dated 15th June 1886

Your Eminence,

You wished to be kept informed about our brother Pierre
Lambert at Saint-Louis de la Sâlpetrière. He is most dutiful in
his offices to his parish and I know no other amongst our brethren who could be said to be more diligent in his service to our
Lord and to the holy Christian virtues that bind us together. He
continues as well to make use of my own services as an advisor
and it will be of no surprise to you, knowing his ardour, that
in this he is as thoroughgoing as can be. If I may be allowed
a degree of flippancy I would say that the word "relentless"
would offer the most accurate description. Of course I welcome
the opportunity to be there for our brother whether in privacy
or in shared conversation and in the latter he has become

145

increasingly willing to engage. This is unusual as he has been so fiercely self-reliant in past years, simmering with passion in his service to our Lord and then with those occasional florid outbursts of unrestrained zeal that first gave us concern for his state of mind. As you know, in recent months this has reached truly obsessive proportions, particularly in his ministrations to a young female inmate of the hospital whom I know only by the name of Madeleine.

You will understand from this letter that Lambert has increasingly needed to unburden himself. He is suffering through some particularly tortuous events which once again concern the same young woman. He has been quite subsumed by the idea that he must save her soul. I have to say that if his account of these events is accurate, it is much more than her soul that is in danger and indeed, we share our brother's fears.

I am not the only one to have been told of these matters. Others of our brethren have been asked to pick at this knot of anguish, one that has gripped Pierre at the very depth of his being. As we try to untangle this, a sequence of events does begin to show. We have of course heard rumours, seen the signs that there are those in Paris who industriously carry out the work of Satan. We shrug, we continue on our way with our faith, our reliance upon the scriptures, in our certainty that the blessed sacraments fill us with the power of the Holy Spirit. We assume that no other power can really make a challenge, that we are righteous in being the only Church and that we are granted spiritual ascendency through our belief and devotion. God, we believe, has chosen us to devote our lives in service to His Church, which is the only Church, and we maintain that charity will always prevail—that it is a fundamental truth. But how complacent have we become? Is the anguish of our brother Pierre in fact his pained gift to us, his warning to be endlessly watchful, forever on guard against an evil that intends to utterly prevail?

We would still be enjoying our complacency if it were not for Pierre's agony of self-reproach. He is convinced that he is about to sin. Of course the confessional serves for the declaration and the due penitence and absolution of sin, whether it is past or future. But Pierre's need for resolution from his "proposed" sin has been so strong that the services of the confessional and myself as Confessor have been unable to contain it. He has had to take up the matter with his brethren and even with me outside of the confessional box and he has required and sought out the most earnest theological debates during our visits to the priory. It has become for him an overriding question of spiritual ethics. Knowing his temperament my expectation is that sadly he will be compelled to find against himself. If ever there was one cast into this world a condemned man it is he.

Eminence, you may already be sensing from my letter that I have trod a fine and problematic line between those words said to me by Father Lambert within the bounds of the confessional and those received through plain speech in our meetings at the priory. It is a similar conflict that now weighs so heavily upon his own conscience. He has been told things in the confessional and he proposes to take this information and physically act upon it, thereby breaking his vow of complete secrecy as a Father Confessor. Therein is his sin.

The young woman Madeleine visits the Chapelle Saint-Louis at the Salpêtrière on a regular basis. In the early years she was always mute and intriguingly she would enter the confessional box and spend her time there in complete silence. Pierre at first was in confusion about this. He could make out the silhouette of a young woman through the lattice, but no words were uttered. Of course he has always had a distinctly unusual congregation. They are the inmates of a hospital for madness and so strange behaviour abounds, from eccentricity to sheer lunacy, and he is well used to hearing more than he can possibly respond to. But with Madeleine there was nothing that could justify a response at all.

On one occasion, because of some trick of the shadows, he remained there maintaining the Sacrament of Penance for a vastly long period of time before realising that the girl had gone and he was quite alone in the box, indeed in the whole building. This intangible quality began to fascinate him. Having once viewed the girl as she prepared to enter the confessional, he was now able to identify her from amongst the many others that make up his congregation. Often he would see her sitting or standing completely still amidst the bizarre posturing and utterances of those around her. It was therefore a momentous occasion when she eventually spoke—and in English. You understand Excellency that this is after two years of silence. Of course I cannot know what those first words were, but one can only imagine Pierre receiving them with joy and cherishing them for ever more. And so Madeleine continued to attend The Sacrament of Penance and the speech did not cease. There were still some occasions when she would revert to muteness, but gradually the communications and the expressiveness increased, and now more often, in French.

Something special had arisen between them. It had been gathering through all the many months sitting there so close but without sight or sound—a most unusual state for our Father Lambert who as we know is such an active and driven man. It was as if she had introduced him to his opposite, and he came to look forward to those times spent with her as an opportunity for quiet personal and spiritual reflection. This brought a sense of peace that he had never before known. It is also surely to Pierre's credit that rather than repudiate it he had allowed this difficult experience to continue and of course, in doing so, he had responded with grace and unconditional love to one of his flock. Ah! "Love". Does he love her? Yes, I expect he does.

It came about over time that she would sometimes remain in the chapel after services and help with such small tasks as tidying up and collecting prayer books. And so the relationship, in its still and understated way, grew and certainly to Pierre's mind his young handmaiden in Christ began to bloom. I believe that we must also give some credit here to Madeleine's physicians who were presumably continuing to treat her. I know that for some time she had been directly under Professor Charcot himself.

She began, additionally, to help in the preparations before the services, drifting around like a pale shadow and I think, increasingly to Pierre, his own shadow, a soft element that he came to understand as a completely new experience of his own being. Though as I write this I remember him stating this very thing, but then stopping for a moment and uttering, "But my mother ..." before pushing the thought away. But what accompanies such strong affection for a person is so often a degree of possessiveness and Pierre, who had made a severe injunction to have nothing and no-one in his life to interfere with his devotion to Christ, now suffered from the kind of worldly and "base" emotions that could only leave his spiritual equilibrium profoundly upset. He felt thrown into the pit of temptation. This was his "time of St Anthony" he would say.

The tide changed and the floods of emotion began to rise when Madeleine informed him that after five years as an inmate she was about to be discharged from the wards of the Salpêtrière. Of course with somebody as uncommunicative as her Lambert had easily and I suspect, happily, assumed that she had no life apart from the chapel or the hospital and had not allowed for any possibility of change. But it was indeed the case that she was to leave. Not only was he faced with this most unwelcome fact, but there was also the emergence of new persons who were to have significance in Madeleine's life, and one very significant other. Madeleine was leaving and she was to be under the charitable charge and protection of a woman; someone of the highest society, the aristocracy in fact, Marguerite the Countess of Bolvoir. It was easy to see from Pierre's later recounting of this to myself and others at the priory that he hated these changes, that he crudely experienced them as attacks and loathed this woman he had never met. To this of course he did not admit, but it was as clear as the peal of a chapel bell—though with a far uglier sound.

In fact Madeleine's departure from the clinical confines of the hospital did not preclude her at all from attending the chapel. She continued to attend the services, The Sacrament of Penance, and still served as Lambert's lay "priestess", his helper around the chapel.

On one occasion the Countess came with Madeleine to visit, or rather Madeleine came with the Countess, as according to Lambert the Countess was not one to be seen to be merely accompanying anyone anywhere; such was her dominant and aggressive personality. Can you imagine she and Lambert together? They did not hit it off. He felt that she was just there to scrutinise a place in which her ward spent so much of her time—and to scrutinise him. She would have surmised that there was the confessional element in Madeleine's relationship to him. He noticed that she made none of the normal genuflections on entering the chapel or upon leaving it, instead giving the altar, to his mind, a dismissive parting glance that was charged with insolence and, as later he mused, with challenge—a challenge to the Holy Sacraments. You will see now Eminence that I begin to touch again upon some of those matters that I referred to at the commencement of this letter.

Father Lambert became increasingly disturbed. He was suffering such great difficulty in having to share this soft and peaceful creature, one who had opened up his life and given grace to his being. The old agonies were now returning, not as arduous spiritual imperatives, but as the emotions of ordinary life, those shared by ordinary people, and primarily that awful ordinary feeling: jealousy. Pierre had become dependent on this girl who hardly ever spoke and he now felt deep despair at her possible loss.

It was though, not just a matter of his own passions. In the midst of his virulent antipathy towards the Countess he was experiencing unease from another source, one which could be related more readily to facts. As they moved around the chapel, lighting candles, placing prayer books upon pews, or reverently preparing for the Holy Eucharist, Madeleine was making occasional remarks from which a narrative was beginning to grow. And undoubtedly adding to his impressions were the most private words said to him from within the confessional. Pierre sensed danger and he became increasingly frightened that something dark, something to be deeply distrusted, was attaching itself to this beloved, pure girl. Worst still, he came to believe that there might even be a plan to despoil and ruin her.

I expect that this was not only due to his apprehension of "actual" danger. It would easily have been compounded by the new state of affairs in which others, now manifestly existing, were destroying his previous delight in there being only her and him. Thus there had arrived an "evil" threat to the "goodness" and "righteousness" of what had gone before. Nevertheless evidence of a more factual kind was gathering.

We must keep in mind that Father Lambert, more than any of us, has been a watchdog for holiness and a fighter against sin. He has watched carefully for the manifestations of sin as they emanate from those groups that gather and abandon themselves to licentiousness and the worship of the anti-Christ. It is now, sadly, my own confession that too often I have dismissed Lambert's urgent and anxious communications to me on these matters. As your Vicar General these are of course my diocesan responsibilities and who else could he come to? At the time it was too easy to reduce it all to his internal struggles. In the confessional we do our duty, we hear the declarations of sin and we know that much of what we hear is repetitive and of little consequence, minor aberrations, sometimes even an artificial filler. We listen, we do what is necessary and on occasions it requires a real effort of will to grace the innocuous with any degree of gravity. But the sin can at times be of great significance. There can be a passionate need for repentance and absolution. Such occasions of course we remember more readily and some of these sins may even still shock us. I myself once ministered to an anguished soul who had fallen power-fully under the influence of so-called "devil worshippers". My understanding is that Pierre too, ministering within the hospital to fevered, damaged minds, minds that many would have dismissed as merely deluded, heard of such things, and in The Sacrament of Penance he once gave absolution to one utterly corrupted; a man who had been enmeshed in a most secret and profoundly evil circle. The knowledge of this, the details of the tragedy, Pierre had retained and now he began to suspect the unimaginable, that his Madeleine might even be drawn into the very darkness that had destroyed the life and sanity of one of his flock.

It was not too difficult for him to begin piecing together a rough structure for this sinister magic circle, a group that he increasingly believed was about to close around and violate both her and the spiritual love he felt they shared. Of course her virginity, a virtue that for us is so attractive to uphold, would be equally attractive to them as a virtue to despoil.

His time as Holy Confessor to the patient who was so disas-trously mixed up with the magicians was long over. It ended in fact with the man's suicide, an event which became yet another reason for Pierre to berate himself and a powerful force in his growing desire to make retribution and to rise up against those who had now become his greatest foe. There was one whom he guessed was at the centre of this evil circle. You know him Your Eminence. You were yourself involved in his excommunication ten years ago. If I were to refer to him now as having once been The Reverend Roberto V. you will recognise and remember. He has, for sure, not gone away. What are we to expect of such people? That when we condemn and punish them for their sins they will slink off in shame and, full of remorse, devote their lives to atonement? Those such as Roberto V. would be merry at such expectations. For him excommunication was a ceremony of supreme validation, an empowerment, a recognition of an exalted position in his congregation of evil.

The clues were there. The Countess had taken Madeleine on a strange excursion. She was to meet an important person, someone who was interested in her and in her future welfare. The account of the trip, the ride in a carriage, the big house outside the city at which the meeting took place, all stirred in Pierre the most unwelcome memories and with them a terrible foreboding. He had heard the description of a similar journey once before and the details of the house were the same as told him by his poor deceased confessant. It was like a dream gradually recalled, a dawning recognition full of strangeness and etched through with fear. And then Madeleine told him of her experience there. Most of the time it had been a pleasant afternoon out at a country house. They took tea on the lawn, walked a little; the Countess seemed happy, different from her normal exactness, a certain frivolity about her. Really Madeleine was puzzled, but what led her particularly to speak to Lambert in her quiet inexpressive tones about this visit was the time during which she was introduced to "the man", the apparent owner of the house, and it felt clear to her that this introduction had indeed been the main purpose of the visit. She wanted to understand from Lambert what had happened; as a religious man she felt he would know. The meeting had taken place in what she could only describe as a chapel, yet she could not easily rest with this description. It contained what seemed to be a large altar, though this was unadorned as if waiting for the necessary artefacts. She was of course familiar with these from her attendance at the Chapelle Saint-Louis and the many occasions on which she had assisted Lambert in preparing for services. The place she was now in was hardly the size of the Sâlpetrière chapel, but it was not small and could easily contain large family gatherings with still room for more, perhaps fifty or sixty in all. There were windows with stained glass, but this was so peculiar and striking. The images within the leading of the windows were still there, but only as silhouettes, as if the colour had been extracted from them leaving the saints now depicted as stark black shapes. This also cut out much of the light giving the chapel an atmosphere of gloom. The floor was stone as may be expected though there were some strange designs painted there that Madeleine could not recognise. Some of these designs were also engraved or painted upon the walls and some of the pillars. The air was heavy with incense. Madeleine had always loved the smell of Benedictine incense, but this had other elements in it as if mixed with perfume and spices. At first it had acidity, a sharpness against the senses, but quite soon, she felt it like an infusion, a heavy warmth that crept through her body from her feet right up to her hair roots. She said her toes tingled.

Pierre, describing this to us at the priory, showed great distress at this point, so that we especially felt the need to give comfort to him. I think that there must have been some drug inhaled in all that perfumed incense and for Pierre the thought of his Madeleine's "toes tingling" utterly contravened the acceptable limits of his imagination. This pale, pure girl, this blessed one who had brought an acceptable love into his life, was describing a flush of sensuality moving through her young body.

This was not though how Madeleine was thinking of it. As she told these things to Lambert and described the scene there was a need to clear her confusion and to understand the nature of this strange place. The meeting with the "important person" took place in the chapel and had been short. In the shadowy interior, through the thick curling smoke of the incense, she had been strangely unable to properly see him—but yes, Eminence, we do believe it to be the one I spoke of. Pierre had persisted in extracting at least some form of description. Large, dark, heavily built, but with a light voice. Not French, perhaps Italian she thought, but of course her experience is very limited. He had spoken softly to her having apparently dismissed the Countess from the chapel. Madeleine had felt strange she said, but had quite liked being with him, and she remembered that as she listened to him her eyes strayed to the windows and the black silhouetted shapes were seeming to move, to congeal together and then to separate and float across the glass. It worried her but simultaneously gave her pleasure. As he spoke in his quiet voice and lilting accent she felt a tickling feeling in her stomach and began to feel warm, though the chapel had been decidedly cool on her entry.

Maddeningly for Lambert, though in response to his insistence so much detail was coming from the normally less than vociferous Madeleine, she could remember nothing at all of what he had said to her. She had the feeling that he had asked her about herself, but that was all. He left the chapel and soon after the Countess collected her and they straight away embarked on the return journey to the city. Apparently, in the carriage, the Countess's mood changed and she became cold and indifferent and this upset the girl and added to her sense of puzzlement about the day. She asked the Countess whether she would be seeing the man again and she felt that her reply, though affirmative, was given in a hostile way:

"For sure you will, and we will see what you make of him next time." It then occurred to Madeleine that the Countess, who seemed much enamoured of their host, may not have been happy at being dismissed from the chapel and had expected to stay. I suppose that given her very restricted life, her lack of sophistication, her inexperience of relationships, someone's jealousy could be hard for her to define, though if one includes Pierre's feelings of possessiveness she seems one way or another to be surrounded by it.

Madeleine had nevertheless, despite her guardian's aggression, enquired as to the date of this next meeting and was told that they would be returning to the house in a month's time and on this occasion would be staying overnight.

Lambert had received now the information that confirmed to him that the girl was to be inducted by these people. Such corruption, such baptism into evil, such terrible sin filled him with immeasurable dread. He said that it felt as if his very entrails had been grasped and were being torn out of him. There was the catastrophe of evil triumphing in this way and thus destroying a beautiful gift from God, one that had come to him surely to be protected and nurtured into even greater goodness. But there was something still worse. He sensed with increasing panic that they were after more than Madeleine's virginity, more than a sexual despoiling and corruption of a young soul. He began to believe that they were after her very life. All the circumstances would suit their sacrificial purpose. A young, uncommunicative girl without a family, without a past, recently discharged from an asylum and into the trusted charge of a black magician's accomplice. This was a girl who could disappear and there would be no pursuit, no great search to find her. She would simply have wandered off, had a relapse, or even have committed suicide. And what a prize she would be to them, a young virgin delivered to the altar.

Your Eminence, these events described are from almost a month ago and so the Countess any day now will be returning to the house with the girl. I consider the situation to be most grave. The intensity of the alarm we feel is matched by the degree of our sense of impotence. The Countess, through the force of her personality and the position held in the government by her husband is extremely powerful. Indeed, as Pierre's intuitions are the only basis for our fears, we have no factual evidence, no grounds to go to the police or to any other body that might offer protection. In the last few days Madeleine, most unusually, has not been seen at the Chapelle Saint-Louis and Pierre, driven by anxiety and contrary to his usual custom, has been in communication with the hospital staff. Madeleine is still under the care of one of the physicians there but has missed her last two appointments.

It is of course, Eminence, not for me to expect any action from you. Despite your seniority in the Holy Church you are in no greater a position to act in this matter than I. Lambert of course remains in a state of great, yet helpless vigilance. The main purposes of this letter are twofold. Our ongoing concerns about the welfare of Father Lambert are surely justified and there is still something related to the girl's confessional and the sin he fears committing, which he declines to share with us.

It has also been my regrettable duty in this letter to inform you of an order of Satan existing in our city which I consider to be more accomplished and sophisticated in its promotion of evil than any we have faced before.

I shall of course inform you of all new developments as they come to light, though these circles are adept at drawing darkness around them.

Asking the blessing of Your Eminence,

I am, Yours respectfully in Christ,
Jean Andrepont

CHAPTER SEVENTEEN

Notes on the case of Madeleine Seguin, now in the care of Dr Jacques Lamond

Notes on the case of Madeleine Seguin
Dr Jacques Lamond, intern to Professor J.-M. Charcot
Salpêtrière Hospital

June 25th 1886

The patient Madeleine Seguin has now been discharged as an inpatient of the hospital and Professor Charcot has entrusted me with her ongoing treatment. She normally returns to the hospital twice a week and on these occasions comes straight to me and we have around an hour in which she can converse about anything that is troubling her, or that she may simply find of interest. Of course she can at times feel most troubled and any glance through her previous notes and the history of her treatment show well enough that it is a truly remarkable outcome that she has left the institution at all.

She was discharged on the 3rd May and has been coming now for her appointments over the last seven weeks and has always been most punctual. I am concerned though to have not seen her on the last three occasions. She has simply not arrived nor sent word of any illness that may have prevented her attendance. It is out of character and puzzling. I am using time now that I had set aside for seeing her in which to write this update of her progress.

Progress it certainly has been. There were times in the first few appointments in which we sat together in complete silence. My attempts to initiate discussion failed dismally and in the end there was nothing to do but allow the silence. Strangely these silences began to feel rather satisfying and, unaccountably, even fruitful. This I cannot explain, but feel quite sure about its value. Initially though, the lack of communication seemed such a waste of time that I questioned whether I could justify seeing her and took the matter up with the Professor. After that I felt at complete liberty to continue as he was so keen for me to do so. Perhaps he has an intuitive sense that I can help. I greatly appreciate his faith in me, but I believe that as well as this she has a special place in his interest and indeed, I suspect, in his affections. She has become a kind of child of the hospital. She was cast into its arms by those who abandoned her at the doors and who never returned. It remains a complete mystery. So, in a way, Charcot became the father, the hospital the mother, and here she has lived with a huge number of siblings. Something has always felt different about Madeleine though, a certain quality which I find most difficult to understand, but which certainly exists and which leads those around her to take a special interest in her, even a proprietorial one. I suppose that to the Professor, this manifested in her becoming one of the most effective subjects of his lecture demonstrations where even the audience, including many of the most august within the scientific community, came hoping that it would be she upon the rostrum. I shared such interest, as it was during a demonstration with this patient that I had my most exciting and valuable insight into the mechanisms of hysteria. I suspect that without this special appeal Madeleine would have just been subsumed into the greater mass of Salpêtrière patients, no more than a listed name and occupant of one of the multitude of beds in the wards.

The acute symptoms of hysteria, most floridly displayed in the first years after her admission, have almost all disappeared.

There is certainly no more of the paralysis that so beset her, though there are just occasions when one of her arms can be seen to hang limply as if in memory of the crippling contractures and anaesthesias of the past. Her senses are operating perfectly, without any distortion or impediment. As I have mentioned, she can be silent for long periods, but this can no longer be seen as hysterical muteness; rather, and I find myself surprised to be writing this, a simple wish not to talk. I can well understand that having lived through periods of grotesque disharmony she might now embrace the peace that comes with sitting in silence.

But speech does occur and what an interesting thing it has been to hear the accounts of her world, told by one who is perhaps for the first time, at any rate since her childhood, able to do so. The fact that on a whim she can move from French to English and back again continues to impress us. After her admission to the hospital her rare utterances were always in English, and this was judged at the time to be a symptomatic feature. The Professor always maintained that French was her principal language and that adherence to English was another manifestation of the neurological disorder. Nearly everything now is in French and without doubt this is her mother tongue. It has become a point of interest for me to observe the occasions of the sudden switch to English, as surely there is a hidden cause, something there in her thinking. If French is the mother tongue is English the father?

The Professor has organised things very well so that there are two people existing in her life outside the hospital who both in their different ways watch over her. One is the Countess of Bolvoir, an acquaintance of the Professor who as a lay person has shown much interest in his work, often apparently, making her own shrewd observations. I have met her myself and found her to be rather cool and imperious, but perhaps my impressions are faulty as she has shown much interest in Madeleine and clearly wants to give her the support of a mature female figure as she goes out into the world. The other is nearer to the girl's age, though still a few years older, and is an artist; someone Professor Charcot commissioned to work on his own house. I just assume that the Professor knows him well enough to trust him to take no advantage. Madeleine's new life is one of relative freedom, but is beset by all the dangers that can befall a young woman living alone in a city; one which can corrupt and destroy innocence and then move on to its next victim with barely a backward glance. The Salpêtrière's first public use was to house the multitude of such victims that filled the streets of Paris; what tragic irony if my patient should now need to be saved from such a fate and could only be secure if once again within its walls.

I believe that Madeleine does wish to speak openly about herself and has progressed in this from the early silences. Her first main communication occurred in her fifth consultation with me. I recorded details in brief case notes at the time, but it is worth reviewing them again now.

Madeleine suddenly and quite calmly ended the era of silence by asking me for a paper and pen. I was so surprised and concerned not to stem her communication before it could develop that I'm sure that I would have provided anything. Anyway paper and pen caused no difficulty as they were already present on my desk. I had imagined she wished to write something down, but instead she began to draw. I do believe that she would have had next to no chance to do such a thing since her admission to the hospital. Drawing has no place in the normal recreational and clinical life here. The only drawing is done by Professor Charcot's man Paul Richer who has made many excellent illustrations of the Professor's work, and indeed by the Professor himself who as I happen to know has some ability as an artist. I am caused now to wonder if we should give our patients more opportunity to express themselves in this way.

Madeleine was immediately engrossed in her drawing, absolutely concentrating on the image materialising before her through the instrument of her own hand. It was no quick sketch either. She drew for at least thirty minutes, just pausing from time to time to look in surprise and wonderment at the development of her work; not with pride, but in the realisation of what her mind and imagination could produce.

Since afterwards she showed no interest in taking the drawing away with her, it has been included amongst her clinical notes and I have made sure that drawings that she has produced since then, it was the first of many, have also been kept for the records. On the last occasion though she did ask if she could keep the drawing. Perhaps she wished to show it to Martens who by then was paying her the occasional visit at her new home.

The drawing that she made was most striking and when it was completed she uttered two further words, "a dream". What a mysterious and fascinating world we encounter when we dream; so full of images. Sometimes there is speech, but always there are the strange scenarios that we view and remember when we wake. It has given me some insight into the pictures that are currently being produced by some of our artists in Paris, perhaps abroad too, but we Parisians seem to lead the way in these things. Normally I take little notice of the latest exhibitions, but one inevitably picks up on what is going on. I suddenly realised that these artists often paint scenes that are reminiscent of dreams, and I expect this is indeed their intention. In this they are presumably showing more interest in images produced by the mind than those that simply relate to the observing eye. They thus become closer in spirit to practitioners of my own profession; we who try to understand the behaviour of our hysterical patients and the strange neurological processes that drive their symptoms. These personal reflections were also influenced by my sense that Madeleine's drawing, which was produced with a paradoxical crudeness yet natural skill, was very alike in its content and appearance to some of these professional works by the artists of dreams.

I may well propose to colleagues that we explore the processes that produce dreams. It may be helpful to us. Some of our patients seem to be in a perpetual waking dream, so if we can discover and understand the pure source of the night dream, we may also be journeying deeper towards the very origins of their illness. Perhaps I am not alone in thinking this. I remember an occasion during my all too short contact with my fellow student Freud when he quite out of the blue told me a dream of his own and he clearly felt that it had personal significance. I was struck by the intimacy of the communication. I will write to him about this.

Madeleine's drawing was of the sea. How or what she knows about the sea I cannot say. Pictures in books perhaps, or even some memory recalled from her mysterious childhood. Later on I came to be sure to have coloured chalks in my office which she was to eagerly use, but here it was black ink only and the sea was depicted by many waves, little frills of water which covered the lower half of the page and which reached up to a horizon drawn straight across with a remarkably firm hand. And there, floating above the sea line, not on water but upon air, was a female figure clothed in a long garment that flowed from neck to ankles and which curved out to one side as if caught by the breeze. The figure's long hair strangely curved towards the opposite side of the page as if she was caught in cross winds or in two worlds; it was disconcerting to see this. The features of the face were minimal; eyes staring straight out and a mouth that was given no expression, but which was slightly open.

Having completed the drawing of the figure, Madeleine paused for a moment and looked up and her features, which had previously been fixed in an expression of firm concentration, suddenly softened and she smiled at me. It was fleeting and in a moment she was engrossed again in her drawing, but from the spontaneity of her look and its utter naturalness I felt a warm calm spread through my body and it seemed for a moment that we shared a world without guile. Purity and

163

innocence are the words that come to mind. Madeleine has been supremely protected from the corruptions of the outside world and in that sense her childhood has been preserved, allowed to drift on unchallenged, free from the trials of modern life. Yet in contrast she has lived in hospital wards with women who have only too extensively indulged in the baser instincts. There was one in particular, an ex-prostitute called Marthe with a particularly violent history, who behaved so possessively towards her that the two were never seen apart. The attendant nuns were so scared of this woman that they left well alone and never interfered. It was before my time at the Salpêtrière but I am told that Madeleine calmly, and of course silently, accepted the friendship and probably benefitted greatly as she was thereby protected from other more predatory inmates. Homosexual contacts between the women, along with acts of violence are regrettably frequent. So Madeleine was the "ward" to the most feared woman in the hospital. In a way the favour was reciprocal as it is said that Madeleine could have a most remarkable effect on her protector and the rare occasions when she spoke, and it was then still mainly in English, were to soothe her and relieve her from her rages. Madeleine was more effective in this than any of the hospital staff with their various treatments. Whether she offered this service in love I cannot say, but her older friend was completely in love with her. There was the terrible occasion after a sermon by Father Lambert in the hospital chapel. In decrying the evil of men, he had invoked the slaughtering of women inmates of the Salpêtrière during the Revolution. Marthe, filled with the violent passion of his delivery, became murderously deluded that she must protect Madeleine and attacked and nearly killed a physician. I have heard of strange liaisons in the animal world. At the Paris zoo there was a celebrated case of a pair of doves that made their nest within the enclosure that housed the lions. The co-habitation was perfectly acceptable to all parties and there was even the suggestion of a growing affection between them.

There was a print that found its way into one of the journals showing one of the birds perched upon a lion's head whilst the other pecked away between its huge feet. The lion, completely relaxed with his tiny friends, dozed contentedly. Of course we humans endow these animal world encounters with our own feelings, but here in the Salpêtrière we certainly had a dove protected by a wildcat, one who loved her passionately and went on doing so until her eventual death; sadly, inevitably and painfully from syphilis.

Madeleine had returned to her drawing with gusto and was now filling in areas within the sea using bundles of lines, several of these distinct from each other, which I came, from my upside down viewpoint, to recognise as human figures. They were placed in the lower half of the picture and were drawn as if submerged beneath the waves. Her earlier radiant smile had been one that related to a shared experience, or at any rate her inclusion of me in the pleasure she was gaining from drawing her dream. Apart from that most welcome moment I felt fairly superfluous to her activity and wished to be included more as I became increasingly fascinated by her vision. I thus moved my chair around to her side of the desk and from a better vantage point could examine these new figures that had entered the scene. By the time she had finished there were four, though I now realised that one of these, in fact the central and largest one and a shape that she had vigorously filled in with the black ink, was a huge fish. As to the human figures, I chuckled aloud because I recognised so clearly that amongst them was Father Lambert our resident priest. A stocky little figure in a cassock and she had drawn him with a huge crucifix hanging from his neck; so big in its size as to bend any ordinary human double. She'd given him wild eyes and a mouth that was wide open as if he was shouting. I was then embarrassed to see, and it took me a while to take it in, I think probably due to my resistance to its unflattering rendition, that a figure on the other side of the central fish was indeed her good doctor, myself! Am I really that skinny and is my beard that scraggly? Oh dear! But at least I was smiling and looking friendly. Lying at the very bottom of the page as if sunk to the depths was a female figure, on her back with open eyes staring upwards, but showing in every way the appearance of a corpse.

I was now understanding that these submerged but visible figures were those of us who had been most important to the girl during her internment. The corpse like figure had on a smock of the kind worn by the female inmates and my guess was that here was Madeleine's infamous protector. I was keen to find out, though also aware of wanting her acknowledgement of my insight, as if she had become a teacher and I a pupil, a strange reversal of our roles as doctor and patient. I pointed at the figure, and without stopping or looking up she murmured her name,

"Marthe."

I next pointed to the priestly figure and said, "It's Father Lambert," and she barely nodded, engrossed in completing the last and fourth figure. This one again, like myself, wore a white coat and the hands were huge and were waving in the air, and she had strangely crowned his head with a tall pointed hat, just like a wizard's.

She whispered, "Dr Babinski," and of course now the wizard's hat made sense; as often as not it would have been Babinski preparing her behind the scenes for her entry into Charcot's amphitheatre and placing her under the spell of a hypnotic trance.

This left just the black shape of the fish unexplained. It sat there fat and huge with eyes upturned. Indeed all the figures, the corpse of her deceased protector, the priest, myself, the hypnotist, all of us were directing our gaze towards the surface of the water and to the female figure floating in the air above it. Madeleine had sat back, appearing to have completed her work, but then she cocked her head to one side, surveyed her drawing, and taking up the pen again she made straight for the dark shape of the fish. With fast scratchy movements she elongated the shape and at one end drew a mouth and at the other a long curving tail fin. Then another fin on the back, large and sharply pointed, and in the mouth she drew two rows of jagged teeth. That was it, she was done. The pen was placed on the desk next to the white sheet of paper now filled with the black outlines of the sea, the waves, the woman suspended in air, the horizon and the dark shapes of the figures beneath the water, and there dominating everything the great black shark.

"Charcot!" she exclaimed in a perfect English accent.

And of course there he was, the master of the deep and in English near enough in name to that fearsome predator of the sea. It warranted a merriment that filled her pale face with colour and then the room with the happy sound of her laughter at this, the joke in her dream.

There was no wish on my part to alter the mood that had been invoked. What better than to see this young woman who has been so ill, so abandoned by her family, now able to enjoy the fruits of her own imagination rather than to suffer them as poisonous terrors. But after she had left and as I sat alone, the drawing still on my desk, I found myself sinking into a more sombre mood. I wished and mentally strived to let the pleasure and lightness of laughter prevail, but to do so would have been an insult to my true sensibility and indeed, as I think of that which I have written, there were moments when I did neglect my thinking as a physician. With this girl it was easy to descend into emotion myself and lose the cool and analytical observation and thinking that must surely be the superior methods for any physician—ones that I have been so fortunate in experiencing in my work with our learned Professor and teacher.

It seemed to me, and it remains my view, and is confirmed by the many consultations that have taken place during her last months in the hospital and since she has left, that those who have wished to help Madeleine have placed upon her the considerable burden of their own expectations. This of course despite their good intentions. Furthermore, the general attitude becomes a proprietorial one. I have now heard much about Madeleine's time in the chapel with Father Pierre Lambert, who seems to have picked her out as some kind of virgin novitiate with a holy destiny. I do imagine that he would love to see her enter a convent and waste the rest of her life in prayer with her knees on cold concrete—by all accounts an activity that takes up most of his own nights. I can only imagine the Professor's absolute dismay if she was ever to hand herself over to the church. I believe he would judge her to be relapsed into illness and wish her re-admitted instantly! But here again is the point: Madeleine does not belong to the priest or to Professor Charcot, or indeed to me, and I confess that something of the understanding I have of this possessiveness of others comes from an awareness of the very same disposition in myself, one that I must surely resist.

Really my patient now needs to pursue a life that is free of hospitals, physicians, hypnotists, priests, and yes, probably countesses as well. I begin to wonder whether her honorary patroness may be joining in with the rest; she was certainly remarkably keen to take up the position. The paradox must be that I, a physician, must help Madeleine to become free of physicians, and as this must be my task I will do all I can to fulfil it. What tragedy if having freed herself from the crippling binds of a major hysteria, she becomes captive instead to the wishes and expectations of those meant to help her.

The clock now shows that her allotted time today has expired. She will not arrive and it is the fourth consecutive unattended appointment. I am concerned, but also aware of a sad feeling, as if I miss her. I realise that these notes, begun as purely clinical, have increasingly strayed into more personal areas and have become more akin to my own introspection. Perhaps this is one of the things about my patient. Her very absence of a manifest sense of personal being over the years has given so much scope to others to fill her with themselves. But this is not enough; we have had many silent, uncommunicative patients. This one conjures up something extra in those around her. As yet I know not how; nor indeed do I know why.

Jacques Lamond

CHAPTER EIGHTEEN

An anxious letter from Louis to Marcel

Letter to:
Marcel Dupont, Marmande, Lot-et-Garonne département, SW France

From:
Louis Martens, rue Lamarck, Paris, France

Dated 28th June 1886

My dear Marcel,

I write to you in anguish. How I regret that we are so far apart—please write back immediately. I need your help, your advice, your sympathy, but also I am so scared. I feel strangely scared for myself, but much, much more scared for my darling Madeleine. She has disappeared. Gone completely and there is no information, no inkling I can find of where she has gone. Are people closing off? Do they not wish to tell me where she may be? It is as if some great iron encrusted door has slammed and she has been trapped behind it and I am left outside, in a cold, wide open dark expanse of nothing, just my fear and my pain. And yet I was with her—I knew where she was—I hoped she was in safe hands; with peculiar people, but surely, as the establishment, the aristocracy, the government? Who can I trust? Dear Marcel, I need your help, your wise words. Can you even travel here? I must dare ask for I believe the situation dire.

She was at a house, this I know. Somewhere on the outskirts of the city, but I know not where. What a fool I was to go along with their ridiculous conditions. I was made not to see where we were going. It was "so private", so much "the residence of a great aristocrat", and so much apparently laden with taboo, that I, a minor artist, was not even to know where I was being taken. So crazy—what would I tell anyway—and to whom? So the blinds of our carriage were kept firmly down, and we stopped not once on our whole journey, one that lasted for two hours at least.

It was this latest confounded commission for the dreadful Countess. "Dear Louis," in her hand delivered note, "that little drawing for you to do—it is now the time to do it, and we may wish you to work it into a painting later. As I promised, it will be a treat for you. Be ready on the corner of Avenue de Suffren and Avenue de Lowendal on the evening of Wednesday June 16th at six pm. My coach will pick you up."

It was as much a command as anything else. But of course all commissions pay and it was a chance to draw Madeleine, and perhaps even in a setting, though contrived by the Countess, to enhance her strangeness and beauty. On the allotted day I packed my chalks and paper and was there as had been decreed.

Inside the coach sat the Countess and a footman. I remembered him before from her house. He was dressed as he was then, the full get up: stockings, doublet, all in silk and some of it pink, and a little white wig, all of which exuded a sinister perversity as his physical form was more akin to a wrestler's and his demeanour that of a thug. And absolutely silent, clearly he was not on board for conversation, more like a dog with its master, absolutely there and silently, and for his existence—attached to her. All this I surmised and when my senses are heightened I can read things strangely well.

So there we sat; she across from me, the footman who is called Lucas next to me, and she is looking flushed, excited really, and yes, beautiful. She looked younger—like someone in love—but surely that cannot be. I felt confused and compressed within the carriage and increasingly worried that I knew so little about this strange commission which carried such secrecy. And then down come the blinds of the windows and on we clatter through the streets as she talks, full of the certainty of her views, her likes and her hates, about the artists of the imagination, and even the impressionists and the history painters, and I feel more and more that I can say nothing. And would she have cared? I felt as mute as the sultry Lucas.

It was getting darker too. I could tell from the reduced light in the chinks round the blinds and then, by the time we stopped, dusk was approaching. I stepped down from the carriage and with such relief was soothed by a strong, warm summer breeze perfumed with all the grace of nature. There were many trees, poplar I think, or perhaps cypress, and the tips of their tall slim silhouettes swayed gently in the currents of the air. We crunched along on gravel as we walked towards a large house and the only one, with no others except for a solitary black shape in the darkness some yards from it, a building that could only be a chapel. There were no lights in its windows. The house itself though already sent out sharp daggers of light through many curtained windows.

I was surprised that by now Lucas had not been discarded, sent off to wait in the servant's quarters, but Madame seemed to have no inclination to be rid of him. He remained, walking slightly behind her like a brooding surly shadow.

As we reached the main entrance another festooned creature appeared, though this one at least in more muted colours, and he ushered us in from the dark of the night to brilliant light and a host of standing people, many of whom paused in their conversation and turned towards us as we entered. There was much recognition and acknowledgement of the Countess.

As Lucas had now suddenly disappeared there were just the two of us, but clearly I was not to be introduced to the gathering. There were no faces that I recognised, so no one from there for me to seek now for help about Madeleine. They looked and they greeted the Countess. Glasses were raised, heads were respectfully inclined towards her, and then the conversations resumed with low tones, the voices engaged but reserved as in the sharing of secrets.

Now the Countess was to put me to work. Clearly she knew the layout of the house well. Unaccompanied, we climbed a richly carpeted staircase, lush in its dark red designs, with heavily patterned wall papers to our sides. On each of the landings, away from the staircase, were three or four narrow steps leading up to funny little dark doors, almost miniatures. We continued up the main stairs until we were surely on the top floor and then veered off to exactly one of these doors. The Countess had led me, the hem of her dress sweeping the carpet; her perfume, reacting to the warmth of her body, seemed to cling to us both. The jewels in her hair-clasp opulently refracted the light of the chandeliers before glowing sombrely when we moved through the shadows. She paused two steps above me before the small strange door. She seemed very tall now as she turned to look down. She smiled and the tone of her voice was thick with indulgence.

"Now Louis you can draw one of your favourite subjects."

She gave a little knock on the door, surprisingly polite, and we entered. And there, sitting alone in a little room, and looking as quiet and simple as some astral creature, was my Madeleine. But it was so very strange. Madeleine showed no recognition. A flutter of the eyelids perhaps, but that could as easily have been a reaction to the draught of air touching her lashes as the door opened and closed. It slightly moved her hair. A heavy curtain around a tiny window swayed slightly, but she was motionless. Marcel, the memory of her sitting there fills me more and more with despair. I fear for her. She was so vacant,

173

so unconscious, so helpless and it was like the time that I first set eyes upon her, at Charcot's lecture, at his great exhibition of his power over her, and her funny weird contortions. Does Charcot himself have a hand in this? She was mesmerised I am sure, in a complete trance and with the Countess looking on with approval. She fussed a little around her, she spoke to her, though clearly there would be no response.

And then she turned to me, quite matter of fact as if all was as normal as in a life class at a school of art.

"Draw her Louis, just as she is." She crossed the room to a light and turned up the wick. I could see more clearly now that Madeleine had been dressed for the drawing. She was wearing a white shift that hung loosely around her and clearly there were no undergarments and the shift was strangely patterned with symbols embroidered in gold thread with one larger sign across the breast, a letter like a rune and this not in gold but in scarlet, and Marcel, as strange as this was, she was beautiful.

A damnable thing, in all my chaos and fear, I can still look at a scene like an artist, still measure the proportions, still wonder about the colours, the lighting, the tonality and the mood. And that is what I did—I drew her. And the Countess remained, sitting in an armchair in that tiny room, looking on with benevolence. I was reminded of the look in the eyes of my mother as she too gazed upon a girl in a ceremonial garment; my sister before her first communion. I sketched for an hour using both dark and coloured chalks and did not restart. There was no conscious intent in me. My hands and my love for the model made the drawing, and the drawing I know was a fine one, one that I handed over to the Countess with a strange feeling of loss, and now I despair that this was my intuition, a sense that I may never see Madeleine again.

"Madeleine will be staying here for a few days." The Countess looked carefully at the drawing, her eyes flickering over the sheet of paper, the thumb and forefinger of each hand caressing it. "She is looking so beautiful at the moment isn't she? What a pity she prefers to be mute just now and not speak to us. We ..."—and then this quickly changed to—"I ... wanted to catch this moment in her life. It is such a special one for her. I could have photographed of course, but that can be so stultifying, so frozen and without emotion. But here we have a rendering of a female spirit by a proper poetic artist and what can be a better combination than that?" She smiled, pleased with her own thoughts. "I do not think that Moreau could have done better himself—though he would certainly have charged more!" She lightly stroked Madeleine's hair. "She is my darling." And I felt a rage within me, a rage so deep that this woman could believe that she has taken possession of my own darling, my muse, the girl that I have painted back into life. But I could only swallow my fury and to be sure, I felt my cheeks were on fire.

There was a bell rope close to the curtain and the Countess, whilst again holding and scrutinising my drawing, reached out an arm and gave an abrupt short tug. Realising that here was the first sign of my dismissal I knew not what to do. I had descended into helplessness. I had never spoken of or been at liberty to tell anyone of my feelings for Madeleine. Only you, Marcel, and how I wish you were here now. I was aghast to see that, without a doubt, any claim I should make for a place in Madeleine's life would for the Countess be a gross trespass into territory that she considered her own, and any such incursion would be met with the most ferocious response.

And through all of this Madeleine seemed to have no awareness of either of us. In her trancelike state it mattered no more to her whether she was with me, the Countess, or indeed the King of Siam. Though as I write now I think of Charcot, or that doctor she sees, or the priest she helps in the hospital chapel, and wonder whether their presence might have turned her head, caught her gaze, invoked a need. With an ache in my belly I felt my own uselessness and her indifference, compounded by the Countess's clear wish to now be rid of me. The drawing had been rested upon a small green baize card table and still she glanced at it as she stood, brushing down the material of her dress with her long fingers as if preparing for a fresh appearance in the rooms below.

"I think, Louis, that we can dispense with a drawing in the chapel. This has turned out very well and serves my purpose."

The little door opened and her footman Lucas, bending slightly to allow for his height, came one step into the room.

"Monsieur Martens is leaving now," said the Countess. "Take him to the carriage and ride with him back to his rooms. Then return. We will keep the carriage here overnight."

The acknowledgement of her order was shown by the slightest movement of his head, but was absolute. He was the embodiment of his mistress's will and his life was in the service of that purpose. Anything that came in its way would be dispatched and, I surmised, violently if need be. But I was not viewed as a threat. Not as long as I obediently returned home as instructed. Lucas waited below the set of tiny stairs and then led me down the main staircase, through corridors, past the drawing room that had earlier been full of conspiratorial guests though was now strangely empty, and then to the main doorway. Here again was the footman to the house, who seeing our approach flung open one of the two great doors. We passed through and onto the steps without and here Lucas paused for his colleague to follow us. Again there was the sound of the crunching of gravel as in the darkness we made our way across the courtyard. The breeze had now become a wind and the silhouettes of the tall thin trees swayed, each in their own time and according to their own size and their position in the dark circle that surrounded the house, and now they also performed as a mournful choir of nature, the air lifting then relaxing their branches.

I walked ahead and behind me followed the two bewigged and thuggish men and I could hear that in their hushed guttural voices they were engrossed in conversation. Engrossed indeed as they therefore failed to see something—a remarkable and strange sight that still baffles me and which adds further to the mystery and uncertainty of the events of that accursed night. I expected Lucas to open the carriage door for me and so I turned around to await him. I was therefore now facing away from the coach and back towards the house whilst the two footmen ambled towards me, still speaking, their heads close together. Right next to the house stood a huge yew tree and suddenly from out of its black shadow sped a figure, small but burly and wrapped in some sort of cloak. It billowed around him as he rushed from the darkness, up the steps and through the still open door. For an instant of time he was struck and illuminated by the bright lights within and I saw that it was not a cloak that he wore, but something akin to the rough dark form of a priest's cassock. And then this bounding apparition was within the house and gone from sight. My two escorts had seen nothing of it and I was in no mood to share my vision with them.

They bade each other farewell, the one trudging back towards the light that still flooded the doorway, and Lucas, the thing of the Countess, having ushered me in to be seated, stepped up after me into the carriage and leaning roughly across me pulled down first the blinds on my side and then those next to him. The carriage swayed as the coachman mounted his seat above, and then there was the sound of the whip cracking above the horses. There was a lurch and I felt us turn sharply and then we were off at a fast pace away from that house that enclosed my Madeleine.

Why was she there Marcel? What was this "great event", and this special occasion in her life that had needed to be for-ever recorded by an artist? Why Madeleine's terrible vacant state—and the strange clothes? I am sick with worry and oh dear God I think now of Huysmans' warning. It is twelve days and still she has not returned to her rooms. I will have to visit

177

the Countess on a pretext—I shall say it is about her husband's portrait, but I fear going there. I should speak to Professor Charcot, but he knows the Countess, he placed Madeleine in her hands. Whom can I trust? I am helpless and feel danger all around. Please do not fail me, Marcel. Send me your views, tell me that you have received this letter, advise me, indeed say what I must do.

Your friend,
Louis

CHAPTER NINETEEN

Louis' despair

Letter to:
Marcel Dupont, Marmande, Lot-et-Garonne département, SW France

From:
Louis Martens, rue Lamarck, Paris, France

Dated 3rd July 1886

Dear Marcel,

The doors of Paris have closed against me. No one helps. My search for Madeleine leads nowhere and all around is indifference. How can this be? She is cared for by an esteemed physician, she is favoured by a Countess, and then, without warning, she is gone, and they have nothing to say. The Countess will not even speak to me. Three times I have called at her house only to be barred at the door by the accursed Lucas, who in his gross manner informs me that his mistress cannot receive me and that I should write to her husband's secretary to make arrangements for his portrait. I give not a damn for his portrait! I wish only for news of Madeleine. Her rooms remain empty and her neighbours know nothing, see nothing and care little. My greatest hope has been for help from the Professor or even Madame Charcot, but my painting commission for them is now over and I have no natural access and feel that I have become merely a stranger, at most an artisan who was simply and briefly once in their employ. Yet I dined with them. Charcot and I spoke together, he speaking with passion into the early hours of a morning, and he wished me to help him with Madeleine, to give her friendship.

Yesterday I went to his house. I know his times, his routines, and I waited for him to leave for the hospital. A carriage was there and as he strode towards it I rushed up to him. My need, my worry spilt all around me and surely this doctor of the suffering would see my state and wish to help. But he looked at me strangely, even with distaste as if I mattered so little to him, and to my astonishment, almost with contempt, he dismissed my concerns.

"Louis, Mademoiselle Seguin is now free of the hospital and must do as she sees fit. If she wishes to move away or to change her address within Paris, then that is her right. You must cease to fret. I did not place you into her friendship for you to become so over-involved."

It was more a condemnation of my fears than a reassurance.

"But Professor, she is young, she is vulnerable, Madeleine is a girl, she was your patient. What if her illness returns? And she would be lost in the city—surely we must find her."

Charcot looked towards his carriage. His agitation and impatience to move matched that of the horse that now shook its head, rattling the buckles and clasps of the bridle and sending a shudder through the shafts. The coachman sat above waiting and impassive.

"Young Jacques Lamond has done good work with the girl. She is less ill now. She will manage."

He took out his watch and gave it a quick and mainly symbolic glance. Charcot always knows the time. He thrust it back into his waistcoat.

"But does he still see her?"

I said this with a new surge of hope. Of course—Madeleine's new physician would surely know where she was. But the Professor's answer only increased my dread.

"The patient no longer sees Lamond, her treatment has ended. And, Louis, you will gain nothing from pestering the Countess. I am in accord with her that her responsibilities towards the girl should now cease, and anyway I understand that she will soon be leaving Paris for the country and will not return until the autumn."

Marcel, Charcot looked strange. He was different. His formality I was used to, though it had been mixed with an affability and even warmth those three months ago when in his study he had discussed his plans for Madeleine. But this now was beyond formality, and I felt his withdrawal as if a hard coldness had set in, and it shocked me and filled me with yet more fear.

It was a cloudy morning and the rain now began to fall, slightly at first, a few lone drops interspersed, but then with more vigour so that it drummed upon the roof of the waiting carriage. Something had changed; Charcot who had seemed so eager to move away and to journey to his work, remained stock still and his eyes were blank and unseeing. I noticed that moisture from the rain was descending from his hairline and dampening the dark hair of his eyebrows. I could only stand silently with him. The horse, eyeing us uneasily, shook its head again and stamped a hoof hard on the cobbles. Charcot remained immobile, like a statue, till quite suddenly his stony gaze was turned towards me, and the look for a moment softened.

"Madame Charcot has paid you Louis?"

The remark was so irrelevant to my immediate concerns that I was unable at first to comprehend.

"The commission—yes, yes, thank you."

"Good," and at that he walked the remaining steps to the carriage. His movement was stately, still with the measured dignity of his position, but there was a slowness, incongruous in the now heavy rainfall, that made a different quality, one that I had never before seen in the Professor, one of pathos. The door of the carriage closed and through the window I saw him take out a handkerchief and dab softly at his wet hair and brow, and the raindrops now running freely down my own cheeks could as easily have been tears and a new feeling replaced my anxiety, it was the terrible wrenching of a loss.

I made the long walk in the rain from the Charcot's house on the Boulevard St Germain towards the Rue Berthollet and so to Madeleine's rooms. Perhaps, through a wonderful miracle, she would be there, sitting in her little wooden chair, by a window, reading or lost in her thoughts. All was quiet when I entered her building and as I mounted the wide stone staircase my steps echoed mournfully through its emptiness, but in my stomach I felt that tightness of hope and expectation that always remains for the lover seeking his beloved, no matter how hopeless the search. I increased my pace taking two steps at a time, up to the top floor. It was a day and a night since I had last sought Madeleine here, long enough for a return from her trip to that strange house, or from explorations of the city, or a discovery of her family. God, if that should happen, might they take her away? And then I was at the door and my hopes collapsed as through that door I could sense the silence and emptiness within and my knock seemed a hopeless tap against failure.

For the first time, I tried the handle of the door. I had always expected it to be locked, but of course Madeleine is without guile, she is an innocent, used to being locked in, not to locking others out. The squeak of the hinges echoed loudly in the staircase as the door opened. The door was green and all inside was green too, a light green with some yellow on the window frames and I had not noticed before how sweet and gentle the colours were. There was still some fruit upon the table, the dish set upon a simple patterned cloth and the oranges had shrunk and a dusting of blue mould was upon the skins. The chair was in its usual place, by the window, the curtains open, so that despite the rain outside the room was light. Her bookcase had become quite full now. There were the poets that I had brought for her and some novels too, and I saw some other books, on travel and distant countries, that I had not seen before and I wondered how they could be there. On top of the bookcase was a folder that had been made, surely by Madeleine herself, from two pieces of card, grey in colour and roughly cut, but neatly secured together by a piece of orange ribbon tied into a bow. With the slightest of pulls the tightness of the ribbon eased, the bow fell away, the ends parted and I lifted the top piece of card. Beneath was a drawing and underneath that other sheets of paper, all drawings that had been made with a pen. Each of these had been dated by a hand that I knew was not Madeleine's. But the drawings themselves? Marcel, could she not have told me that she drew? Me, Louis, her artist friend. I knew they must be by her. Some were charming, but others strange, each one as if telling a separate story with mythical creatures, yet without resembling those figures that we know and that have been moulded into familiar forms by artists over the centuries. These were the mythical creatures of Madeleine, surely the products of her dreams both of day and night, and often one feminine form, ethereal and hovering, or seeming to drift helplessly above ground in a wind, whilst other more earthly figures prowled beneath and then, in other drawings, far more sinister, were dark creatures, crouched and glowering in the lower corners of the sheet. I shuddered as one of these forms struck me with the unwelcome memory of Charcot's devilish little elemental, his pet monkey. And I thought of him again standing, oblivious to the rain, with the blank, dead look of a stone statue, and then his slow, resolute walk to the carriage as if he was turning away and retreating from something that could no longer be borne.

He was in the pictures, I could see, and I was there too. She has a gift for drawing, the sure signs of a natural talent though without training. My bow tie was evident and my pointed beard, and that waistcoat, Marcel, that you always joke about as I wear it so often. I looked for the Countess, but was unable to see her, though if she manifested as one of those skulking and grotesque figures it would surely be fitting. I was less sure of some characters. In two of the top drawings there was a man, prominent and in the centre of the picture, dark of hair and with a curly black moustache and he seemed to be supporting the floating female with the top of his head. There were animals too, crudely drawn and perhaps copied from her books on travel and foreign countries.

I sat in a chair at the table with these drawings spread out in front of me and sunk into even greater despair as I realised how little I really knew Madeleine. In that moment when I first set eyes upon her and her eyes had met mine, those lovely lost grey eyes, I had the wonderful experience of belonging, it was uncanny, as if she and I had always been destined to meet and that we could have the most ideal love, one that is granted to few I know, but that is life's gift to the most fortunate and its reward to the most brave. But what was the truth? I hardly knew her. A few visits to her rooms and some precious moments when, with her new found ability, she would speak, talking of the views from her windows, her visits to Father Lambert at the hospital chapel, the new clothes bought for her by the Countess which she would show me whilst laughing as if they were an amusing novelty. Of her hospital visits to Lamond she never spoke and I asked nothing as I sensed that her time with him had a special quality that contained a value that was quite new to her; one of privacy.

And, Marcel, sitting there with these thoughts, and it fills me with shame, I realised that I was nothing special—not to Madeleine. I am but one figure in her life, a friend yes, but nothing more. The Countess, Father Lambert, Lamond, and indeed Charcot, will all know her better than I. I have pursued an illusion and my loss is doubled as the person has gone, and also the dream. And what is left? I have heard nothing from

Dujardin, and there has been no further invitation to a Mallarmé Tuesday evening. Would I go anyway? I would be tongue-tied, my thoughts frozen amongst such powerful minds, and what if they were to ask me—"What of the Salpêtrière, Louis? What of Charcot's lectures and your new friend?"

My life in Paris now feels empty as if something that enhanced all, which gave to me the most wonderful energy, an enthusiasm to work and to meet people with the utmost confidence, has deserted me and left me scorned and abandoned. Oh, as surely as Madeleine was abandoned all those years ago! And worse, I feel fearful. In my own room I jump at the sound of the creaking of a floorboard, the slamming of a door on another floor. When I walk outside, through those streets that once excited me and that I have felt blessed to know, I feel fear and those who pass me seem sharp-eyed inquisitors, hostile to my very being—"What are you doing here, Martens? Go back to Belgium!" And I have become afraid to cross the roads and it is not the traffic upon them. I fear a road if it is empty and its very emptiness brings terror and I am unable to cross over. I stand transfixed and then I dash wildly, or sometimes I attach myself to a passerby as a child to its parent. I know now, Marcel, that I am unable to remain in Paris. I am also too fearful to journey out. It is my request to you as my dear friend to come for me here and to fetch me to your house in the country and to allow me to stay with you for a few days. I hope that I will then be fit to travel home to Brussels.

You will understand the urgency.

With thanks,
Louis

CHAPTER TWENTY

A second letter to the Archbishop of Paris
from his Vicar General

Letter to:
His Eminence Joseph-Hippolyte Cardinal Guibert, Archbishop of Paris, Hôtel du Châtelet, rue de Grenelle

From:
Rt. Rev. Msgr. Jean Andrepont, Vicar General of the Archdiocese of Paris

Dated 5th July 1886

Your Eminence,

It is with regret that I must inform you of events that I know will cause you great concern and that will also draw upon your considerable experience, I would like to say for their resolution, yet I fear that any true resolution may be beyond our earthly endeavours and I believe that in these matters we will be left, as is at least our consolation, solely in the hands of God. There will be one element that I know you will be able to act upon as it is within our own jurisdiction, indeed within our own family, yet if I may so venture, I believe the decision that will be asked of you will weigh heavily upon you as it bears upon the future of our brother Father Lambert, one who has raised such strong responses in us, and with such contrasts in both our praise and our doubt.

We are faced by circumstances warranting all the fears presented in my last letter to you, and that take us even further into the realities of an evil which is being practised in Paris and that transgresses anything we have known before. And there exists in this a mastermind, one who was originally within the body of our Holy Catholic Church, but now thrives in his excommunication and the exercise of the most heinous and savage assaults on holiness. How can this be when we live in a new world of science, an age which even challenges our own belief in God and in which ancient superstitions and primitive rites should surely have crumbled to nothingness? Yet perhaps therein lies the true culpability, that the understanding of material things, the great advances of science, have caused the rejection and neglect of occult forces that in our own church we have ritualised, made safe for our congregations, but that find their absolute compensation, their unlimited expression and freedom in the practices of witchcraft.

As to Father Lambert, the sin that he feared has indeed been committed and he has violated the Seal of the Confessional. A grievous sin and one which brings upon him ex-communication; and what do we then make of a situation in which Lambert as an ex-communicate is liable to be judged in the same manner as his greatest foe, Roberto V.? In such considerations I can only offer my prayers to the wisdom of Your Eminence and to all those who will now decree our brother's fate.

Pierre Lambert's suspicions, indeed his great fears as to the safety of his young parishioner, the young woman Madeleine, have only too tragically been proved justified. Lambert himself is now resting at the Priory and is in a state of utter exhaustion. His duties at the Salpêtrière chapel I have of course passed on to others who are available, but a permanent replacement must be found.

For two weeks we were unable to make any contact with Lambert. He was nowhere to be found and the chapel doors remained closed to any who arrived to worship. Neither was there any message left by him to give us indication of his movements and his state of mind. We were left only with his earlier stories of the sect in Paris that he so greatly feared and his acute anxiety about the safety of the woman, so we were sure that in these lay the cause of his disappearance. We were tremendously relieved when a week ago Lambert re-emerged, though our pleasure was severely undermined as he had the appalling appearance of a man who had been dragged through the inferno, and indeed such a comparison is as close to the actual truth as it is to metaphor. As well as his ghostly pallor, the lines of his face seemed even more deeply etched than ever—you will recall his appearance Excellency from your own meeting with him some years ago. Small in height but stocky and with dark curly hair and eyebrows, the large head with the face and its dark brown eyes intent and with the frown lines of one who had suffered deeply and that should belong to a man of a much greater age. Now the hair is still thick but is a steely grey, always unkempt, and those lines upon his face track at even greater depth the arduous force of his convictions and the pains of his recent torment.

It was in fact I who found him. It has been my duty to visit regularly his chapel and to do what I may to alleviate his absence and there he was in his Chapelle Saint-Louis, close to the altar, on his knees and deeply in prayer. The large expanse of the chapel loomed emptily and silently around him and even the constitutional solidity of his form seemed depleted, with his cassock hanging loosely as if it too bewailed the trials of the preceding days. When I saw him I was taken up by a great swell of love. I should always wish to love my fellow man and who would not hold in special regard one who is a colleague in our Church and one who is so dogged in his pursuit of righteousness? But the strength of my feelings when I perceived Pierre, hunched, battered and communing with God, took me by absolute surprise so that I called out to him, despite him being in prayer, and rushed across the central floor of the chapel to embrace him. For a moment reaching up he returned my embrace, but then stood up, stepped back and made his announcement.

"You may not wish to handle me too warmly, Jean, for I am excommunicate."

Of course the violation of the Seal of the Confessional brings upon the sinner that immediate consequence and it is prior to any deliberations by his Church superiors, but when I am to describe to you, Eminence, the circumstances of this sin, I believe that though Pierre must face the results of his actions, you will not struggle to find, fully in your heart, the well of forgiveness.

He has felt obliged to write down his own account of the events, so I should now describe to you those actions of his, carefully referring to his written words, but also my own memory of how, later that night, he slowly spoke to me as he re-visited, with grave thought and emotion, every scene and interaction that had come to pass.

The young Madeleine, though no longer an inmate at the hospital, and despite the hostility towards the Church that Pierre had seen emanating in such menacing fashion from her guardian, the Countess of Bolvoir, still valued her visits to the Chapelle Saint-Louis, the time she spent assisting Pierre and when all was sufficiently ordered in her mind, in conversing with him as well. And he of course adored this—I fear that this is not too strong a word for his emotions towards Madeleine, and he ministered to her about the scriptures and also about the rigours of ordinary life with a sense that this was in every way God's calling to him and that for once in his life his duty to his fellow man and to God could be fulfilled in a spirit of tranquillity. Indeed, at these times I believe that our brother was in no less than a state of bliss. Yet the doubts and the fears were relentlessly building and the girl's account of her trip away with the Countess festered amongst his thoughts as he increasingly was convinced that the man that she had met there, and who to his suppressed rage, had spoken so that her "toes tingled", was Roberto V. So that the pleasures and fulfilments that came to Pierre through his closeness to Madeleine turned increasingly to stomach-churning anxiety and mixed with that, a simmering rage. Roberto V. was no longer simply a man of evil who should be contested through God's will—as indeed is the opinion of us all—he had, with the darkest irony, become Pierre's great rival. Eminence, I must ask for your forbearance here as this is my own observation. Father Lambert would never admit to such emotions, which would be too base and worldly for him to contemplate as a source for his actions. But how interesting it is that one who should indeed be seen as a rival—though in the battle for righteousness and spiritual truth—should increasingly manifest as a more human and personal enemy. No doubt within us all lurks a rival waiting to surface and to challenge us and when we risk losing our spiritual superiority in the fight, we may then find ourselves greatly weakened. In fact Lambert was to need all the spiritual justification that he could still muster to fight the desperate battle that lay ahead.

Madeleine now presented him, in all her innocence, with the news that she and the Countess were to journey once more to the house in the country and that this time she was to take with her those items of clothing and toiletry that would be needed for a stay that would be for at least one night. And though he pressed her, she felt unable to say when she would next be able to attend the Chapel.

For Lambert the writing was now vividly upon the wall. He had no doubt that the previous visit had been a test, a trial run, an interview even, all in preparation for this, a diabolical event in which the girl was to be the subject of a ceremony of magic of the most evil kind. Madeleine's very innocence and sexual virginity were the qualities that made her so perfect for their purpose and Lambert, well versed in the ways and aspirations of the Satanists, could not resist the persistence of an idea, though he tried to rationalise that such a course would be a step too far even for Roberto V., that the rite of the human sacrifice of a virgin was their intent. And at the same time he felt terribly alone in his fears. The girl suspected nothing and had enjoyed her strange visit to the big house and had even rather liked her host. Pierre had evidence of nothing, but still in his memory were the confessions from all those years ago of the male Salpêtrière patient who had been driven mad and even to death through his involvements with V.'s sect; one that then had been in its relative infancy, but now had grown in power and was preparing for the ultimate offering to Satan. And what if he had come to me or shared his fears amongst our own holy community? What credence would we have given? This I wonder. What words of consolation would we have offered our poor brother caught up in the rigours of his own conflicts, his never ending war against sin, his constant need to atone for the wickedness of mankind? "Satanists in Paris—of course no doubt about that, but human sacrifice—come now Pierre, your imagination tortures you too greatly!"

Lambert concluded that the only way was to act alone, to completely trust that his suspicions were founded, and to plan and prepare to save the girl from her fate. For many hours, through the night and into the dawn in his Chapelle Saint-Louis, he prayed, and then the sun sheared its way through the chapel windows, and he watched its beams arrow across the cool stone of the floor, and raising himself he prepared for the contest ahead. He needed little, just the cassock that he wore and some money which would be necessary for travelling. The latter was easily obtained from the recent offerings of his congregation. He placed it all into a pouch and left. Father Lambert is perhaps the last person that I would ever expect to see hailing a cab. He would rather walk across Paris in bare feet, but now it was a necessity, and so leaving the chapel he found a cab and gave to the driver his instructions. Madeleine had been excited and carefree in telling him the details of her forthcoming trip and he knew that he should be there waiting in his own cab for the Countess's carriage to arrive at Madeleine's apartment, where she was to be picked up and then transported out of the city.

All was as expected. He waited within his cab until the arrival of a black carriage drawn by two horses. The driver got down from the carriage and entered the girl's building. Lambert noted that the windows of the carriage had the curtains drawn from the inside. It was only a few minutes until the driver emerged with Madeleine close behind him and carrying a small bag. She had tried to do something sophisticated to her hair. Usually long and over her shoulders like a young girl, she had arranged it now so that it was tied up into a style that seemed like an attempt to mimic the elegantly coiffured manner of the Countess, and though the attempt, given her experience and the means available to her, was clearly an utter failure, the poignancy of her wish coupled with her natural beauty, swelled Lambert's heart and gave even greater strength to his compassion.

He had instructed the driver of his cab to follow Madeleine's carriage, keeping to enough distance to avoid suspicion, and so the journey began. A long journey, heading west through the city and then out into fields and woods and onwards through villages, but making no stops. Our brother is not a widely travelled man and so had no recognition of these, yet he was aware that they crossed the Seine on three different occasions and felt quite sure that the last crossing was the bridge near Saint-Germain en Laye. After that they were in the countryside again and to Lambert's dismay the large carriage with its two fine horses increased its speed so much that his own cab, drawn by just one horse, and undoubtedly not from the finest stables, was unable to keep up. He heard his own coachman curse and yell out to him from his seat above—that this cab was his livelihood and this journey would surely destroy it and kill his horse too—he would go no further. Lambert strained to look

192

out of the window; they were far from anywhere inhabited. The land immediately around them was open and flat but the road ahead was soon to plunge into a forest into which the carriage with Madeleine, so far ahead now, had disappeared.

Madeleine was lost to him. Our Father Lambert is, as we know, the most tenacious of men. He prepared to dismount from the cab and resolved that he would walk, even run in the same direction and to put his faith in God. But he then located somewhere, in a rarely utilised area of his mind, the more worldly values of mankind. He had money with him and perhaps this would be the key. He offered a huge amount to the coachman, enough for sure to buy a new horse at least and certainly enough to return the grumbling driver to his position and to send the coach lurching onwards. Lambert then insisted on sitting with the driver so as to have the best possible view. This met with considerably more grumbling and bad humour, but was allowed.

Eminence, it seems clear to me that they were heading for somewhere in the region of Poissy. You will know something of the area. It contains a number of fine houses, some quite hidden and standing in their own grand isolation, and all spread out across a large area of land. By now they were out of the forest and the carriage of the Countess had surely turned off the main road—Lambert knew that time-wise they had been travelling far enough for this to be the case. So, which turning should he now choose? It had become a matter of either good or bad fortune. Or, thought Lambert, of prayer, and he sank deeply into communion with Our Lord, beseeching His help in finding his prey, and it was indeed with the vigour and resolve of a hunter that he presented himself to God; as one that, with His Blessing, would destroy a beast of evil that plagued the world. And God heard his prayer. Or perhaps it was something that Pierre had once heard that had lodged in the unconscious part of his memory. Either way, we should give thanks to God, for seeing a particular sign, one that pointed to a narrow driveway that led through a wooded area, the sense arose in him that this was the turning that they should take, and thus the uncanny spawned a welcome reality that brought with it immense relief. They espied in the distance, in a clearing surrounded by huge trees, a stately house with separate buildings, one of which was in the shape of a chapel, and there, at rest in the courtyard was an elegant black carriage and its two black horses.

Pierre immediately ordered his own driver to rein in the horse and they halted within the shadows of some trees, still a hundred metres or so from the house. He was relatively confident now that the copious supply of coins that he had with him (I can only imagine that the collection accounts for the Chapelle Saint-Louis will show a marked decrease for the past month), would secure the compliance of the driver in almost anything. In this case it was to get off the track and return to the road and await there until Pierre's return and to wait for as long as it took, all night if necessary. The driver of course grumbled and protested but Lambert felt quite sure that with more money already owing and with that amount increasing by the hour he would indeed wait and that the accumulating hours would offer too great a reward to be sacrificed. The greater worry was that the motionless cab might be spotted by any occupants of the house should they drive by. The only remedy for this, and it was hardly secure, was for the cab to wait not in the driveway but on the main road.

Pierre then carefully made his way towards the house. He kept as close to the side and as much in the shadows of the trees as he could and probably the shapelessness and dark colour of his cassock helped, but then a footman, a burly and uncouth looking fellow, came out of the house and looked directly up the driveway so that Pierre had to throw himself into a hedge. It seemed to him that he may well have been seen and all he could do was wait, now hidden by the hedge, and there were sharp thorns amongst its branches so that he was in great discomfort whilst he listened for approaching footsteps on the gravel. He stayed there for at least an hour, not daring to move. He was on the point of cautiously emerging when he heard a new sound and realised to his great alarm that another coach was approaching. It was coming from the direction of the road and towards the house and would pass by him so closely that he had to squeeze himself even further into the thicket where the thorns were now scratching his face and drawing blood. He did of course think of the agonies of Our Lord and became even stronger in his resolve. He was also feeling angry now. Angry at the threat from these people to Madeleine and at the power they had in this situation, a power that they had no right to exert, but one that had placed the girl and indeed, himself, in such danger. As the coach came past he looked out from his hiding place and was greatly surprised by what he saw. Without doubt the coach contained the figure of the Countess. In the seconds it took to pass by he saw her profile through the window, completely still and gazing ahead and, he thought, as if carved out of stone. So Madeleine must have been quite alone in the carriage that he had pursued. He was sure as well that there were two others with the Countess, probably men, and that one of them was bewigged as in the traditional dress of a footman. Then they were gone and continuing on to the house. He had smelt the horses as they passed and felt the heat from their bodies and now in the distance he heard them snort and there was the distinct sound of the carriage wheels on the thicker gravel of the courtyard and then the squealing of its springs as it came to an abrupt halt. He heard the opening and the slamming of its doors and voices drifted towards him though the words were indistinct. Now feeling safe enough to peer out he did so, and there were the two carriages, both large, black, and glistening, standing side by side and then for a moment a glimpse of the three people entering the house— the Countess, a footman, and a younger man who carried a small case and a portfolio. The great door of the house closed behind them.

Pierre's wish was to gain entrance to the house; he believed that there would be no alternative but to confront his foe, with all directness and face to face. He also knew that between him and Roberto V. lay the driveway, the courtyard, the immensely solid and absolutely closed entrance doors, the staff of the house and whoever else might be on guard there, and not least, that in that enormous place he had no idea where to find him. But first his imperative was to gain access. Having achieved that he would perhaps, even in captivity, be brought before Roberto, but this was by no chance certain. He could find himself cast and locked up in a cellar or worse and then Madeleine would be lost and beyond all help. He was at least confident that the diabolical plans of his foes would be best suited to the night time and that it was therefore acceptable to follow his instinct to wait for the dusk to further settle, and then under cover of the growing darkness, to reach the courtyard and get in close to the house.

And so he waited, and then feeling that the risk could be taken, he rushed first to some thick undergrowth beneath a huge yew tree that grew close to the house. There he again waited peering at the house from the shadows and wondering how he could ever get inside.

He was to have a stroke of great luck. The entrance doors of the house swung open and three men emerged. At the front was the young man with the portmanteau, the same individual that he had seen earlier entering with the Countess. And there too following behind was the footman who had accompanied them. He was deep in conversation with another footman, the one who earlier had gazed up the driveway and sent him jumping to hide in the bushes. The young man at the front walked alone towards one of the carriages and Pierre compared the anxious look on this man's face and the unease that showed in his walk with the ambling easy gait of the two footmen as they followed behind. And then Pierre saw that the house door had been left open. Surely for the footman's return, but that would not be until the carriage had been reached and the passengers, he assumed them to be the young man and the Countess's servant, seated and the carriage doors secured. And so without thought, on the impulse and seizing the moment, he dashed from his cover, and with the backs of the three men still towards him, he ran the few yards to the door and through it into the brightness of the lights within.

And there was not a soul to be seen. He was absolutely alone. He looked into a large reception room which had recently hosted a gathering, as all around were the remnants of refreshments and the many used wine glasses that were still to be cleared. He was standing in a large vestibule which also led into a wide hallway with several doors along its sides, and to his right were the lower curved steps of a staircase that he knew would wind up to at least four floors. To quickly locate either Madeleine or Roberto V. was beyond any possibility as there would be twenty rooms or more and then also the attic rooms; there was no chance of any success in searching through the house and only too soon would he be caught and either thrown out into the night, or more likely still, locked away somewhere with all the justification of him being reduced to a trespasser and common thief.

The realisation of the impossibility of the task and the wildness of his optimism left him standing there transfixed in the glaring bright light from the chandelier which now swayed above him, touched by the breeze through the open door. And then he heard the muffled calling of voices, the slamming of carriage doors, the crunching sound of horses' hooves upon the gravel, and he knew that at any moment the footman, by all appearances in truth a bodyguard and a sentry, would be back in the vestibule and standing right next to him.

Necessity coupled with the greatest anxiety can cause the human mind to eliminate the superfluous and reach the only possible conclusion with the most incredible speed. This was Lambert's pronouncement to me as he looked back at that moment. He realised that he might simply have frozen, but instead his course of action flashed before him. He must head for the chapel and that he would be able to find. The chapel was a separate building, but he had noted the short covered walkway that connected it with the house and the side of the house from which it extended and it was of course all on the ground floor. His sense of direction he knew to be good. He dashed through the large reception room whose far door opened upon another hallway and he could see that this must surely lead to his destination. The door at the end offered great hope as it bore the signs of being an exterior door. He looked behind him and could see no one, but he heard the sound of the main doors being closed and knew that there would only be seconds before he was discovered. He rushed along the hallway, seized the iron handle of the door, turned it and the door swung open and he felt the gentle bite of the now cool evening air.

Lambert's inspiration had been that of course V. would himself be making for the chapel. As it was the day of the ceremony V. would most probably arrive with others, but at least there could be the chance to disrupt and deter them from their plans by his unexpected presence, or, and this was his greater hope and with far more chance of success, V. would be there early and alone to prepare for the service.

Pierre quickly traversed the walkway between the house and the chapel and pushed open the heavy chapel door. At first he could see nothing. All was gloom inside, but a few candles flickered at the far end and on the altar table, and as his eyes adjusted he just perceived, standing in front of the altar and silhouetted against the light from the candles placed upon it, the large and bulky cassocked form of a man.

The man turned to see who had entered and Lambert recognised the features; the smooth baldness of the head above a wide brow and immensely thick eyebrows and the curling side whiskers that framed the heavy, clean-shaven face with its disconcertingly fleshy and sensual lips. The two men stared at each other but before any words were said or challenges made, through the chapel door, with a brutal snarl upon his features and wielding a club, burst the footman. The club swung and struck Lambert upon the shoulder with such force that he was felled in an instant, his whole body striking the stone floor with an impact that for a moment rendered him unconscious. He thinks now that it was probably only minutes that he lay there, but when he opened his eyes and peered through the shadows, there was only one other there. The large silhouette was exactly where it had been before, unperturbed and again turned away from Lambert as it attended to some items upon the altar. And then from the dark shape, looming massively now in the candlelight, came a voice, surprisingly light and gentle, the French with just the slightest inflection of Italian.

"That servant is such an oaf. I must apologise for such thoughtless aggression. He is though acting in accordance with his nature, and it is true—he is paid purely to protect me."

For a while there was silence. The figure continued to address its tasks and Lambert, fully wondering whether his shoulder was broken, rose to his knees, but then in pain and exhaustion, fell back so that he rested, sitting upright and supported by the hard end of a row of pews.

"But surely since you have taken such trouble to enter here, you have something you need to say." And with this Roberto V. turned again to face his unexpected visitor.

There was one statement first and foremost and Lambert, though stunned and in great pain, had no difficulty in making it, indeed he found the resource within himself to declare it in such a way that his voice echoed and his indignation rebounded across the stone walls of the church.

"There is here a young woman of my own flock and she belongs not with you and I forbid you to carry out on her your vile enactments!"

"Of course," replied Roberto, once again turning away from Lambert and facing his altar. "Of course. I know of you—it is

Father Pierre Lambert is it not? I have heard about you and this 'attachment' between you and a girl called Madeleine?" The light voice was inflected by the slightest lilting tone of a question that was no question at all, but in truth a barely disguised cynical and self-satisfied musing.

He turned once more to face Pierre. "What am I to do with you, Father?" He stepped away from the altar and moved towards him. "Shall I say to you that the girl you seek is here? We have many guests with us tonight. It is true that it is a special night for us, one to which you were surely not invited, though you have burst in upon us in such impolite fashion. We will have a ceremony—I do not believe that it is against the law of the land. Your Madeleine may just be here. Yes, I suppose that she could be here, but then maybe she is now gathering amongst my own flock—and do I always know who they are?—I am sure, Father Pierre, that you do not always recognise all of yours."

"I know that Madeleine is here and that all that you do tonight will be devoted to her destruction!"

Pierre now found a strength returning that was purely fuelled by his growing rage and his utter indignation that any creature upon earth could bear malice and wish harm to one who had suffered and lost so much of her life and who was now on the very verge of claiming for the first time her right to happiness. And so he made the declaration that he had heard ringing inside his head and that had accompanied all of his thoughts and plans those past days as he searched agonisingly through every possibility, every chance of saving her, until each dropped away into uselessness and this one alone remained.

"She is no longer of use to your purpose. You require a virgin, a maiden intact, and she is not so!"

For an instant Roberto lost his sinister affability. It was clear that such a remark was completely unexpected and through the dark self-satisfied cloak of his composure there showed the momentary expression of one whose plans, made so carefully and with such confidence, might just, against all arrogant expectations, be flawed. And then, with the expression of a returning certainty, and a soft laughter as at a joke of only reasonable quality, "Very good try, Lambert, but really I know, a mark of your desperation. And how can you so besmirch this girl that you think so well of? I can assure you that we have no doubts about her virginity—the Countess has been keeping a very wary and protective eye upon her since she left those safe confines of the hospital."

"Not wary enough! It was an acquaintance of her own who did the deed!"

Roberto's mocking laughter now changed to take on the vocal characteristics of a sneer, but a tone that again betrayed a growing uncertainty.

"And you think you can be so sure of this?"

Pierre sensed the shift in Roberto's manner, a concern, a new wariness, the response to a new and unexpected, unwanted element. And there was too a change in the dynamics between them. Roberto was losing his air of superiority and yet his loss seemed tempered by an interest, a fresh inquisitiveness; the beginnings of a new idea.

"How can you be so sure, Father Pierre?" The voice was at its softest, even seductive. It was as if Roberto was searching for a new structure, a new way to encapsulate the possible fragmentation of his plans. "Unless you convince me," and this was delivered purely as information as if emotion had now become superfluous, "we will still continue with our service. Too much has been invested here tonight to drop everything because of the lies of a love-struck priest!"

Of course Roberto V. had no trouble in assessing the more earthly drives that had propelled Pierre into his satanic chapel. The statement, though still retaining the light, almost melodious tone, oozed sarcasm. Lambert could not hold back. He knew that to save Madeleine and to defy evil some substitute gratification must be offered and that there was little else that could satisfy his foe than the damning of himself and all that he held holy. It was the manifestation of a terrible paradox.

He rose up, stood and faced V. fully. In a voice as loud and strong as when he pronounced God's Commandments in the Chapelle Saint-Louis, that place which over the years he had battled so valiantly to keep pure, he declared:

"It has been confessed to me in the Sacrament of Penance!"

Lambert could see that Roberto had sensed something coming, perhaps a new factor to bring him solace in the midst of his growing recognition that his great plan might now be thwarted. And here there was something at least that he could seize upon, bear witness to, and in his dark soul, take credit for—our brother's sin—the violation of the secrecy of the confessional, a sin that brings the ultimate penalty of excommunication and that placed Lambert, the most ardently spiritual of men, the fighter against sin, in the very same place of Christian destitution that V. so wilfully inhabits himself. For a moment he seemed even to forget about the girl.

"Father—but should I still address you so?—I assume that your life as a priest and your services to your God may well be coming to an end. So this perhaps is your final act for the Church?" His attention was then brought back to Madeleine. "Though I dare say, one not purely motivated by the wish to save an innocent child of Christ. She is a very nice girl isn't she? One so beautiful and I do believe, very clever too. And what an interesting history and now there she is with a full new life before her, so much to catch up on after all those crazy years in the Salpêtrière. Absolutely budding and ready to bloom, and yes, Father, for those very reasons, our perfect sacrifice."

Lambert knew that there was no more that he could do. He was a captive himself and had now showed and played the only card of value that he held. He watched V. turn away from him, the heaviness of his figure belied by a lightness of movement. Both men wore cassocks, but whilst Pierre's was plain and heavy, V.'s was shiny black and silken with trimmings of fur. Its folds unravelled and swung around his legs as he walked again towards the altar. The air was thick and heavy with the pungent vapour of spices. V. took a taper and placed it in the flame of a massive black candle. It was held upon a stand wrought in a nightmarish tangle of iron, and as Pierre looked down at the hardened puddle of black wax around its claw-like feet his vision became confused and it seemed as if the structure was floating above the dark mouth of a hole. For a moment he believed this and against all reason he wondered where such a hole should lead, and it seemed to him that it must surely run deeply into the bowels of the earth, far deeper than the foundations of the church. V's hand was touching the stand, resting upon one of its curves, and then his fingers seemed to gently stroke the wrought iron and suddenly with a flare the taper ignited, dimmed, and spluttered back to life.

Several small brass crucibles were distributed around the chapel, some resting on the altar and others hanging from chains against the walls. From most came streams of white smoke which slowly ascended, hovered and then dashed off upwards or sideways as if averse to some invisible encounter until, regaining composure, they continued their inevitable lift towards the beams above. Pierre's fascination with the black hole now broadened to include these white plumes of smoke and the strange contours that they spun in the air, so that he looked up and as they reached the beams it seemed to him that they took on a new life, for on touching the wood they became animated again, slipping in and around the rafters like white sloths, and for a while he was sure that the roof of the chapel, filled with fumes and lit most dimly by the light of candles, was full of pale undulating creatures and he was repulsed and yet he laughed. Had it been a minute or an hour? Pierre had become so lost in his visions that he could not tell, except that he saw V. still standing there with the lighted taper. And V. was also laughing, softly to himself as he now walked across to the far side of the altar to ignite the wick of another black candle and Pierre had the conviction that the two great candles made a pair, were companions, and that one was male and the other female, and it felt unaccountably pleasing to him.

V. then moved towards the pulpit. The dark mass of his form seemed to float across the floor and then to levitate until he stood there, in the pulpit, looking down upon Lambert, who looking up saw that just behind the figure that now loomed above him was a painting and it was of Christ our Lord nailed to the cross, but crucified upside down, and that at the base of the cross, where there would normally be the figures of the Virgin and those suffering at the death of Our Saviour, there were instead a gathering of dark devilish creatures revelling in the tragedy. And our Brother Lambert was so shocked at the sight of this image that the beguiling and hallucinatory trance that had almost enveloped him was blasted away like the rending of the tabernacle veil and he was seized by a profound hatred of this high priest of Satan, one who had desecrated a chapel, a house of God, perverting and subverting it with the aim of unadulterated malevolence. All that was good and beautiful, all that was pure must be defiled. He saw too, sil-houetted in the chapel widows, the black shapes that had been substituted for the richly-coloured saints, just as Madeleine had described. On the walls were the faint outlines of magi-cal symbols, but there were few of these and he was surprised that despite all the foul desecrations he could still feel in the chapel its essence as a place of worship. It was a different wor-ship to that of Roberto V., and one imbued with the history, seeped into every stone in the walls, of centuries of Christian prayer. And it struck him that V. had not been able to create his own temple, but had needed, like a parasite, to feed upon the Christian spiritual essence, one that had accrued through year upon year of worship, within those walls, upon those cold flag stones and amongst the hard and sharp and painfully honest receptacles of the pews. And perhaps this was also the inescap-able personal history of his tormentor, one who had himself been a priest and a man whose whole devotion to Satan could not be seen as generic in its own right, but showed instead its dependence upon a drastic turning away from Christ; the disavowal of a love for Our Lord that must surely once have filled his heart and his soul.

And to his enormous surprise Father Lambert, looking up at the satanic priest who from the pulpit looked down upon him, felt a surge of compassion that rising in his breast suffused his whole body and brought tears to his eyes. At that moment something profoundly changed. He has described it to us as his own epiphany and his understanding of a new meaning of love. He realised that he could no longer forcibly fight to keep apart the good and the bad, the love and the hate, Christ and the Devil and that it was only through the eternal and inevitable struggle between these that love, through its very survival, remained supreme. That love could only be valued through its acceptance of the sins that so opposed it. And so for Lambert there was a new calm, a new strength and a new understanding of this man before him, but also with great sadness he realised that he may not be able to save Madeleine and that it might now be inevitable that she would perish.

But Roberto V. was not finished. Here, in the chapel with Pierre Lambert, he was in a situation that seemed to stir in him a new interest. He lent his elbows upon the rail of the pulpit. His hands were clasped in front of him, the fingers, far too slender for a man of his size, were entwined and seemed to gently flex as he began to speak softly and eloquently to Pierre, propounding his own philosophy, his praise of the altar upon which he now worshiped, his triumphs, the devotion of his followers, the uselessness of the Christian religion, its gross faults and its terrible histories.

And Pierre knew that he had now to draw on all his remaining strength, physical, mental, and spiritual. Already he was dreadfully tired. There had been his vigil in prayer the night before in the Chapelle Saint-Louis, and then the enormous stresses of the day, his pursuit of the carriage that brought Madeleine, his long and uncertain wait in the undergrowth, the attack by the footman and now here in the chapel, the sheer and relentless weight of the dark soul of Roberto V. Night had closed. The large trees that surrounded the house and chapel allowed no moon or starlight and the chapel windows became almost as black as the distorted silhouettes that they framed. Only the fat black candles gave light, which still refracted through the pale streams of smoke from the crucibles that curled up and coiled around the beams of the roof. Pierre again remembered Madeleine's experience and the sense of intoxication she had felt when in the chapel with V. The aromas that thickened the air were now unbearably intense and he knew that they must surely contain drugs to subvert the mind and destroy his rational thoughts. In his mind's eye he watched these thoughts become bundled up like little packages of words and then, through the actual organs of his eyes, he watched the little bundles float up with the smoke, high into the darkness of the roof and into nothingness. He feared that he would cease to exist and just clung, like a drowning man will desperately grasp the hand of a rescuer, to the idea that it could only be that he was drugged. Or was it the effect of V.'s words? That soft intonation, the hypnotic rhythm of the sentences, the calm insistence of his creed. And he spoke to Lambert from the pulpit, and for such a time as he may have once spent, many years ago, in just such a position, preaching to a Christian congregation.

Lambert realised that his encounter with Roberto V. had taken on a new form, one he had not considered, and that it was now just between the two of them, seemingly diametrically opposed, and he realised that without doubt this had now become for V. a kind of duel, and in this he had no choice but to respond. At the same time he knew that his own weapons for the fight were not as they had once been. He saw that this was already a battle of wills. His challenger, and he found himself thinking, his rival, was an occultist whose intense self-training, strength of intellect, development of willpower and abandonment to Satan, made him the most dangerous of foes.

Previously, Pierre would have used his own will to declare his fierce knowledge of the scriptures, his conviction of the uselessness of evil and his mission to destroy it. But now, in the midst of his epiphany, his revelation was that he had nothing to prove. And strangely he remembered a little painting that had hung upon a wall in a corridor of the seminary at Bordeaux where he had spent his final months of study; a painting that he had passed so many times with hardly a glance and yet he could now recall its imagery as if it had once been a subject of great study, and he saw there the figure of Christ forgiving the sins of those who decried, blasphemed, and tormented him and the gentle gaze from that face that had watched him hurrying past through the corridor and had found access to his mind and his memory through just the corner of his eye. He had nothing to prove and the onus was all upon Roberto V., and his own response could only be compassion for a man who had so profoundly lost his love of mankind and who had now to protect himself within a citadel of profanity. And so when V. had finished Lambert made his answers, from the heart.

The priest of darkness descended from the pulpit and rested his heavy body upon a pew close to Lambert, so that they were both side by side, looking ahead and watching the smoke from the crucibles, and these Pierre no longer felt to be a threat. If the intoxication did not dissolve the intent and the purpose of V., why should it do so for him? And he even sensed that it offered something; his mood and his thoughts were becoming as fluid as the sloths that had curled around the rafters, but this was no longer a vision that caused him fear. The streams of smoke were like softly undulating waves born by the air and as he allowed his senses their freedom, he was sure, and it pleased him greatly, that he was watching the rhythms of life and that they were set to their own graceful music. He knew that in breaking the confidence of the confessional he had committed a great sin in the eyes of the church, but he believed now that he could at least absolve himself—he wondered at and then relaxed into a new experience—freedom from guilt.

So he spoke from the heart. It is at this point, Your Eminence, that I can no longer rely on the precision of Father Lambert's written account. I have been helped so greatly by the meticulous detail that he felt was required, but I do believe, and I imagine that he would agree, that what then passed between the men was far more than just words and that there were times when the communication took place on a different level of consciousness. Both men are well-versed in the occult and the methods of its practice, one as a practitioner and the other as exorcist, and the power of the human mind when trained can pass all expectations. Certainly a dialogue of a kind took place and Lambert in his account refers to texts from the Bible and also to the writings of the saints and learned theologians. No doubt Roberto V. drew upon his own sources of learning—there have been many scripts since antiquity to promote the Devil's work.

Lambert gives no measure of time to describe the length of their discourse. Perhaps time itself was in abeyance. Eventually after a silence had come upon them, V. rose and stood aside from the pew and suddenly the two of them had completely returned to the material world.

"I have no choice but to believe you about the girl. You would not have confessed to me your breach of the sacrament and thus humiliated yourself if it were not true." The thickly intonated sarcasm returned, "It was well done, Father, and I absolve you."

He was already moving towards the door and as he did so he looked down at the silken material that rippled around him and shook it a little so that its folds fell into place. He paused at the door and turned. "The girl is not a virgin so she is of no use to me. Take her. Though I cannot speak for the Countess

Bolvoir. She obeys me but she is a strong-willed woman. She may still kill her out of spite. So take the girl now and be gone—I want no bodies to dispose of." The door, of its own accord, swung closed behind him.

Shortly afterwards a servant appeared with Madeleine and the two of them were quickly escorted through the courtyard and to the driveway. The moon had now risen so that it was high in the sky and clear of the trees and Lambert guessed it to be nearly midnight. It would probably have been the time of their ceremony.

The servant turned back to the house and they hurried along the driveway and to the road where sure enough the cab awaited them, with its snoring and soon to be grumbling driver. As they returned to the city Madeleine slept. Pierre found a rug to cover her legs and had no qualms as he placed his arm around her, steadying her and holding her close to him.

Eminence, I shall rest my pen there for now. I know that there will be much discussion of these matters and of Father Lambert's position in the Holy Church. I have conveyed his story as faithfully as I can and in as much detail as he would have wished. You will have sensed from my account that my sympathy for Pierre Lambert is profound. I find him to be a man much changed and truly now, though having sinned, he has grown closer to God.

Forgive me, Eminence, if you should find my judgement to be at fault.

Asking the blessing of Your Eminence,

I am, Yours respectfully in Christ,
Jean Andrepont

CHAPTER TWENTY ONE

Félicien Rops corresponds with the Countess

Letter to:
Marguerite Countess of Bolvoir, Faubourg Saint-Germain, Paris

From:
Félicien Rops, 19, Rue Gramont, Paris

Dated 6th July 1886

My dear Marguerite,

Oh! I received your letter of fury. What can I say? You had promised me a time to sketch the pretty young Madeleine and this
I did with not a little sense of inspiration. She really has some
special mysterious quality of the kind beloved by artists.

One thing led to another. The girl seemed to wish to experi-
ment and to find out about love and so she, a virgin, entrusted
me with that first experience. All I can say, Marguerite, is that
your "ward" seemed most satisfied after my attention to her
youthful needs and that I carried out my duty in this respect
with due tenderness.

Should you ever wish to speak to me again I remain your
affectionate and grateful friend.

Félicien

CHAPTER TWENTY TWO

Jacques Lamond writes to Sigmund Freud

Letter to:
Dr Sigmund Freud, Bergasse 19, Vienna

From:
Dr Jacques Lamond, Boulevard de Port-Royal, Paris

10th January 1900

My dear Freud,

First of all congratulations to you on your completion and publication of *The Interpretation of Dreams*. How things move on. Though we often peer through strained eyes, we are now beginning to see some discernible shapes, rough structures as yet, but enough to give us some bearings and the wonderful reassurance and encouragement that come with new under-standing. And of course, I have in mind your work, your own investigation into the inner workings of the mind, and indeed the turmoil that besets the unfortunate hysteric. I agree with you too, that in understanding the processes that exist within the hidden depths of our patients we at the same time throw light upon factors that are shared by all mankind, from the hys-teric to the healthiest and worthiest members of our society. The majority of us can maintain our reality, our normalcy, our relative health. For others the disruption within destroys the chance of a calm and ordered life without. And my dear colleague, what you must have put yourself through to write this book on dreams since, as much as you have referred to the fact, I believe that even more so, this has been a labour focussing on your own dreams, the hidden thoughts and emotions that they express and so, surely, testing your own stance in the world of plain reality.

Of course we work with our patients who cannot benefit from the benign reassurances of "reality", but who are condemned to live in their own dream-like worlds; sadly indeed and too often, the realm of nightmares.

So, in dreaming we experience those manifestations of the unconscious mind that you have so vividly described. Under cover of sleep, our normal mental functions laid aside and rested, the nether world becomes active, just as the creatures of the night come out to hunt after sunset, and the ideas and wishes forbidden in our conscious waking can prowl about and seek their satisfaction.

Five years ago in *Studies on Hysteria* you and your esteemed colleague Breuer declared "Hysterics suffer from reminiscences". I love that; so succinct and even poetic. You were telling us then that these reminiscences had been rendered, put asunder into that place that you have called "the unconscious". But in your dream book you show how we not only find in the unconscious those terrifying and painful reminiscences, but also the most alarming elements that lie hidden in our minds. "If thine eye offends thee"—pluck it out and fling it out of sight. No spiritual, moral or intellectual resolve, but a reflex response of the mind to its own unacceptable contents. And you say that those creatures of the night that are freed in dreams to seek their pleasures are the manifestations of our human instinctual life with the sexual instincts the most powerful of them all.

I would like to venture an idea of my own for your consideration. Indeed I hope that as well as gaining your consideration it may also offer you some stimulation and pleasure as my communication comes mainly in the form of a narrative.

Those years ago dear Freud, indeed it is now fifteen of them, when you and I first met at one of Professor Charcot's Friday lectures, he brought on his case studies, and there was that particular one, a young woman, who was quite a "rave" at the time amongst the intelligentsia (along with those of lesser intelligence but greater wealth), all who were drawn to the displays of the Professor's magnetism and learning. I expect (hope!) that you will remember from my earlier letter that she came to be entrusted to my own care at the hospital and I found her case to be increasingly fascinating. The degree to which I felt involved, I have to admit, was considerable, and therein you will see, lies the core of my thinking. Like you, with your dreams and your "self-analysis", I too have had to learn much from the shocks and embarrassments thrown up by my own personal responses.

This young woman, my patient, had no childhood records with her when, at the age of seventeen and completely mute, she was admitted to the Salpêtrière Hospital, to all intents and purposes an orphan, with no details of parents or family. Some provision in a secret and mysterious way was made for her, as regular payments for her upkeep were sent from a trust fund. The original source of the money, a person whom we could only imagine to be a parent or family member, remained completely anonymous. That the girl was born out of wedlock within a wealthy and shame-ridden family was at the time my only guess.

This lack of attachment in the life of the girl, with connections to the past rendered only as existent through annual payments to the hospital, the very remoteness of her forbears and their dismissal of her, carry a remarkable incongruence within the total story that I am about to describe. How is it that one so cruelly repudiated by those who were her relations by both blood and law, should create such a magnetism around her as

213

to attract the obsessive attentions of a group of influential and in some cases, outrightly powerful individuals, and how could she bring this about when being almost completely withdrawn within her own strange inner world? That it was also the case that those drawn to her came with their own distinct agenda for her future will become strikingly evident. Particularly I have in mind Charcot himself, the wealthy and influential Countess of Bolvoir, and most intriguingly, the resident priest at the Salpêtrière.

You will remember the imposing and sizeable chapel at the hospital—the Chapelle Saint-Louis. An interesting building with its inner space divided into different seating areas, each segmented in to wedge shapes around the central area so that throughout its history there could be various segregations— men from women, patients from staff, the more deranged patients kept from the rest. And there presided Father Pierre Lambert. Professor Charcot was our esteemed conductor of scientific affairs in the lecture rooms, wards and laboratory. In the Chapelle Saint-Louis the man of influence and rank was Pierre Lambert. But what a difference in the relative displays of these two men. Charcot, immensely learned, but with his light touch and rococo gesture and Lambert decidedly gothic; everything heavy and weighted down by his religious fervour, whilst still it soared upwards in his spiritual ideals. And he too with a considerable learning, though of a kind that you and I as men of science might well resist calling true knowledge. A man devoted to his religion and to his calling and a man decidedly intent on the saving of souls. So, what better place could he be in than the Salpêtrière? Perhaps no active sinners as he may have lived and worked amongst as a priest in the slums of Paris with their vagabonds and women of the night, but many of those same women came to populate the wards of the Salpêtrière, and certainly in that place were hundreds of women lost to the world. Do you believe that the history of an institution may be imbued into its very walls, there to seep out in later years? I have often wondered whether our priest was the vicar of such history. He seemed to embody the past of the hospital like a tormented ghost still haunting its ancient corridors. And if Lambert was not a ghost himself he certainly looked to be a man who was haunted, as if the insane who were once chained to the walls screamed out their fear and agony just to him, and those women massacred during the "Terror" begged him for retribution against the mob.

You have shown us that there is an unconscious, a veritable Salpêtrière of the psyche which harbours ideas and emotional ventures we can scarce dare even think of. It occurs to me that there must be some kind of agency, akin to the parents' authority in childhood, that operates in the mind to keep all that stuff tightly battened below. I wonder what you think? We see how, at times of revolution and great uprising, the "parents" of the state are thrown over, the mob becoming as the primitive instincts, unbridled by any restraint. The Salpêtrière was host to such a dreadful event in the September Massacres and Lambert knew it well.

To save a soul. I wonder, Freud, if it is so different to the object of our own endeavours. We hope that our patients will be "saved" and we apply our energies and our scientific knowledge to relieving their torment. We do not consider God as part of that process, but we do know that to bring science to triumph over illness a great investment may be needed from us as individuals. Lambert did not use science; he drew from his experience of his God, but he too must have used his own human resources, even more I would venture, than us. Just science or just God will never be enough.

For twelve years Lambert was consumed by his need to save Salpêtrière souls. And of course he could not save them all. So what does one do when unable to do everything? At least do something. If not all souls why not put everything into the saving of one soul? Which brings me back to the source of my fascination and the point of my communication. You will no doubt already be ahead of me. My patient, the young woman whom I shall call M. was his chosen soul. I came to see this through vague allusions that she made when she was moved to speak, and these, along with her speech, gradually became clearer, though there were also reports from the hospital staff that at times of liberty from the ward, and these were increasingly with the Professor's blessing, she was finding her way across to the chapel. No doubt our intense religious was sending her powerful telepathic messages! The impetus grew out of her original simple attendance at the services, which I knew that she liked, and of course the priest's version of our own provision—the confessional—though quite what she confessed given that she was still mainly mute, I find it hard to imagine. What I can imagine is Lambert talking to her through the grill of the confessional box with that silent soul absorbing all of his fervour.

So her visits increased as did their special relationship. But why did Lambert choose her? And why did Charcot choose her as his special subject and with his audience exalting her as their favourite hysteric? And also the Countess, seeped in her own predatory nature and whose unnatural obsession with the girl turned out to contain the most malevolent of intentions. I should mention as well a young artist, one of those who were soon to be known as "The Symbolists", who was absolutely besotted with her.

And why should I have spent many hours at night awake and thinking of M. and how I might best understand and help her? More so than any other patient. I must admit as well to a certain proprietary force in my own feelings and if you have detected a degree of jealousy in my comments about the clearly proprietary attitudes of the priest and the Countess, then I have to confess that you are right. There were times when I was beset with the most unwelcome but irresistible idea that we were all fighting over her. I even grew to resent any mention that she made of the visits she received from the young artist.

So, if I may return to our science and the theories that you have so admirably expressed, you have put forward a theory of the instincts that has as its main driving force the instinct of sexuality. With consideration to the remarkably strong relations I have described and the feelings and wishes that have been directed towards a seemingly quite ordinary hospital patient, may I now venture to suggest the importance of a different instinct? I would suggest a raw and most primitive instinct which has as its aim—possession. To possess the "other", if for some reason, apparent or mysterious, the "other" engenders that desire. It is much as we so easily observe, an infant or young child will without fail wish to possess its mother—exclusively. I do believe that it exists in your book in those ideas that you associate with the mythological story of King Oedipus, but can it not be that such an instinct to possess will also forge its way into our need for others, with no dependence upon sexual desire but as a relentless force in itself? It is of course only a short distance that separates such intentions towards people from humanity's all-encompassing need for the possession of things inanimate; from the love of a special book to the greed for the greatest accumulation of wealth in which, with a strange irony, the possessor can ultimately become the possessed.

And in respect to the patient M., might it also be the case that there should be some relation between her deprivation, the complete absence in her life of those to whom she might justly feel possessive, and the insatiable possessiveness that she somehow engendered in others?

My own work continues apace and is mainly now in private practice. I meet from time to time with a small group of colleagues and we discuss our ideas, and of course your work is often mentioned and we speculate as to whether your psychoanalysis will spawn a whole new movement.

It is more than six years now since Charcot's death and I am so happy to see his great gifts to science developing fruitfully and in ways that have perhaps required a new generation and the greater freedom of thought that it brings. I was sad that you were unable to attend his funeral—it was, fittingly, quite an event—but of course with patients to see, a growing family and such a distance to travel I know that it was not possible. And I understand that he lives on for you, most affectionately, in the name that you gave to your first son.

I am, as ever, so glad that we met those years ago and that I can continue to know you and your developing thought through your published work, and that my occasional letters might offer a little interest and at least revive memories of those days of early discovery.

With cordial and respectful greetings,
Jacques Lamond

Ps. This is not the completion of the tale of my work with my patient M. There was much more to come. Perhaps in my next letter.

CHAPTER TWENTY THREE

A family visit

Letter to:
James Fournier, The Langham, 135, Central Park West, New York City, USA

From:
Susan Fournier, Gulab Sagar Home for the Orphans, Fort Road, Jodhpur, Rajasthan, India

Dated 4th April 1938

Dear Jim,

The train journey from Delhi to Jodhpur laid me low in a hotel room for a week. Apart from the heat and the amazing discomfort (I'd spent too much on my flight and couldn't travel first class), my stomach completely refused to accept the culinary difference and made its protest in the most volatile and aggressive manner. I'll spare you further description. Suffice to say that on leaving the train I was in no way fit to go straight to our Aunt and with the help of a station porter and several others on the way, each of whom helped lighten my purse, I found a reasonable hotel, collapsed on the bed and slept for forty-eight hours and even the heat couldn't wake me. You were so right by the way. I thought I'd just about survive coming here in

April, but I've left it too late and summer has well and truly kicked in, and heck, we are in the middle of a damn desert. I tell you the Mojave has nothing on this place.

But let's look at the positive, and despite the heat it's glorious. Once I'd woken up I gave myself two days to look round the city and of course, explore. They call this "The Sun City", for obvious reasons, but it has a golden glow anyway which I guess is down to the sandstone that they use for lots of the buildings. They are building an immense palace right now out of their local chittar sandstone and it will be amazing. The current maharajah started this off and they say that he did it to give work to thousands of locals, but he'll also be getting an out-of-this-world residence. India is quite a place, believe me. And there is the biggest one of them all, the Mehrangarh Fort. It takes your breath away. You look out from Jodhpur, and there it is up on a hill, watching over the city. So, I've done the trip. It's about four miles out from the city walls and you take a road winding up to it through the desert and when you actually get there it's even more amazing with its own bunch of palaces and temples and galleries. I can see why the British have been so fascinated by this place—and its riches!

But here is the thing. I have more than located our man. He is embedded in the architecture! Just close to the fort is a place called the Jaswant Thada. So let me try and describe this because it even compares with the Taj Mahal—ok not in size, but its beauty is exquisite. It's made out of marble, but the way that they did it was to cut the marble really thin, which must take huge skill, and so the polished surface reflects the sun with a beautiful warm glow. Cool marble and blazing sun combine, there may be some kind of alchemical thing going on there; anyway it took me right into the spiritual realms, not least because of the setting with mountains around, a tranquil lake right next door, the gardens, the gazebos. And then they create these really intricately-carved patterns in the marble which is called Jali work, it's like gorgeous icing on a cake.

One funny little thing—once when they had a funeral pyre there, a peacock, having really lost its sense of direction, flew into the flames with predictable results, and the bird now has its own memorial and even that's beautiful!

So, the Jaswant Thada was originally built as a cenotaph by the Maharaja Sardar Singh and is a memorial to his father, and the father is—guess who? Our man! Charcot's friend, Jaswant Singh II, Maharajah of Jodhpur, 1873–1895. So this magnificent building is in his memory (I guess the Salpêtrière is Charcot's cenotaph!).

But this is not all. There's another palace called the Rai Ka Bag, this one much older, built in the seventeenth century and also pretty magnificent, and this turns out to have been the same Jaswant Singh's favourite place of abode. He actually used to like to live in a large octagonal bungalow in the grounds. It's also where he hosted an Indian mystic whom he clearly thought a lot of. So I've been finding out quite a lot about our Maharajah. He's generally thought of as a good ruler, and as we might expect, given his interest in Charcot's work, he was a reformer and a man who brought on the scientific advances with things like the railway and the telegraph. However he might well have had some interesting interactions with his anti-religious friends in Paris, because clearly the spiritual was essential to him.

The mystic who stayed with him at Rai Ka Bag was a gentleman called Swami Dayananda and he's an interesting man too. Actually to call him interesting feels a little frivolous as this was a man of great spiritual stature and I can see how our Maharajah thought so much of him. He was the first main advocate for Indian independence and also a reformer; a man who kept in many ways to strong traditional values, to the Vedic law and an ascetic way of life—celibacy, yoga, devotion to God (I don't know what the Maharajah with his eight wives made of the celibacy), yet he was a champion for gender equality and really wanted girls to have as much of an education as boys, and that was a real battlefield at the time, probably still is. He also had an ongoing "Lutheran" battle with the Hindu establishment which he saw as enmeshed in idolatry and obsessed with its own importance and with keeping possession of the scriptures. Not surprisingly he made enemies. The irony is that what got him in the end were not the various political assassination attempts, but something comparatively mundane—and it happened whilst he was staying with our Jaswant Singh.

I suppose we must imagine that the Maharajah with his wealth and position was a man who, despite his spiritual and scientific interests, still enjoyed worldly pleasures. At any rate when the Swami was staying with him he caught the Maharajah with a dancing girl and gave him a telling off and read him the spiritual riot act. I don't know how Jaswant Singh took this, but it's known that it didn't go down well with the dancing girl. A version of "hell hath no fury" I suppose and the spirit of hell really took hold of her, because what she wanted after this holy man's insult, was revenge. So she persuaded (feminine charms again?) one of the Maharajah's cooks to be the vehicle and got him to lace the Swami's bedtime glass of milk with poison. He went to sleep but when he awoke the agony became terrible. Dayananda knew that he had been poisoned, but even with his yogic powers it was too late to do anything. The Maharajah did everything he could, but a month later, chanting mantras and on the morning of the religious festival of Diwali, the great Swami passed away. He had already forgiven the cook and given him money to flee the kingdom to save himself.

What happened to the dancing girl (Salome, Judith, Delilah?—it reminds me of all those Symbolist paintings of femmes fatales), I do not know. And of course neither do we know what all the feelings of the Maharajah would have been, but a degree of guilt seems likely. And all this was three years before that visit to Charcot that connected him to Madeleine.

Anyway, dear brother, I'm sounding at times like a tourist writing home, and I suppose in a way I am, but I think that it's all of interest. And now, to the main purpose—our Aunt is well, though I now use the title "Aunt" with some reservation as she seemed so amused to be addressed as a relative. It was as if the term had no relevance for her and was just some peculiar cultural artefact. I was a little embarrassed at this though there was nothing unfriendly about it, just her amusement which left me feeling silly. I think I blushed in fact.

Well, for us at any rate she is family. So—family resemblance? She's of medium height and I expect that at age seventy-three she's shrunk a bit. She is slight of build and that's in her movement too; she slipped into the room where I was waiting with a lightness that to me belied the occasion. I suppose I had expected a threshold appearance with gestures, acknowledgement, and a great big embrace, and I had practically killed myself over a week getting to Jodhpur, but suddenly there she was just standing quietly in front of me.

Travelling to the orphanage was easy; it's near to the outskirts of the city and after two days of recuperation and sightseeing I was starting to feel like a local. When I first arrived, the staff, they are young Hindu women, made me welcome, but with a funny kind of hospitality. When we meet family and good friends and are greeted there is a kind of emphasis on being "made" welcome, and it's a personality thing, an effort that can really gratify. This was different and it's paradoxical because I know that I was being made welcome and it was sincere, but I still felt that I could have been anyone. But then maybe that's the point: it's universal, ubiquitous.

First of all I was ushered into a large room with wicker chairs and also some big old upright chairs in polished dark mahogany. The windows were shaded and the whole room was in shadows and it was so cool given the blazing heat outside. A couple of flies buzzed around. There was a big, motionless propeller high on the ceiling that seemed redundant. A youngish woman, all in white and with covered head, showed me in and said that they had received my wire and that

Mataji would see me soon. So, there you are, Aunt Madeleine is now Mataji; I gather it's a respectful name for Mother. And I'm sitting there in this very still room, all alone apart from the flies, and I'm rehearsing my lines, and then the flies settled and it was absolutely quiet; I heard not a sound in the whole building and with those thick walls, nothing from without. And then there she was, and I hadn't even heard her come in.

So I blurted out:

"Hello Aunt Madeleine, I'm your niece Susan from the United States of America." Which was when I got the amused response, followed straight away by a kindness, and all expressed in just a look. The eyes are grey and clear. For a moment they roamed over my face before settling onto mine and I knew then that she felt at least a little pleasure in my visit.

For the rest of her appearance, I can say that she just doesn't seem that old, certainly not seventy-three which is what you told me. The hair is very straight and silver grey—she wore no headscarf, and it's tied back in a bun. Pale soft skin with very few lines. I think that the oldest thing about her is her eyes. I don't mean by this that they seem dead, far from it. If I didn't know better I would say that they were mocking, giving me that embarrassed feeling again, but I think that really it's their look of a kind knowingness. I guess that they have seen and understood so much. Babies can have eyes which look old too, but they are doing the opposite because they are having to learn so much, like a movie camera, each new frame trapped, stored and thrown back into the brain for editing. Well Madeleine's eyes reflect what has already been seen. And also infants don't veil their eyes, they don't hide the fact that they are looking, which is all that they use their eyes for anyway; so if the eyes then show an emotion it's going to be seen and maybe that openness is something Aunt M has too.

So I gave her the "Hello Aunt" greeting and got the amused response and I did feel taken aback and she saw it and reached out and placed her hands upon mine, cupping them around.

It felt so nice and I immediately began to cry. So ridiculous, but it had been such a long journey and then I'd been reading all that stuff about her again whilst I was travelling, her own life journey and all those incredible events when she was just a young woman, a girl really, and the characters, and I was thinking or rather feeling—"You survived all that. All these things happened to you and here you are, the real thing and I'm touching you."

Her voice was soft and light and I could just make out a lilting hint of a French accent.

"You've had a long, long journey, Susan, and thank you so much for coming to see me. And no one has even brought you tea yet. We will see to that soon."

She pulled one of the wicker chairs close to mine. It screeched a little on the stone floor and the sound echoed through the corridor outside. Her hands now rested together in her lap.

"I expect that you came on the same train lines that first brought me here over fifty years ago. But I think probably with very different intentions. Well at least I imagine you have intentions, because you have travelled so far to see me."

And she seemed to find this really funny.

"Anyway, when I came here myself I was only aware of what I was travelling away from. A negative purpose perhaps, but it got me here, and then later there were un-thought reasons that emerged, though perhaps it can all just be seen as a simple matter of destiny."

But then she looked expectantly and it seemed as if the one to give their reasons first, whether thought or un-thought, should be me.

"Well," I said, and already it was difficult because it felt selfish, "we—that is my brother James and I—and all the family, but I guess especially us—we wanted to find you. We wanted it so much. You see we know such a lot about you—well about your life in Paris, and you were related to my family, you were of my family and yes, we think you know so little of it.

225

You might not think that you still have a family. Back then there was Charcot instead, and the priest, and the artist, and all those doctors."

Here the serenity found space for surprise, and real surprise, and perhaps displeasure or maybe she was just perplexed.

"These people," she said, "you speak as if you know them yourself. Why do you bring them to me now? Has there been a family detective at work?"

And then, back into her repose, her hands still together with one resting upon the other in her lap, she became quiet and the eyes glazed a little as she searched within herself, as if it were she who should answer her own question.

"You have come here because you need something, but perhaps too you feel that I need something. Would you like to tell me what it is and then I will tell you whether I am ready to think about Charcot and the others? And it's also time for tea, I think." And she called out towards the door, and the voice, I think in Hindi, made a tinkling echo as it reached through to whoever awaited its command.

"Shall I call you Aunt Madeleine? It feels right."

The fingers of one hand slightly lifted and then lowered as if to say that that would at any rate do for the moment. Her face was impassive.

"In the family tree I come out as your niece. I'm thirty years old and I'm a US citizen. I'm a journalist based in Paris, where I work for a news agency, something like Reuters, but I do a lot of freelance work. And don't worry, none of this is to do with me trying to publish a story about your life, but I guess it is to do with the kind of drive I have when I recognise a story. I grew up in the United States and my brother James lives there still, near our parents, and we've both been gathering bits and pieces about you over the years. I'm the reporter who investigates and he's the historian who gathers it all together. For both of us it was the fascination of finding an unknown family member who came with a real history. I know that there's my own wish to identify in there too, with Europe and Paris and art and psychoanalysis. But later, other reasons for doing this started to come."

Aunt M rose from her chair and walked slowly and softly towards the window. She stood facing it and the thin lines of horizontal light flitted through the slats of the shutters and turned her into a grid of bars of brightness and darkness and as I noticed this I saw just to her right a picture that had a luminosity and brightness that contrasted with the pale shaded tones of the wall. It was out of character. There were some other pictures in the room, spiritual themes, large, faded and heavy; if they could have made a sound it would have been of the creaking of their old frames. But this other little picture—bright and light. The sun had moved a little so that now I noticed the dust motes dancing in the strips of light from the window and how they seemed to be dancing to the rhythms of that little picture.

She saw me looking. "It's my indulgence," she said. "I brought it with me when I came to India for the second time and when I came to this place they allowed me to keep it. One day I asked if we could have it on the wall, it's such a happy and good picture. So much more joy in it than these others—such gloomy things—so we put it on the wall here. Of course they did not know the memories that it holds for me, or anything about European art, and there was no need to tell. As I say, it is my indulgence, but I know that it is a good thing. These days it is me that they ask if we need to change things in the rooms, and I'm usually happy for change, but everyone seems to like this one to stay just where it is."

She smiled. "I believe that he has become very successful. We were very close for a while after I returned to Paris and he was well thought of even then. He was different to Louis who I had known years before. Louis painted me so that it certainly looked like me, often very much like me, but it was also full of him. As I looked back I saw that it was me suffused with Louis. But Henri painted me and we just laughed as it seemed so

227

unlike me, yet he would protest otherwise, and I would tease him that he didn't know how to draw, which of course was not at all the case. So unlike me, yet there was something of me there, and something of him, but not too much of either, so that his pictures of me felt that they lived in their own special place, and I could still live in mine. Along with my doctor, Jacques Lamond, Henri and his art helped greatly to free me. After we parted I left Paris for the second time and journeyed back to India and to here with my little picture."

She turned and walked back to her chair. Whilst she had been speaking a girl had brought the tea, quietly laid it on a table and retired, stepping backwards through the doorway with her gaze respectfully, even reverentially, upon the figure of Madeleine.

She poured the tea and it felt a good moment for me to offer something of the information that I had brought and which was likely to be quite unknown to her.

"Louis Martens never seems to have made it as an artist. We tried hard to track him down but without much luck. We know that he returned to his native Brussels. It was his friend Marcel Dupont who had the success. He did well with impressionist landscapes and later also made his mark as a writer on art. He died a few years ago, but had achieved enough success for a Parisian publisher to bring out his writings and correspondence. He was a prolific letter writer as was Martens and the two of them were hard at it when Martens was in Paris and of course it was you who was nearly always the main subject, for Louis at any rate. It was so fortunate for us, as in that collection of letters was a great deal of your story in those years 1885 and 1886. It was also in Father Lambert's Salpêtrière archives and, in his own mind at least, the evil that threatened you was linked with something awful that happened there during the Revolution a hundred years before. We had some luck with the hospital archives too and were able to see some case reports. I'm sorry that your Doctor Lamond died five years ago, but long before then he'd become a distinguished psychoanalyst."

I realised that I was bringing so much of the past with me in this visit to Madeleine; memories distant in years and from far away in Paris, but no less powerful for that. At the mention of Lamond's death her eyelids flickered and her forehead, so remarkably smooth for one her age, puckered just in the centre and she looked downwards as if to collect her thoughts and, I expect as well, to calm her emotions. Then she looked up and sighed as if resigning herself to the inevitable sadness that must accompany the review of a long and deeply-lived life, and perhaps also the sigh was of resignation to this intrusion that I was now making into her life. Without the hardness of a practised journalist I might have called it a day there and then and just drunk tea, that and the fact that I had travelled five thousand miles. However having decided to allow the memories, she smiled a little and was calm and her gaze was clear and steady and at that moment I fully realised that I was in the presence of a refined and powerful mind and no doubt, in the terms of the Hindu culture, an advanced soul.

"I am not surprised that Jacques Lamond became successful. About the same age, but such a different man to Louis. Very serious, but he cared, and he discovered something that I believe helped us both. He understood me far better than Professor Charcot, but you know it was Charcot who in the end came to the rescue. He must have felt so terrible at trusting Marguerite Bolvoir—such an error of judgement. Of course she came with all the trappings: a Countess, great wealth, a sharp intelligence and a genuine interest in his work, in fact I suspect flattery played its part there too, great men so often require great praise. Charcot knew nothing of her plans until he had Father Lambert pounding on his door in the early hours of the morning with me huddled and hidden in a coach outside. The Father had freed me from the greatest and most imminent danger, indeed I believe that I would have died, but the danger remained. The man whom the Countess worshipped and served, no longer had any use for me and so was no threat, but there was a malevolence and rage in her that Father Lambert knew as an evil that would only find its consummation in my destruction. And I was now of course a great risk to her reputation. So Father took me to Charcot, and do you know that in all their years together at the Salpêtrière, it was the only time that the two of them ever properly talked. Such antithesis between religion and science, and so unnecessary, but then just for a few weeks they were united. Charcot knew he must act and that the Countess was too powerful for him to involve the police; her husband was one of the most senior officials in France. So he contacted his friend in India, my dear Maharaja, and you know whoever it may be that you have come to talk of as my real father, I will maintain that my father is truly Jaswant Singh. He even came from Jodhpur to Paris to collect me and for seven years I lived in his home, not far from here, just a few miles."

Madeleine seemed radiant with love as she spoke of her Indian father protector, and of course this is something we've had no inkling about, though Jim, you had wondered whether he'd played a part in getting her to India; he'd figured so strongly in one of Louis' letters as a friend of Charcot's. And then there was her later return to Paris—we knew nothing of it—and the little picture on the wall?

"I returned to Paris for Charcot's funeral in 1893. I wouldn't have gone myself, but the Maharaja was determined to go and determined as well that I should go with him. He believed that my education into life in Paris had never had a fair chance and that now it should. Like a good father he was ready to let me go. At first when he left it was agony. The Countess, now a widow, was living abroad and was no longer seen as a danger to me, but I missed him so much. That separation from him tore me apart and brought back terrible memories, ones that I now know caused my illness, my so-called 'hysteria'. By then Jacques Lamond was working in private practice, and he agreed to take me on again. I saw him every day for two years. He is a very good man. I remember that at the time when I discovered that he had recently married I was quite put out and jealous, and when he saw the strength of my feelings he was shocked, but it all became 'grist to the mill'."

Do you know, Jim, when she spoke of her affection for her analyst—something we both know plenty about—I do believe that she coloured a little and looked rather coy. I guess the erotic emotions never depart, not even for the elderly and the spiritually advanced! And the mood was still there …

"Anyway, later I had someone of my own," and she glanced again at the gay little picture on the wall. "We were close for a number of years, very close for a while, but these things can fade, others come along and life can throw out snags to catch one lover and leave the other solitary and travelling alone. That is what happened, but perhaps I had some hand in it. I had never forgotten India and never ceased in my wish to return. The Maharaja died two years after Charcot, but he had always known that I may return and left me well provided for."

I mentioned that she had said little about Louis Martens and yet, more than anyone, it was his correspondence that we'd relied on and he'd been so besotted with her.

"Louis was a nice young man. He had such plans for me and I was happy for him to bring me books to read, though I had to humour him quite a bit. I think the thought of me reading Baudelaire's *Fleurs de Mal* made him quite excited, but actually I much preferred Mallarmé's poems. Difficult to fathom, but I always felt that they weren't intended to be understood in the normal way. I'm sad that Louis was not successful as an artist—when I knew him he was always so full of hope and confidence, and then his group of artists, the ones that came to be known as the Symbolists, quite took Paris over in the 1890s."

I had benefitted greatly from Madeleine's readiness to speak to me of these memories which, though mixed in their pleasure and pain, carried the utmost intensity and that had, as their outcome, the most remarkable survival. And I began to sense that we had reached a place, for now at least, at which further questioning from me would be incongruous to the intimacy she had shared and the grace in which it had been granted.

There was a silence now and it was comfortable and we drank our tea and I felt myself relaxing back into my chair and into the quietness. All was very still. One of the flies lifted itself from wherever it had rested, buzzed a little and then was quiet again. The sun, from which we were so protected, had continued its long searing arc around the building, and must now have faced the other side as the sharp bars of light had given way to a soft even glow that left the room seeming darker than before. From outside through the corridor there was the sound of a door being opened and of voices. Madeleine placed her tea cup on the table next to her and sat straight in her chair, the hands together in her lap, her back straight and independent of the cushion behind. For a moment her eyes closed and though her body seemed so alert I feared that I had tired her too much and was about to ask if she needed to rest when the eyes opened again, very clear and grey and looked straight at me, fixed as if waiting for a reaction, but to what I knew not, except that I gradually heard a new sound, one that grew louder and louder, coming down the corridor and towards us, and this was very different, an absolute contrast to the peace that had prevailed just moments before, and I was alarmed, and still she looked at me, waiting for something, and then a horde burst into the room and all around us was chaos and clamour.

Through the door came a seeming multitude of children. Twenty to thirty of them and all ages, boys and girls, and they were each and every one overflowing with excitement and their excitement and joy had one source—the graceful, elderly lady sitting now amongst them as they shouted and vied for her attention. And she laughed and rose from her chair to accept the arms of the younger ones which were clasped around her knees and the claims for attention from the older children, and with each of her hands tightly grasped, she made her way to the door. One of her young assistants entered the room and clapping her hands together called for calm and quiet and, rare in my own experience, a quietness did prevail, so that Madeleine, who now of course already had other concerns and duties on her mind, turned back to me.

"This is our work here—our children who live with us and whom we teach and who have no parents as such, so there is much that we have to give. We dedicate our lives here to children—you may wish to stay, Susan."

And I, who had felt so emotional when I first met Madeleine, and had cried, and who now felt little more than a child myself, in that moment surrounded by children and in the presence of their loving mother, lost my adulthood and stood shocked and helpless and utterly humble, regressed, unable to answer her question. And she saw and knew, and smiled warmly.

"You know that we are all children here, and you are so welcome to stay with us."

And I will stay for a few weeks. You'll need to wire me some money though, I'm practically spent up. I'll have much more time to talk to Madeleine now, though of course she may decide that she has had enough going over the past. As to the family tree, she seems hardly bothered. I expect her memory has reclaimed much of it anyway. But tomorrow I will still tell her the tale of a wealthy upper class French family and the girl-child who was born illegitimate to its son and heir, and the shame that was brought down on that family. And how we come into the picture because in disgrace he left and came to America for a new life—leaving his daughter abandoned to the devices of those that wished she had never been born.

Before I parted with Madeleine that night, if you can call it that, bed-time is eight pm here, I offered her everything we have, the documents, letters, the copies of the case reports. I said that we felt so much that she'd been at the centre of all of this with so many people treating her, writing about her, pursuing her, thinking and imagining things about her, all with their own beliefs about who she was, and that we felt that in some way, in giving her the documents we might be giving her back her life, that only she could be its author.

She didn't need the papers, didn't want them. Of course she got herself back, or maybe it was the discovery of herself, long ago. But she did thank me and she said she knew what I meant and that it was the thing that she and her Dr Lamond had discovered all those years ago and that had been so important to them both.

Give my love to all at home and pass on my news.

Love,
Susan

ACKNOWLEDGEMENTS

With many thanks to Clare Yates for her very helpful and expert recommendations concerning the text and to Bryce McKenzie-Smith for generously reading the manuscript and allowing me the benefit of his literary acumen. My thanks also to Paula Charles, Michael Yates, Sean Jefferson, Dee Fagin, Carol Leader, and Robin Ray, who all offered valuable encouragement along the way, and to Professor Brett Kahr for his enthusiastic support in bringing this to publication.

My wife Candida has emotionally supported my endeavours throughout the writing of this novel and I am most warmly grateful to her.

ABOUT THE AUTHOR

William Rose was born and continues to live in London. He has had, for many years, a special interest in both the art of the Symbolist movement and the early development of psychoanalysis, two areas of cultural purpose that in their own very different ways, aimed to free the human psyche from the limitations of repression.